Brance moved

along a h[...]be-
hind him [...]ln't
been foll[...]ked
behind h[...]ed
aside a wa[...].

*He stepped through, and the panel
swung shut behind him. In the center
of a small, windowless room stood the
crate from customs. It had been opened
with frantic haste, the sides ripped
away, the delicate paint containers and
sprayers kicked aside, the bale of
fabric split open.*

It was hollow. In the center an animal
huddled—seated, after a fashion, on an
oxygen tank, its forelegs extended stiffly, its
eyes closed, its ears drooping lifelessly, its
lustrous fur ruffled and matted. The oxygen
mask hung limply over its frothing snout.

"Dead?" Brance demanded hoarsely.

*The eyes opened. The creature
shook the mask off, took a great, shuddering breath. Its ears jerked, it
lurched forward onto its four hoofs
and struggled upright. The long neck
slowly uncoiled. A husky, whispering,
blurred voice asked, "Whose funeral
is this? Not mine, I hope."*

Brance flung himself forward and embraced the long, silken neck. "Franff!"
he sobbed.

The Light That
NEVER WAS

LLOYD BIGGLE, Jr.

DAW BOOKS, INC.
DONALD A. WOLLHEIM, PUBLISHER

1301 Avenue of the Americas
New York, N. Y.   10019

For
Elizabeth A. H. Green
who will understand
this substitution for the violin concerto
once rashly promised.

First Printing, April 1973

1 2 3 4 5 6 7 8 9

PRINTED IN U.S.A.

* 1 *

There were riots on the nearby world of Sornor, and on Mestil the renowned Galactic Zoological Gardens had been closed to protect the animals from an enraged populace. Gerald Gwyll found the news irritating—not because he cared what happened on Sornor or Mestil, but because he had been vicariously exposed to the same lengthy report and commentary three times that day, on three successive rocket trips, by news-grubbing seat partners who kept the volume on full while Gwyll was trying to read.

But the antipathy of man for beast, with all of its vice versa implications, seemed remote and irrelevant when Gwyll stepped from the underwater ferry into the dazzling clarity of the bright sunlight that flooded the island of Zrilund.

A long, zigzagging stairway led to the top of the cliff, and when Gwyll reached it he turned and looked back. The last of the tourists were huffing their way up the steps, and behind them the white pier lay abandoned, a gleaming finger directing the eye to an empty horizon. Beside it the ferry rested motionless on the flat, crystalline blue of a somnolent sea. The sky was a brilliant, deep azure; the curving chalk cliff a blinding white under the slanted rays of the late afternoon sun.

It was the light that halted him there, where perspiring, complaining tourists bumped him as they struggled past. Magnificent light. The scene fairly screamed, *"Paint me!"* and nine artists—he took the time to count them—were doing just that. Their easels stood in a row on the rise of ground beyond the wide graveled walk that led to the stairs. Their turbaned heads bobbed comically as they worked.

A hand tugged at Gwyll's arm. He looked down at a small boy, of earnest, freckled face and pleading voice. "Take you to see the artists, sir?"

"I've seen artists," Gwyll said sourly. "I can see artists now."

"*Lots* of artists," the boy persisted. "And the famous places. The fountain, the mushroom church, the philpp trees—"

5

"Do you know where Bottom Farm is?"

The boy made a face. "That'd be way over in the swamp."

"It would be," Gwyll said in grim agreement. "How do I get there?"

The boy jerked a thumb toward the low pavilion where the tourists were congregating. "Hire a wrranel 'n cart, I guess. It'll be expensive, 'n you'd best hurry. None of them drivers is gonna wanna take you to Bottom Farm if he can get a load of tourists to haul around town."

Gwyll eyed the carts skeptically. One at a time they lurched away, passengers clinging precariously to their hard benches. The wrranel was an ungainly, horned beast that seemed to take two jerking steps backward for three forward, and the rattling carts jounced and swayed as they bumped over the rough stone paving.

Gwyll shuddered. "How far is it to Bottom Farm?"

"It'd be six, seven miles, at least."

"At least," Gwyll echoed. "I'd like to get there today and with my stomach intact, so I think I won't hire a cart. Are you game for a seven-mile hike?"

"I dunno. Would you be there long? It'd be dark before we got back."

"You wouldn't have to wait for me—just show me the way. Do you know a man named Arnen Brance?"

The boy shook his head.

"His address is 'Bottom Farm,' and I have to see him today." He took a coin from his pocket and flipped it into the air. The boy caught it. "Down payment," Gwyll said. "Five more like it if you'll take me to Bottom Farm."

"I better ask Ma," the boy said, fingering the coin wistfully.

"Do that. I'll go with you as far as the fountain and wait for you there."

They gave the waiting wrranel carts and importuning drivers a wide berth and strolled along a narrow street between old stone buildings. Gwyll recognized it at once. He'd seen it in a hundred good paintings and more that were intolerably bad than he cared to remember. Several of the latter were on display in shopwindows, along with paintings of other Zrilund subjects and a clutter of souvenirs: cheap claptrap for tourists who didn't know anything about art but knew what they wanted to pay. Gwyll gazed aghast at a particularly lurid rendering of the Zrilund fountain and turned away with a shudder.

"I guess you don't like art," the boy chuckled.

The fact was that Gwyll loved art—good art—and because he knew that there would be little good art without the

6

striving of a great many artists to become great, he possessed a benign tolerance for sincere mediocrity. He respected any painting, even a bad painting, that was crafted with integrity. It was only artists that he hated.

The street turned sharply, widened, and separated into two looping branches to embrace the carefully contrived greenery of the town oval. Wrranel carts stood in rows about the perimeter, and tourists milled everywhere, almost, but not quite, outnumbering the artists. For the first time in his life Gwyll grasped the awesome significance of an old Donovian curse: *An epidemic of artists*. Zrilund was said to have originated the expression, but a hundred other towns and villages of the world of Donov claimed it or something like it: an epidemic, a blight, an affliction, a scourge of artists; a pollution of artists; a seizure of artists; a rot of artists.

They worked with frenzied movements, stretching, craning their necks or stepping aside for an unobstructed view and then darting back to their easels with poised sprayers. Most wore the traditional artist's turban, but a few hardy individualists were bareheaded under the hot sun. One panoramic glance at the paintings in progress revealed to Gwyll every technique he had ever heard of, every type of equipment even including knives and brushes, and every school of painting.

Then he glimpsed a flash of color and forgot the artists.

Fountain at Zrilund! Several great artists had painted it, and thousands of bad artists, and paintings, copies of paintings, photographs, prints, and filmstrips were available wherever pictures were sold. Harnasharn Galleries never had less than a dozen inexpensive originals in stock, for not even Harnasharn could afford to ignore the tourist trade.

But the greatest of the paintings, even Ghord's "Fountain Lights," paled beside the breath-taking, chromatic turbulence of the original. Scientists had tested and analyzed and experimented and explained but never quite accounted for the fact that the rare combination of mosses and fungi and algae in and about the Zrilund fountain turned its quiet mist into brilliant, swirling color.

The boy's shout was lost in the din set up by laughing tourists and snarling artists. He darted away; Gwyll stood motionless, stunned by the overwhelming beauty of blending, ever-changing colors. They made him aware as never before of an intrinsic weakness in even the greatest painting: only by implication could it show change and movement.

Suddenly the boy was tugging at his sleeve. "Ma says okay," he shouted.

Gwyll turned away reluctantly.

A seven-mile walk into a swamp seemed a fitting climax to a day when frustration had relentlessly piled onto frustration. It began with a crudely crated painting that arrived in the galleries' morning shipment. Gwyll was accustomed to hastily unpacking such unsolicited and unauthorized offerings, taking one brief look, and repacking them. One look at this one had sent him shouting for Lester Harnasharn, and Harnasharn took one look and said, "Get him. Today."

Gwyll caught the next rocket, and seven thousand miles later he was talking with an artist named Gof Milfro, in the resort and art colony of Verna Plai, in Donov's southern mountains.

Milfro hadn't painted the picture. A onetime friend of his named Brance, an artist who'd taken up farming on Zrilund, had sent the painting to him and asked him to get an authoritative opinion on it if he knew anyone capable of rendering one. Old Harnasharn had once done him a favor—Harnasharn had succored thousands of artists in times of dire necessity, even deplorably bad ones. Unlike Gwyll, old Lester *liked* artists. So Milfro, asked to obtain an opinion on what was obviously a very good painting in a radically imaginative style, had sent it to Harnasharn by way of returning a favor. No, he didn't think Brance had painted it. He hadn't any idea who the artist was—didn't know anyone who painted that well—wasn't even sure anyone *could* paint that well, the thing had made him drool just to look at it. If Harnasharn was able to make a good thing of it, well, fine, and being as he was behind in his rent and not eating regularly . . .

Gwyll gave him an advance against a possible commission in the event that Harnasharn made a good thing of it. He returned to Donov Metro for further instructions and found Lester Harnasharn sitting where Gwyll had left him, gazing at the painting.

"What'd you come back here for." Harnasharn demanded. "Get over to Zrilund and get that artist under contract. Move!"

Gwyll had moved, but first he took the time to look up Arnen Brance in the Harnasharn files. The galleries maintained a permanent file on every artist who'd ever exhibited on Donov and a great many who hadn't, and one glance at the strips convinced Gwyll that Brance wasn't the artist he wanted.

Harnasharn agreed. "Adequate craftsmanship, no imagination. With a different approach he might have gone far, but all he could do was slavishly photograph things in paint."

"So why go to Zrilund?" Gwyll asked. "The artist could

have sent the painting to Brance from halfway across the galaxy. I can place a call—"

"Go!" Harnasharn thundered. Then he added kindly. "Look here, my boy. The galaxy doesn't produce a dozen really great artists in a generation. This may be one of them. Don't come back until you can bring a signed contract and every painting he has—even if you have to go halfway across the galaxy to do it."

Gwyll went. Another four thousand miles by rocket, and he arrived at Nor Harbor shortly after noon and learned to his horror that the only transportation to the island of Zrilund before morning was the underwater tourist ferry. He had an hour wait and then a tedious and sweltering boat ride, with the ferry prowling about the ocean floor in pursuit of exotic curtains of exquisitely colored sea slime, while perspiring adults and children clambered over Gwyll in the hope of seeing something interesting and the pilot's voice droned on tirelessly, "On your right, ladies and gentlemen, an unusually large specimen of the *liffu*, a strange aquatic reptile that carries its young in large bubbles attached to its spine. If you'll look closely—"

And now a seven-mile walk into a swamp, and with no assurance that Brance would know who the artist was or even that he would be home. The previous frustrations could have been a mere warming up for what was to follow, but at least the awesome beauty of the Zrilund fountain provided a measure of compensation.

They turned their backs on tourists and artists and hurried off, first along the narrow Street of Artisans, now a decrepit row of rooming houses and boarded-up shops, but fifty years earlier a picturesque way made famous by Etesff's celebrated painting. They passed the mushroom church, which both Garnow and Morvert had immortalized, and walked out the long avenue bordered by misshapen philpp trees that Zornillo had once caught in just the right light and a thousand frustrated imitators hadn't.

Zrilund was no longer an artists' colony, though no local resident would have admitted it. It had suffered from prolonged overexposure, and its great days were gone forever. It survived precariously on its past reputation, a shoddy tourist center, a haven for picture hacks, and Gwyll considered the paintings produced there degrading to the cheap souvenirs that were sold beside them. The serious artists had gone elsewhere. It seemed a shame that Zrilund's perfect light was not being put to better use, but Gwyll was forced to admit

9

that he would find it difficult to get excited over yet another rendition of these familiar Zrilund scenes, however masterful.

The stone road abruptly became dirt and gradually diminished to a cart track between tall hedges. For long stretches it was so narrow that the prudent driver would have walked ahead to make certain that the way was clear before venturing a hill or a turn. The boy skipped along at Gwyll's side, chattering merrily; Gwyll walked in silence and pondered the gloomy landscape. The road meandered, rose and fell, but the general direction was downward from the steep bluff on which the town lay. They left the hedges behind, and Gwyll looked out across dismally flat, waterlogged land that wore a pale, delicate, bluish fringe of vegetation.

"What do they grow here?" he asked.

"They *try* to grow kruckul," the boy answered indifferently.

Gwyll had never heard of it and wasn't interested enough to ask what it was. He searched vainly for a glimmer of the quality he had seen in the painting—the fantastic shimmering of light and color, where the trees, or something like trees, gleamed phosphorescent, where the sky was a turbulent mist, and the grotesque landscape hung suspended over clear, motionless, non-reflecting pools. He saw only bleak, soggy fields. He sighed, wondering where his pilgrimage would take him next.

They walked on. The road became sticky, oozing water filled their footprints just behind them, and they began to slip and slide in the bubbling mud. Scum-covered water filled the ditches. The fields were undivided, even unmarked, but Gwyll could not imagine anyone caring where one farm ended and another began. The dwellings were hovels perched in solitary squalor wherever the ground humped a few feet above the sodden plain.

Behind them the sun had already dropped below the horizon, and Gwyll began to wonder anxiously how quickly darkness descended on this cursed place.

"There!" the boy said suddenly, pointing.

"Is that where Mr. Brance lives?"

"Ma says that's Bottom Farm. It's the last one on this road. Can I go now?"

Gwyll hesitated. The boy seemed honest, but even if he weren't, or if he were mistaken, there wouldn't be time to search farther before darkness fell, and the boy's mother might worry about him. Solemnly he counted out the money.

"Are you gonna stay here?"

"Not if I can help it," Gwyll said grimly.

"Well, I guess I could wait."

10

Gwyll shook his head. "You run along home. I can find my way back. If Mr. Brance doesn't live there I'll just have to look again tomorrow."

The boy grinned and hurried off, and Gwyll slopped his way toward Bottom Farm.

The muddy path had grown progressivly worse, and when he passed the last farm before Bottom Farm it dwindled to nothing. A network of small streams lay before him. He made his way over the first on a flimsy bridge built of half a dozen slender logs. Four logs spanned the second stream, and the third had only two, as though the builder had grown tired of the job or—more likely—run out of wood. He halted aghast as soon as he was close enough for a good look at the house. It was a mound of sod with a tattered cloth hanging in the misshapen doorway. The one window he could see was overgrown with grass. Gwyll had never imagined such a primitive existence.

He approached the house and called out timidly, "Hello."

The cloth jerked aside and a face framed with frowzy red hair and beard appeared in the opening. "Yes?"

"I'm looking for Arnen Brance."

"You certainly are if you walked all the way from town, and I guess you did. You've ruined your shoes, fellow."

Gwyll looked down at his feet. His shoes were solidly coated with mud, and his legs were sloshed with mud almost to his trousers. He flushed, though he could not have said why he felt embarrassed. After that tramp through the swamp he couldn't have looked otherwise.

"I'm Brance," the bearded man said. He grinned. "I can't remember the last time anyone wanted to see me that badly."

"I'm Gerald Gwyll, of Harnasharn Galleries," Gwyll said. "You recently sent a painting to Gof Milfro, and he—"

"*Harnasharn Galleries?* I don't understand."

"Milfro sent the painting to us."

"The devil he did! The next time I see him I'll flay him alive. I'll do worse than that. I'll—I'll *paint* him alive!"

"Did you paint that picture, Mr. Brance?"

"No, I didn't, and Milfro had no business sending it to you."

"Who is the artist?"

Brance stepped from the hovel and confronted him belligerently. "Why do you want to know?"

"I want to offer him a contract."

"I see." Brance's eyes were deeply, coldly blue, and Gwyll had the sensation of being impaled and dissected. He managed to meet them firmly, though he took a step backward. "I can't help you," Brance said.

11

"Do you have a grudge against this artist? There are few painters who wouldn't welcome an offer from Harnasharn."

"Here," Brance said suddenly. "Come in and have something to drink. Your feet are soaked, and the way back is just as long and muddy as the way out."

"Longer than you know," Gwyll said grimly. "If I don't find that artist, I may be looking for another job."

Brance held the cloth aside, and Gwyll resignedly took a cautious step into the dim interior.

"I've only got the one chair," Brance said apologetically. "Sit down. I met L.H. once, a long time ago. He told me I was an art dealer's nightmare My craftsmanship was adequate and I had no notion of what to do with it."

"L.H. says what he thinks."

"He was right, too. I never sold a painting, but that was only because I refused to paint souvenirs. Drink this."

Gwyll took the mug and sipped cautiously. The liquid was cool, fragrant, spicy-tasting.

"Our local product," Brance explained. "Kruckul-root tea. The stuff also makes a very good bread. Here—I'll cut you a slice."

"Thank you. Do you grow it yourself?"

Brance nodded. "If we ever develop a strain that'll give us a better yield, we'll do very well with it."

"It seems like an odd occupation for an artist."

Brance laughed. "Ex-artist, you mean. Why odd? Ex-artists must eat. The old duffer who owned this place was a friend of mine, and when he got fed up with it and offered it to me I grabbed it without apologies. I'd given up painting, and I wanted to go to the most inartistic place imaginable."

"You found it," Gwyll said fervently, resisting the impulse to stomp the drying mud from his shoes and legs. In the dim light he could see little of the hovel's interior. He slowly munched the bread, which, like the drink, had a strong, spicy flavor. Brance hovered nearby, almost invisible in the gloom, recounting the nutritional virtues of kruckul roots.

Gwyll swallowed the last of the bread and drained the mug. "Thanks. I suppose I'd better get through the worst of the mud before it's completely dark."

"You won't," Brance said. "Both moons will be up in another hour or two. Better wait."

Gwyll shrugged resignedly. "I'm in no hurry. I probably won't be able to get back to Nor Harbor before morning. Why won't you tell me who the artist is?"

"Because I can't," Brance said slowly. "Because I don't dare. Did you mean that about looking for a new job?"

"You said you'd met L.H."

"He was being nice at the time, but I can easily imagine—look here. You seem like a decent enough person. Will you swear to keep this between yourself and L.H. and make him swear to that before you tell him?"

"Yes—"

"Come along, then."

He led Gwyll from the hovel. A smaller mound, a sort of outbuilding, stood a few paces to the rear, and there Gwyll blinked in a sudden flash of light as Brance lit a candle. He brought out a crude palette and a piece of art fabric stretched over a thick frame.

"You take the candle," he said.

In the candlelight Brance's eyes gleamed wildly, and it occurred to Gwyll that the man had behaved somewhat irrationally from the beginning. "You asked for it," Brance said. He laughed gleefully. "Follow me."

Carrying the candle awkwardly—he had never seen one before except in paintings—Gwyll stumbled after him into the thickening darkness. They halted beside a stone-walled enclosure, a square that measured three or four strides across. Gwyll's candle revealed nothing within it but creamy mud.

Brance leaned over and wedged the art fabric between the wall and a protruding rock. He placed the palette on another rock and slowly backed away.

"Don't hold the light so close!" he hissed. "Here—let me have it."

The mud stirred. What looked like a quivering puddle of slime spread slowly across its surface and reared up suddenly. It assumed a shape, became a bloated oval of pulsating, mud-encrusted jelly, and flowed toward the palette.

A sudden wave of revulsion left Gwyll trembling. His stomach revolted against the nauseating stench, and his mind utterly rejected the disgusting, blotched, shimmering mucosity of the creature's body. The mere thought that such a slimy mass was *alive* appalled and horrified. He clenched his teeth until his jaws ached, but he continued to watch.

It reached the palette and reared itself above it, a froth of foul scum through which the lips of the paint cups seemed dimly visible.

And then it began to paint. A multitude of fine filaments darted to and fro, and on the fabric a speck of paint appeared, and then another ... five minutes passed, ten minutes, the picture grew with infinite slowness. When finally Brance blew out the candle a mere square inch had been covered. The colors were only dimly distinguishable in the

13

feeble, flickering light, but already Gwyll could recognize the *texture.*

He did not want to believe. He said, "You mean—that *thing*—painted—"

"It won't work long when there's a light," Brance said.

Gwyll repeated weakly, "That *thing* painted—"

"The painting Milfro sent to you. Yes."

He tugged gently at Gwyll's arm and led him away.

"I can't believe it," Gwyll muttered. "It paints in the dark?"

"It doesn't see as we see. Obviously. It must perceive some light that's invisible to us. Certainly it paints things that never were—that couldn't be, in the universe we know. I've never been able to identify anything in its paintings, and yet I've felt from the bginning that it must be painting what it sees. I suppose my human prejudices won't let me credit it with the imagination of genius."

"What is it?"

"Scientists have a thoroughly unpronounceable name for it, but to the natives it's just a swamp slug. It's never been found anywhere except on this island, which is probably why so little is known about it. I took photographs to the zoology professors at Nor University and none of them had ever seen one. They offered to buy it. Said they'd like to study it." He laughed harshly. "They offered me ten dons for it, which seems like a rather low price to pay for a great artist—but of course they didn't know about the paintings. They thought they were making a very generous offer for a rare but inconsequential kind of gastropod, and they seemed offended when I told them to come over and catch their own. Maybe it's just as well that they didn't try. The natives tell me the things used to be common, but these days you almost never see one, what with more and more of the swamp being drained and cultivated. This is the only one I've ever seen."

"Do you have other paintings?"

"Seven," Brance said. "Seven plus the one I sent to Milfro. It was a long time before it got the idea that the whole fabric could be one composition, and even now it doesn't often produce a large painting. With four of the eight I had to cut the fabric down to fit the part that it painted."

"Does it work all night?"

"On a dark night. Tonight it'll stop when the moons come up. It paints slowly, as you saw, and the next night it won't always start where it left off. It took me four years to get those eight paintings. Drat Milfro—I just wanted an opinion, not a visitation. Anyway, L.H. can't fire you for not putting this artist under contract. Sorry I can't offer you a bed, but

14

the only one I have you wouldn't like. I can't even lend you a light to walk back with, but I'll go as far as my neighbor's with you and see if you can borrow his."

"That's very kind of you."

"And remember your oath!" Brance's voice cut savagely through the darkness. "If a word of this leaks out, I'll kill the person responsible."

Gwyll started back to Zrilund Town with the feeble beam of the neighbor's small handlight picking out the uncertain borders of the road. His memory was still replete with what he had seen and smelled, and after a couple of miles he finally lost control, and along with it the scant lunch he had eaten on the ferry and the nutritious products of the kruckul root.

At Zrilund Town he did something he wouldn't have had the courage for as recently as that afternoon. He pried the fat com agent from his dinner to open the Zrilund Communications Center, and he kept him waiting—and fuming—until he got a clear channel to Donov Metro and routed Lester Harnasharn from his bed.

Harnasharn, looking ludicrous with a night covering perched jauntily on his bald head, did not even seem perturbed. "Did you get him?" he demanded.

Gwyll hesitated. The com agent stood looking on, and there were possibly dozens of people listening in. "There's a very substantial matter of ethics involved," he said.

"I understand. He's already committed himself elsewhere."

"Not that kind of ethics. I think it's a matter that you'd want to handle yourself."

"I'll leave at once."

"There's no hurry. The only boat scheduled from the mainland operates at eight in the morning—which is afternoon to you."

"Then why did you get me out of bed?"

Because I haven't been to bed, and once I get there, if I can find one, I'm not getting up in the middle of the night to send a message. Anyway, I thought you'd like to know."

Harnasharn chuckled. "Thanks. What happened to you? Is it raining mud on Zrilund?"

"That's as good a way to describe it as any."

"I'll dress for it." He chuckled again. "Before you look for that bed I suggest you find a bath." He cut the connection.

"I'd suggest the Zrilund Town Hostel," the com agent said dryly. "Fourth right from the corner. Hylat'll let you have the bath and bed and maybe a bit of supper, which you look as though you could use."

Gwyll thanked him and paid for the call. The bath and bed

15

would be welcome, but his stomach wasn't yet in condition to tolerate any thought of food.

Twenty-one hours later, Lester Harnasharn perched on the edge of Brance's pen peering in fascination as the slug hung over the art fabric, filaments tirelessly in motion.

"If I wasn't seeing it with my own eyes—" he muttered.

Brance said nothing. Gwyll, holding the candle, was too preoccupied with his nausea to speak.

"Are those things *tongues?*" Harnasharn demanded.

"They could be," Brance admitted. "I've never been able to locate its head, but that doesn't mean it doesn't have one. I guess *tongues* is as apt a description as any."

"It dips each one into the paint, and then—where does it mix the colors? On its tongues, or right on the fabric?"

"I don't know. It may mix in some secretion of its own, which would account for the unusual texture. I do know it won't use any kind of paint that doesn't have a vegetable base."

"Vegetable? Did you give those paintings a spray set?"

"Of course."

"And it sees something that never was," Harnasharn mused. "That must be it—I think. Those paintings certainly give me the impression of looking at something I've never seen before, or of looking at something familiar in a way that makes it seem like looking into another dimension." He turned angrily. "But they're *art,* confound it! Splendid art! I don't care if the being that created them is human, or a slimy worm, or a hunk of rock. Harnasharn Galleries has never demanded an artist's pedigree. Of course I'll exhibit those paintings, and I'll be proud to do it."

Brance laughed sardonically. "Will you exhibit them anonymously, or are you planning a reception to introduce my slug to the critics?"

"What do you suggest?" Harnasharn asked. "The slug belongs to you, so legally the paintings must be your property. The contract would have to be drawn in your name and you'd have to sign it. For all of its obvious talent, the slug's signature, even if it could produce one, would have very little legal standing."

"Brance could sign the paintings," Gwyll suggested.

"No." Harnasharn shook his head emphatically. "A painting signed by a person who did not paint it is a fraud, regardless of the circumstances. I'm willing to exhibit a slug's paintings if I think they're good enough, but not if they're signed by anyone but the artist. I won't knowingly admit a fraud to Harnasharn Galleries."

"I wouldn't even try to sign them," Brance said. "The texture is so peculiar that the mere touch of a brush or spray botches it. I've tried to finish some of its aborted efforts, and you couldn't imagine the mess I made of them."

"Very well. Then we'll have to exhibit anonymously. I'll make you an outright offer for the eight paintings; or I'll contract to exhibit them and handle their sale at auction at our usual commission with the option to buy any or all at the highest bid price less commission; or—and I recommend this—I'll give them a special showing and then place them in our permanent exhibit on a deferred-sale basis and hold them until bids reach the figures we agree upon. I'd guess that in five years they'll be worth several times what you could get for them now. And of course I'll advance you a reasonable amount. What do you say?"

"It sounds like a very fair offer," Brance admitted.

"Have you ever heard of Harnasharn Galleries making an unfair offer?"

"No. But the problem, you see, is that I don't know if I want to sell. This is the only great art that I'm ever likely to own. I'm selfish enough to want it for myself. Anyway, why expose such beautiful things to the vulgar gaze of the crassly stupid?"

Harnasharn seemed amused. "You aren't the first artist who's delivered that particular lecture to me."

"Then you should have your answer ready."

"I do. 'A thing of beauty is a joy forever,' as the old proverb says. You're selfish enough to want the paintings for yourself. I'm generous enough to want to share them. I simply point out that beauty, shared, doesn't diminish or depreciate. You can share it and still keep it for yourself. Let me exhibit the paintings on a deferred-sale basis, giving you the option of recall and making any sale subject to your approval. It's as simple as that. While we're waiting for an offer you're willing to accept, you can share this beauty by way of our permanent exhibit and in reproductions and filmstrips."

"If you put it that way—"

"I do. If you have something to write on I'll make out a contract. It wouldn't be prudent to try to name or describe the artist, so I'll simply refer to paintings of a certain style, and we can include any future output under the same description. I assume that there will be more. How long do these things live?"

"According to local tradition this one is still a baby, and I've had it for six years. The first settlers found huge slugs

17

here, but they were so repulsive that they were killed the moment anyone saw one."

"Where can I write?"

"There's a table of sorts in the house?"

They turned away, and Gwyll took a final, shuddering look at the dim form of the slug as they moved off: slimy body hunched over fabric, the multitude of filaments tirelessly weaving, weaving, extracting from the darkness the dazzling essence of pure light.

2

They were two old men with years enough between them to know that failing eyesight sometimes enables one to see more clearly, and their friendship had stood firmly since the days when the Government Common was a wrranel pasture. Below them the gardens were vibrant with color, and across the common a few artists had gathered to paint the odd, purplish effect of the long shadow that Donov University's tower cast on the massive, creamy marble of the Cirque, the World Management Building. To their left stood the delicate, fluted façade of the Donovian Institute of Art; to their right, the graceful silhouette of the World Library.

It was a scene worth painting, and because the artist Garnow had once done so, from this very balcony, it was also famous. World Manager Ian Korak knew it so perfectly in all of its detail that he still enjoyed it despite his near blindness. On this day, however, his clouded eyes were deeply troubled and his thoughts were not of the view.

He said meditatively, "My friend, we have to face the fact that diplomatic posts on Donov are either a haven for the weary or a sinecure for the incompetent. Ambassadors come and go without even bothering to present their credentials. The so-called permanent embassy staffs have such a turnover of personnel that there isn't one individual among them whom I've known long enough and well enough to call a friend and with whom I can have the kind of confidential discussion one needs to have on sensitive subjects. One of the worlds where the situation is most critical is Mestil, and the new Mestillian ambassador only arrived yesterday. That's one problem. The other is that these diplomats haven't been home for years and know only what their governments choose to tell them. Even if they were fully cooperative, it's doubtful that I could learn much."

Master Trader Har M'Don ruffled his massive stack of white hair and asked querulously, "Then why try?"

"Because I'm worried. Because it seems as though a disease has infected this sector of the galaxy, and a disease as virulent as this one may be contagious. Neal Wargen has

19

organized all the available information, and he thinks the riots have a pattern."

M'Don smiled. "Don't most social phenomena have patterns?"

"Is hatred a social phenomenon?"

"Hatred is beyond my comprehension. I don't hate anyone or anything."

"At our ages, my friend, any kind of emotion is a luxury. I'm wondering if the emotion of hatred, at least, isn't a luxury the human race can no longer afford. Humanity is extremely old, and it should have outgrown such emotions as you and I have outgrown them, but it hasn't. There are animaloids whose capacities in many ways exceed or at least splendidly complement ours, and we should have accepted them as partners in the scheme of things before they asked. The day may come when humanity needs every partner it can find. But we didn't accept them, and they did ask, and then they demanded, and still humanity is attempting to ignore them—except in this sector, where they're being exterminated."

M'Don said doubtfully, "You're exaggerating, aren't you? Any decent-thinking person would have to concede that the animaloids are treated shamefully, but—equality? Could an animaloid with hoofs operate a computer?"

"Of course—if a computer were designed to be operated by an intelligent animal with hoofs. We design them exclusively for the digital or vocal capabilities of humans, and then we call the animaloids inferior because they're physically incapable of using them. Worse, all too often what we unjustly consider inferior, we hate. Before any species indulges in such a wasteful luxury, it ought to ask itself what might happen if the hatred were returned."

"There's more than one way of looking at that," M'Don objected. "Remember the Aamull massacre? And that business on Xeniol—come to think of it, they called that a partnership, but very few of the human partners survived."

Korak nodded. "Which is only to say that some animaloids are as vicious as some humans, and on both Aamull and Xeniol the animaloids received justice. Why can't those who aren't vicious receive justice?" He pushed himself to his feet and stepped to the edge of the balcony. "I worry about this. We humans have developed so many divergent types of our own, as we spread across the galaxy, that we should have been more tolerant of other species. But we found, among other things, beings that looked amazingly human and had a minimal intellectual capacity, and creatures with intellects at least equal to ours that were obviously, sometimes disgustingly, animal in appearance. To our eternal shame we've accorded the brainless humanoids more respect than the intelligent animaloids. Fifty years ago animaloids on Mestil petitioned to have the franchise based upon intelligence rather than appearance. They're still petitioning, or they were until the Mestillians answered the petitions with mass murder. Other places, other requests, and they ask so little: The right to use public facilities on an equal basis with humans. Denied. The right to laws based on their own customs and capabilities. Denied. The right to share in the making of the laws that govern them, to share in the determination of the taxes they pay and how the money should be spent. All denied. The most serious thing of all is that our language—all human languages—lack a word. How would you describe a close friendship between a human and an animaloid?"

"What's wrong with *friendship?*" M'Don asked.

"What's wrong with *brotherhood?*" Korak demanded.

"Nothing, I suppose. Except—"

"Except. Except that the concept of an animaloid being brother to a human grates. It doesn't fit. Yet there are such relationships, many such, and no known human language has a word for them. I had the matter investigated. We need a word to describe 'more than friendship' between human and animaloid." He slumped back into his chair. "Wargen thinks there's a pattern to the riots. You have offices on a number of the riot worlds. Have they supplied you with reports?"

"Of course. It never occurred to me to examine them for a pattern, though. Events differed so drastically from world to world—on some there was a long series of disturbances that eventually culminated in rioting, and on others there wasn't a hint of trouble in advance. Do you want those reports?"

"Yes, and I'd like every scrap of additional information that you can obtain. If there *is* a pattern, knowing what it is might prevent a tragedy here. Or elsewhere."

"How could it possibly affect Donov? We have no animaloids."

"Madness takes strange turnings. It's already affected more than animaloids. Did you hear about the Galactic Zoological Gardens?"

"Yes. Very well. You shall have the reports."

"Thank you."

M'Don got to his feet. "I've never had an animaloid friend. Probably few Donovians have, since there are no animaloids here. In my case, though, I've traveled so extensively that I must have had many opportunities, and I can't recall even speaking with one."

"Did you ever want to speak with one?"

"I don't know. I honestly don't think I'm prejudiced on this

21

subject, it's just that until this moment I've never even thought about it. If I had, I might have made the effort. I'm sure it would be an interesting experience. Animaloids must have a unique view of the universe."

Korak smiled. "Everyone I've talked with who has had the good fortune to know an animaloid well insists that such a friendship adds an entirely new dimension to one's awareness of one's self."

"Then it's unfortunate that we have none on Donov. I'll send those reports as soon as I can assemble them." He turned away, turned back again. "I think maybe you're right. We need a word."

In the mountains of Donov's southern continent, the picturesque town of Verna Plai lay—some said floated—in a valley celebrated for its mineral springs. It was Donov's most famous health resort, and it also possessed an art colony of note. The rugged, scenic mountains that surrounded the town, with their geysers and steaming springs, provided spectacular subjects for painting.

Art colonies came into being on Donov wherever there was anything that more than one artist wanted to paint. The Verna Plai colony was unique in that tourists had discovered the town long before the artists did, and Verna Plai tourists still tended to have an overwhelming interest in their own bodily functions and an abysmal lack of interest in art.

Most artists were wanderers, but every colony developed its small group of perms, of artists who remained there, often in dire poverty, because they loved the place. At Verna Plai one of them was Gof Milfro.

He painted faithfully for as many hours each day as he could hold his sprayers level, and once each week he took an armful of paintings down to the Plai. There he made the rounds of those merchants who condescended to display paintings, cheerfully verifying his assumption that none of his had been sold. Then he wandered about the hostels looking for an unwary tourist whose digestive processes had been loosened sufficiently to unblock a petrified aesthetic sense. Having failed in that, he occupied himself on the steep climb back to the artists' colony with a searching review of his acquaintances to determine which one might be the best subject for the small loan he needed in order to exist for another week. Since he had never been known to repay one, artist creditors were as difficult to find as tourist customers. Somehow he survived and continued to work tirelessly—ragged, hungry, uncomfortable, but for all that indomitably cheerful and irrepressibly optimistic. He was an artist.

22

The day he received his windfall from Gerald Gwyll, Milfro laid in a few needed art supplies, paid off a fraction of his arrears in rent, and then made the rounds of his fellow artists. Starting with a neighbor, Jharge Roln, he poked his head through the open door, said, "I just dropped in to pay you the five dons I owe you," and tossed him a coin.

Roln caught it and stared at him blankly. "You don't owe me five dons."

"Haven't I ever borrowed five dons from you?"

Roln shook his head.

"Well. *Someone* must owe you five dons. Consider it repaid. I've borrowed from so many I can't remember them all, so I'm paying back five dons to everyone I meet as long as the money lasts."

When Milfro was contentedly broke again he made his way upstreet to a cavernous bistro called The Closed Door because at one time in its ramshackle history it had none. It was a favorite gathering place for artists, who had their own private annex, and there Milfro occupied the chair of honor.

He had earned that distinction several years before, when the caterer had incautiously permitted him to do a painting in payment of a long-overdue adde bill. He astutely performed the painting during the caterer's absence, and he painted the thing on the wall so that it could not be rejected. He portrayed himself, in the armored costume of a warrior of another world and time, mounted on a stampeding wrranel and pursuing a terrified tourist with a paint sprayer. What the caterer thought of this was never recorded. The other artists delightedly took turns in adding themselves, variously costumed but always on wrranels and armed with artistic impedimenta; or in contributing to the crowd of panicky tourists prize specimens that had aroused their ire during their visits to the Plai. The painting expanded in both directions and became a vast, panoramic mural.

The mural's fame grew. Tourists began to trudge up the hill for a look at it. They found the walk as healthful and stimulating as the mineral baths, and they came again—and again. The caterer's business expanded almost beyond his credibility. He did not overlook the source of his prosperity, however; when the enormous main room became so crowded with tourists that there was no place for the artists, he added the annex, reserved it for artists only, and served food and adde at cost—which inspired the artists to continue and expand the mural. At both ends of the room it turned corners, turned again, and met in the center of the opposite wall where a crowd of angry tourists was shown pursuing wrranel-mounted, terrified artists.

A firm dealing in art reproductions heard of the mural and sent a representative. A contract was negotiated, and soon the caterer began receiving royalty warrants. Whenever one arrived, he chalked up the amount in the artists' annex and served free food and adde until it was exhausted. His competitors did not complain; the number of tourists taking daily walks up to the artists' colony had enhanced everyone's profits.

As for the man who started it all, Gof Milfro had his seat of honor and, like the others, free food and adde whenever there was a royalty warrant. Otherwise he borrowed and begged and had an unexpectedly rare windfall when a tourist paid him a pittance for a painting that had required a month's work. Somehow he survived and continued to work tirelessly—ragged, hungry, uncomfortable, but for all that indomitably cheerful and irrepressibly optimistic. He was an artist.

On this day, despite his pleasure in distributing the Harnasharn largess, he was a worried artist. As he took his seat of honor at the end of the long table, he asked, "Is there any news from Sornor?" He got no answer, so he raised his voice and asked again. Other than a momentary lapse in the conversation, the only response came from a young artist who called, "What's with Sornor?"

"I'm worried about Franff," Milfro said.

"Who's Franff?"

"More of an artist than you'll ever be."

"Oh—that animal."

"Animaloid!" Milfro snapped. "Which by definition is what you probably think you are, an intelligent animal."

He was prepared to enlarge upon that, but an altercation at the door caught his attention. A woman in tourist costume was attempting to enter, and a waiter firmly blocked her way. "Artists only, ma'am."

"I only wanted to speak with Mr. Milfro," she said.

Milfro got to his feet. "Yes? Oh, it's you."

The waiter moved aside, and she stepped into the annex, a tall, dark woman of flashing eyes, appealing smile, and indeterminate age. She looked about curiously and exclaimed, "No murals? It's very generous of you artists to beautify the building for others before you do it for yourselves."

"Just because we're artists doesn't mean we like art," Milfro growled. "Did you get to see it?"

"Yes. For two uninterrupted hours! I'm on my way back to Donov Metro, and I wanted to thank you before I leave."

Milfro removed his turban, bowed slightly, and said, "You're entirely welcome—I don't remember your name."

"Mora Seerl." She spoke to the other artists. "I'm a visiting critic from Adjus. This is my sabbatical year, and I'm studying at the Institute and visiting as many of the art colonies as possible. I wanted to do a detailed study of your mural, but every time I came here the place was so crowded I couldn't get near it. Finally I told Mr. Milfro about the trouble I was having, and he spoke to the caterer, and the caterer let me come in after closing."

"Best caterer in the universe,' Milfro murmured. "What'd you think of the mural?"

"It's charming! I haven't seen so many portraits in one place since I arrived on Donov. I had the impression that Donovian artists don't know how to paint portraits. Several of your tourists are priceless, and of course the whole concept is absolutely ingenius. Unfortunately, all of that wall space, and all of that paint, and the tremendous amount of effort and skill involved in applying it, are aimed at showing pictorially the two types that among all the people of Donov are the most utterly lacking in pictorial qualities—artists and tourists."

She thanked Milfro again, delivered a smile of farewell that embraced everyone in the room, and rushed away. Milfro resumed his chair. "An artist can't even have a joke," he announced disgustedly, "without some stupid critic trying to take it seriously."

Jharge Roln had come in and seated himself at the far end of the table. He called to Milfro, "About Franff—"

"What about him?"

"Know an artist named Orn Evar?"

Milfro nodded.

"I hear he has some kind of a connection with one of the riot worlds. I don't know which one, but it might be Sornor."

"Thanks," Milfro said. "I'll go see him now."

The ramshackle dwelling where Evar lived was the spiritual sibling of every other ramshackle dwelling in the colony. Milfro clumped up three flights of creaking stairs to the attic, where Evar enjoyed the unusual luxury of private quarters and even had a weatherproof skylight improvised out of a hole in the roof.

The door was ajar. Evar sat morosely in front of an easel, tears streaking his face. Milfro stepped into the room and stared at the painting on the easel.

"What's *that?*"

"A *fvronut,*" Evar blubbered.

"Of course it is. What's a fvronut?"

"Animaloid on Stovii."

"Oh." Milfro regarded the painting with interest. "Really,

that's nicely done. That's quite the best thing you've ever done. You might be very good at portraits. I doubt that there's a market for this one, though—not many tourists would want a painting of a hideous, earless, long-snouted, toothless, leather-skinned—"

"It's not hideous!" Evar shouted hotly.

"It's not? Excuse me, of course it's not. Beauty in the eye of the beholder, ugliness likewise. It really is the best thing you've done."

"It's the most beautiful creature I've ever known," Evar said, blubbering again. "It's more than my equal, or yours, and it saved my life. If it's ugly in the painting that's my fault. I wasn't—" He sniffed. "I wasn't equal to the subject. Now it's dead. The riots. I just heard."

"But it isn't," Milfro said. "You have the painting, you have your memories—"

"No. It's dead."

"Look. I have an animaloid friend on Sornor. Franff. The best friend any young artist ever had and a great artist himself. The situation on Stovii couldn't be worse than that on Sornor. I'm afraid Franff has been killed, but he's not dead. He'll live as long as he's remembered, and no one who knew him will ever forget him."

Evar sniffed again. "If you don't mind—"

"Sure thing," Milfro said. "Sorry to have bothered you. I'll close the door."

He did, and then he opened it. "Say—if that fvronut was better than either of us, and beautiful besides, and saved your life—why do you keep calling it 'it'?'"

He closed the door again, very gently, leaving Evar staring after him.

A sheaf of riot reports arrived from M'Don, and Neal Wargen, the World Manager's First Secretary, had planned on devoting a full day to them. Instead he found himself sourly contemplating a call for help from a precinct police commander. A smuggler was leaving a glittering trail of illegal jewelry across an inland province of the southern continent.

Wargen controlled his temper and asked for a data report on *persons—missing and surplus*. On his way to the port he read the tabulated facts concerning everyone on the world of Donov known to be where he wasn't expected or known not to be where he was expected, and the sad tale of a tourist missing from a chartered tour group caught his attention. On a world specializing in tourists and vacationers, a lost tourist represented an affront to the national honor, but a smuggler eager to put distance between himself and customs officials might not be aware of that.

Wargen caught the next rocket to Port Ornal, the southern continent's spaceport, where he picked up the file on the missing tourist. From there he flew to the precinct capital, and a few inquiries in the role of an importer looking for outlets for hand-fashioned trinkets quickly satisfied him that the smuggler was still in the hinterland. He followed his trail posing as a tourist shopping for distinctive presents for his aging mother on the world of Lycol.

Outsiders frequently erred in assuming that fortunes could be reaped in smuggled jewelry on a mineral-poor world where jewelry was inordinately expensive. The frugal Donovians mostly regarded such trinkets as something to be sold to tourists. They rarely purchased any, and those who did, and who wore the jewelry, were talked about. The missing tourist's trail was as easy to follow as a wrranel stampede.

By midafternoon Wargen had caught up with the culprit, a shabby little peddler who had somehow maneuvered false-bottom luggage through customs. Wargen dispatched an anonymous tip to the local police, waited unobtrusively until he saw the peddler arrested and his satchel confiscated as evidence, and hurried back to Port Ornal. He returned to Donov Metro on the late afternoon rocket, stopped at his office to dictate a report, and finally reached home two hours late.

The Wargen mansion stood at the head of a small valley, and Wargen daily blessed his grandfather for having had the foresight to buy the surrounding steep hills; otherwise, their stark majesty long since would have been smeared with some alien world's cockeyed architecture. The huge castellated building was one of the worst examples of alien excesses on Donov, but the view from within was superb. The valley mouth opened like a vast window on a breathtaking panorama of Donov Metro.

On this evening his enjoyment of the prospect was brief. His mother greeted him coolly and asked, "How could you! On Ronony's rev night!"

Wargen groaned. "End of the month reports, you know. I wasn't paying any attention to the time."

"I don't believe it. I don't believe you can sit all day in that stuffy little office and not pay attention to the time. Go and get dressed."

Wargen groaned again. "Long trousers and sleeves, I suppose. It's enough to make a man go asteroid hunting."

"You *know* you'll enjoy it when you get there. And by the way, if that little Korak minx is there—"

"Charming child, isn't she? What about her?"

"Nothing, Pet. Hurry and get dressed."

Wargen grumblingly permitted himself to be rushed into rev dress and swept off to Ronony Gynth's, and he continued to grumble until the moment Ronony's steward stepped forward to greet them. In actual fact he was more eager to attend than his mother was, but it would not have done at all to have her suspect that.

All of Donov had heard of Ronony Gynth, the mystery woman. Few had ever seen her, and fewer still were aware that she headed the world's largest and most active group of spies. Wargen was an ardent admirer of her work while at the same time taking great pains to ensure that she knew nothing of his, had no inkling at all that the charming World Manager's First Secretary was much more than he seemed—was in fact the head of Donov's Secret Police.

Not even Wargen's mother knew that.

★ 3 ★

Lights wreathed the fabulous hilltop mansion, and Ronony
Gynth's guests, brilliantly cloaked, immaculately garmented,
glitteringly adorned, filed into the enormous, gold-festooned
rev room, where the steward announced them with the
mellifluous tones of a trained melodist.

The guest of honor, the newly arrived ambassador from
Mestil, His Emissary the Grandee Halu Norrt, sat on
Ronony's private balcony with his wife and staff and studied
the clustering and drifting and eddying throng with intense
interest. Ronony sat nearby, artfully concealed by shadows.
Rumor had it that she was an invalid, that she suffered a
disfiguring disease, that she was grotesquely fat and disgustingly lazy. Whatever the cause, none of her guests had ever
met her. She never accepted invitations, and she attended her
own revs only as a secluded spectator.

She pushed her earpiece aside and touched the ambassador's arm. "The young man near the entrance—that's Neal
Wargen, the World Manager's First Secretary."

"Ah! The Count Wargen! And the lady?"

"The countess, his mother. He's a full citizen of Donov, as
was his father, and the fact that he's Korak's First Secretary
is vastly more important here than his being a registered and
certified count somewhere else. All the best people call him
'Count,' though. See the girl who's watching him? That's
Eritha Korak, the World Manager's granddaughter. She has
a mad crush on him, much to his mother's disgust. The
Koraks have always been commoners, wherever they've been,
and they have no status at all."

"But on this world, where there is no official nobility, isn't
the World Manager rather beyond status?"

Ronony snorted. "World managers are merely civil servants with exaggerated responsibilities. On Donov—oh, all
right, beyond status, but that doesn't make the people want
to have anything to do with him socially. Or with her."

"He serves the people of Donov, not you carpetbagging
interlopers and vacationers from other worlds," the ambassa-

dor said lightly. "How many citizens of Donov do you number among those 'right people?' "

Ronony did not answer. A few late-comers swept through the entrance, and her portly steward stepped forward to greet them. She picked up her earpiece and turned a dial on the console at her elbow. The steward announced the new guests and turned them adrift, and a gathering wave of servants pounced on them to offer food and beverages.

Again Ronony pushed the earpiece aside. "There are complaints because there's no reception line. People had counted on meeting you."

"I'm tired of answering questions about those poor animals," the ambassador growled. "And how would I know what's causing the riots? I haven't been home for nine years. Don't they realize that an assignment to a vacation world is supposed to mean a well-earned vacation?"

Ronony said soberly, "I do hope the rioting is finished. Fortunately the onus is spread somewhat because so many worlds are involved, but even so—couldn't there have been controls on the news media to stop this daily agitation?"

"The situation developed so rapidly that it took everyone by surprise, at which point it was already too late to impose control. The Lord Censor probably felt that the resultant rumors would be more harmful than the facts."

"What *is* causing the riots?"

"If I knew, or if I had any notion of a remedy, I'd be on Mestil instead of here. It's a nasty dilemma, and I can't begin to understand it. Everyone knows that our animaloids are invaluable, and still our subjects riot against them. I'm only grateful that I don't have the responsibility for solving the problem." He leaned forward and changed the subject. "Very pretty. A splendid party. But—no music? No dancing?"

Ronony smiled. "Music has an unfortunate tendency to cover up conversation."

"Ah! And you do this every month, and yet your guests have never seen you. Amazing!"

"I could have twice this attendance, but by limiting the invitations I make them that much more prized."

"And you actually obtain all that vital intelligence at these revs?"

"Occasionally I obtain vital information here, but I always overhear a great deal of careless conversation that can lead to important information if used properly. My organization uses it properly."

"Remarkable! Donov is such an *insignificant* world."

"A silly world. It has no army, only the one space cruiser its membership in the Federation requires, and not even an effective police force. It doesn't threaten anyone and it has nothing that anyone would want. I have fat dossiers on at least a dozen high Donovian officials and politicians, I could blackmail them easily, but why bother? No, our operation is valuable for precisely that reason. Donov is unimportant, everyone relaxes here, and people who relax tend to become careless—and that applies to the diplomatic staffs as well as to important government officials and the prominent people who vacation here."

"I'll take every precaution to keep my staff from becoming relaxed," the ambassador promised. "And—no one even suspects?"

"Of course not. I have to use unpowered pickups—there are people who carry detectors as a matter of course, even on Donov, and one beep would shatter everything I've accomplished. That means I can't cover the center of the room unless I contrive some kind of low-hanging decorations, but most of the confidential talk takes place along walls or in corners."

"But you only listen in on a small part of it."

"All of it is recorded and studied later. Occasionally I'm able to monitor something vital that requires immediate action. For example—did you know that someone on Mestil has been smuggling out filmstrips of the rioting?"

"*What?*"

"A Donovian importer named Colyff has somehow obtained copies. I've been listening to his conversation as much as possible. He's inviting his friends to see them."

The ambassador scrambled to his feet. "I must let the First Lord know at once. Do you realize—"

"Fully. I've already sent a message, and I'm taking steps to obtain the filmstrips. Please sit down, you're attracting attention." She leaned forward. "There's someone I don't know. Did you catch the name, Carlon?"

"No, ma'am." The servant, who had been hovering discreetly behind her chair, hurried away. A short time later he returned. "His name is Jaward Jorno, ma'am. He is escorting the Dame Lilya Vaan."

"Strange. I've never heard of him."

"I understood that he has not been in Donov Metro for many years."

"See what you can find out about him." She turned to the ambassador. "Watch the little Korak girl. She's still trying to summon courage to speak with Count Wargen. Sometimes I regret that I have to collect information. It would be so amusing just to be able to watch."

The Countess Wargen had the rare gift of being at her regally impressive best in a crowd. She swept forward on her son's arm, and the milling revelers magically parted before them. They moved so easily that Lilya Vaan, attempting to intercept them, was left far behind. Wargen whispered to his mother, and they turned and waited.

Lilya pushed through to them and breathlessly introduced her escort. "Jaward Jorno, the Countess Wargen and her son, the count."

Jorno cocked his head alertly as his wrist touched Wargen's "Wargen? Wargen? Say, aren't you—"

"The World Manager's First Secretary," Lilya purred. She knew better than to keep the countess standing in the center of a room, so she drew Jorno back, they exchanged pleasantries, and the Wargens swept away. As Wargen continued to make polite responses to those he met, he searched his memory. To his certain knowledge Jaward Jorno had not been in Donov Metro for years, not officially and publicly. Wargen wondered what he was up to.

He seated his mother in the terraced conservatory off the main rev room and stepped back as a line of servants formed. One rolled up a serving tray, the others deftly filled it as they moved past, and with a disapproving scowl the countess found herself contemplating one of Ronony Gynth's sumptuous dinners. She loved to eat, but she despised the lozenges that inevitably followed overindulgence. She asked, "Aren't you hungry, Pet?"

"I'll have something later," Wargen said. He excused himself and left his mother pondering her tray of food amidst the lavish conservatory greenery.

As he returned to the rev room a hand plucked at his sleeve. "You're a liar!"

"You're a fiend," Wargen answered calmly.

Eritha Korak met his eyes sternly and pouted. She was small, attractive without being pretty, and possessed of an inner radiance and a mind and spirit wholly alien to the self-indulgent society of these expatriate or visiting millionaires and noblemen. At the age of ten she had debated foreign policy with full fledged ambassadors, and at the age of fifteen her private tutors confessed that she had completed all the university courses they were qualified to teach. She had found no new worlds to conquer since then. Society did not know what to make of her. As the World Manager's granddaughter she was entitled to certain social concessions, but she had very little wealth and seemed uninterested in men despite the fact that men of all ages found her fascinating. The young women of her acquaintance hated her thoroughly.

"You promised to speak with Grandpapa," she said accusingly.

"And I did speak with him," Wargen assured her. "I did and I do. I speak with him almost every day."

"About me?"

"I never promised to speak with him about you. I merely promised to speak with him."

"You—you *fraud* you!"

"However, I did chance to mention this strange passion of yours for a career in art. He was opposed to it."

"Was and is," she said bitterly. "He says I have no talent. His eyes are so bad that he can't make out shapes at all, and yet he says—"

"Have you?"

"Talent? No."

"Then why do you want to study art?"

"Because I like it. Because I want to know something about it, and the only way to really understand a painting is to take one's own hand and—" She looked back. "Your mother is glaring at me."

"That's because she thinks you're a minx."

They walked away side by side. "I am a minx," Eritha said. "I'm also a very bad artist. I've flunked the entrance exams to every accredited art school on Donov, and the non-accredited ones don't want me either. They're afraid I'll exhibit my work as evidence of their inept teaching, but I wouldn't. So I'll have to go to one of the colonies and learn by doing, and Grandpapa says if I do he'll cut off my allowance. Do you think he really would?"

"I'll guarantee it."

"That's what I thought. Why is it that if I stay at home and fritter away my time I'm considered respectable if not actually meritorious, and if I try to learn something that will enrich my outlook on life I'm a wanton?"

"The problem," Wargen said, "is that most of the non-artists on Donov hate art, and all of them hate artists. You can't associate with artists without having some of that rub off on you."

"But—Grandpapa?"

"He's responsible for Donov being an art center, and there must be moments when his conscience is restless about that. In your case, though, he just objects to anyone wasting his time. Did you know he once was an art student himself?"

"No!"

Wargen nodded gravely. "He discovered that he had no talent, so he dropped it—just like that—and studied government." He touched her arm, and they moved toward the

33

center of the room. "To him, the most pathetic figure in modern society is the person who neglects his talents while trying to exercise talents he does not have. It's a double waste." He dropped his voice. "You have undeniable talent as a minx. Why don't you exercise it and find out what Jaward Jorno is doing in Donov Metro?"

Instantly she turned aside, but—talented minx that she was—she did not head for Jorno but moved in the opposite direction. Wargen turned his attention to the other guests, smiling, touching wrists, pausing now and then for a brief conversation, but even while murmuring social inanities he managed to listen attentively to the conversations around him. When he heard a woman's voice remark, "Gerald Gwyll—that's Harnasharn's assistant—was in Zrilund last week," he turned abruptly. The vision of a representative of the most famous art gallery in the galaxy among what easily could have been the worst artists in the universe gave pause. Wargen was instantly curious as to what Gwyll had been doing in Zrilund.

He recognized the speaker, a portly matron whose enthusiasm for art was exceeded only by her abysmally bad taste. His sudden attention momentarily flustered her, but he favored her with his most disarming smile and asked politely, "How are things in Zrilund?"

"Gerry says the place is falling apart, but the fountain is beautiful as ever. I don't know if I should go back for one last look at the old scenes or if I might find the experience crushing. It used to be so charming."

"The saddest words of tongue or pen," Wargen murmured. "It used to be or it might have been." The woman tittered. "I understand there's still quite an art colony there. Even falling apart, Zrilund has the best light on Donov—which is saying a great deal."

"Art colony, hell!" the matron exploded. "It's just a tourist trap. There hasn't been a decent artist working there for years."

"It's really not fair to say that," Wargen observed thoughtfully. The fact that Gwyll had talked about his trip to Zrilund without mentioning any artists made the situation preposterous. Harnasharn wouldn't send an employee all the way to Zrilund without an extremely good reason, and if a particular Zrilund artist were involved, Gwyll would have been promoting him at every opportunity. "The younger artists travel about a great deal," Wargen went on, "and probably all of them want one shot at Zrilund if only because of the light and all that hoary tradition. And as you say, the fountain is as beautiful as ever."

34

The bystanders were listening respectfully. "Maybe that's where Harnasharn got the paintings for this anonymous exhibit that he's scheduled," a man suggested.

"No!" The matron tittered again, and the man flushed. "No Zrilund artist would consent to being exhibited anonymously. You're sure about that? Anonymous exhibit? Well, really!"

Wargen excused himself with a polite smile and moved on, filing a mental reminder to have a look at the exhibit. Eyes followed him, conversation faltered as he approached and welled up behind him, and revelers maneuvered to place themselves where he might notice them. The Count Neal Wargen was a prize for any hostess's guest list. His presence assured the eager attendance of prominent families with marriageable daughters, of businessmen and politicians who wanted a favor from the World Manager or thought that in the future they might want one, and of a large group of people who merely liked Wargen and enjoyed his company. Wargen knew all of this and bore his burden cheerfully.

A friend intercepted him—Emrys Colyff, who stood with a small group of men talking in conspiratorial undertones. He spoke introductions, and Wargen touched wrists politely while memorizing names and faces.

"Has the W.M. been giving any thought to the effect these riots might have on Donov?" Colyff asked.

"I haven't heard him mention it," Wargen said, "but I'd be surprised if he's been thinking about anything else."

"I've got ahold of some filmstrips of the Mestil riots— never mind how. Can the W.M. see well enough to make use of them?"

Wargen shook his head. "He'd ask someone to look and then tell him about them."

"He can hear, can't he?" one of the men asked. "Just hearing those things would be the most shattering experience of his lifetime. Hearing *and* seeing—"

Colyff nodded soberly. "If I get them to you, will you see that the W.M. hears them and has someone describe them to him?"

"Certainly. If possible I'll do it myself."

"I'm worried," Colyff said. "This is going to be bad for business—in times of trouble people tend to stay home and look after their own interests—but there's more than that at stake. I'm worried that this madness might spread here. I know we haven't any animaloids for anyone to blow his top about, but I can't help thinking—madness finds its own object, doesn't it? We have a lovely world here. I'd like to keep it that way."

35

"Send me the strips," Wargen said. "I'll do what I can."

As he turned away someone firmly barred his path: Jaward Jorno, slender, superbly conditioned, outstandingly elegant even in that vast room of elegance, handsome, so youthful in appearance that Wargen, who knew his age, found himself doubting it.

Jorno murmured, "Count Wargen? I'd like to ask you a favor."

"Please do," Wargen said with a smile. It happened a minimum dozen times at every rev.

"Do you have any influence with your boss?"

"I can—sometimes—influence the order in which his mail is read to him."

"I need to see him. Tomorrow. It's urgent. That's why I came to the Metro. I spent the whole dratted afternoon at the Cirque and couldn't get past the first receptionist."

"What did you want to see him about?"

"A private matter."

"Is that what you told the receptionist?"

Jorno nodded.

"Then you'll never see him. He thinks of himself as a *public* official, and he's pleased to discuss public business with almost anyone, at almost any time. He considers private business none of his business."

"I see."

"I'd suggest that you draw up a memo demonstrating how your private business touches the public interest."

"If I gave you such a memo, would you see that it reaches him?"

"Certainly. That's my job."

"Thank you. I'll consider it." He turned away, paused, looked at Wargen again. "It *is* a public matter, you see, but I'm not certain whom the public might be."

Jorno moved off, and Lilya Vaan pounced on Wargen. Big, overbearing, too often vulgarly loud, flamboyant in appearance, her first rev on Donov would have been her last had she not been giving it herself. But her magnificent home had the most fabulous rev facilities in Donov Metro—each level of the enormous building had its own rev room, and they flowed together by way of cascading ramps. To this she added vast wealth and a peerless gall in bagging prominent guests and celebrated entertainers. Her invitations were even more prized than those of Ronony Gynth. Behind her formidable façade, Wargen found her touchingly shy, generous, and kindhearted.

"Look," she said. "My cousin Telka is after me to twist your arm."

"She wants to see the W.M. on private business?"

"Nope. She wants you and your mother at her next rev."

"If I'm free I'll be delighted to attend. As for Mother, I seem to recall some kind of unfortunate accident—"

"You *seem* to recall?"

They stared at each other and then burst into laughter. Years before, at one of Telka's famous seafood revs, the countess had been served a cup of govo chowder that on close examination proved to contain one live govo. Since such a thing was physically impossible—no govo could survive its conversion into chowder—the countess instantly concluded that it had reached her chowder cup aided by someone's malicious intent. Rage was beneath her dignity, but no Wargen would properly ignore such an insult. She summoned Telka and sweetly apologized for arriving before the food was cooked, and then she remained for the entire rev—she was the last to leave—and periodically during the evening she asked if her chowder was ready to eat yet, and when it was brought to her she scrutinized it elaborately and pretended that the govon were still alive. Telka, reduced to tears, fled her own rev long before it was over, and the countess had ignored her invitations ever since.

"Perhaps between the two of us—is she by chance serving govon?" Wargen asked.

Lilya patted his arm. "She wouldn't dare!"

A food bar rolled past. Wargen sniffed deeply and remembered that he hadn't eaten since morning. He found an unoccupied chair at the center of the room, signaled, and a moment later was savoring Ronony's famous spun salad. Passersby ignored him—the right to eat undisturbed in the midst of a rev was a foundation stone of Donovian etiquette—and in his concentration on the food he did not at first hear Eritha guardedly calling to him. She stood a short distance away with her back turned.

"He came to Donov Metro," she said disgustedly, when she finally caught his attention, "for the aesthetic pleasure of viewing beautiful women such as I."

Wargen waited until the next passersby had moved on. "It might be interesting to know whom he talks with while he views those beautiful women," he said softly.

"If you were polite, you'd say, 'such as you.' "

A short time later he saw her join a group of women on the balcony, where she had a sweeping view of the entire room—as did Ronony Gynth on her private balcony opposite, but Wargen did not look in that direction.

He satisfied his hunger and resumed his circuit of the room, greeting friends and listening, listening. . . .

"I'd hoped to have a few words with the guest of honor. Why is he hiding?"

"To avoid having to answer questions. Why else? Those poor animals—"

"I don't know. Here on Donov we can't really appreciate their point of view. I mean, what can you do with an animal that talks back and demands equal rights?"

"Isn't that the Count Wargen?"

Wargen turned, smiled, moved on.

An old university friend captured him for introductions and demanded, "Still on that humdrum government job?"

"Still on it."

"Well, the offer's still open. Any time you want a position that's both interesting and profitable—"

"But I don't need the money," Wargen smiled. "I come from a long line of bandits who accumulated vast fortunes at the expense of the public on several worlds, so I feel that I owe something in return."

"You're giving your time in return for the public money your ancestors misappropriated?"

"Not exactly. On this world, anyway, I'm merely trying to make it difficult for anyone else's ancestors to misappropriate public money."

His friend considered that with a frown. "I say—that's not really sporting, is it?"

Amidst the ensuing laughter someone proposed a toast to Count Wargen, which he acknowledged gravely before excusing himself. He had seen Jaward Jorno in close conversation with a member of the World Quorum. He passed by without seeming to notice them, but Jorno noticed him and fell silent as he approached. Ronony's steward was diplomatically moving the guests toward the terrace. "The finest lumeno player in the galaxy," he chanted. "Never before seen on Donov. Take your places, please. The finest lumeno player—"

A huge lumeno console was in position, the virtuoso waiting patiently, and as Wargen stepped onto the terrace for a closer look at the instrument, the warming up exercises began. The virtuoso rippled his fingers over the keyboards, and color patterns surged back and forth across the dark valley below.

Lilya Vaan moved to Wargen's side. "It's Sorlin," she said enviously. "He really is the best. I had no idea he was available. He has the largest lumeno console ever seen on Donov, and he says he's never had a better place for an exhibition. He's been a week setting the lights. I wonder how Ronony happened to get him. Are you staying?"

"I'll see how Mother is feeling."

He turned toward the conservatory, and along the way he was intercepted by Eritha Korak. "Medil Favic," she said. "The attorney. He's going around looking for World Quorum members, and when he corners one he gives Jorno a signal and Jorno comes and takes over the conversation. He's talked with seven of them. Anyone trying to find out what they're talking about is in danger of being trampled, because at least six of Ronony's goons are doing the same. Will you have another try with Grandpapa? About the art?"

"Then you'd be leaving Donov Metro," Wargen said. "I couldn't get along without you."

"Cad!" she muttered and flounced away.

The countess was standing when Wargen reached her. "A new lumeno virtuoso," he told her. "Ronony imported him just for tonight. He has the largest console ever seen on Donov, and Lilya is beside herself with envy. Shall we have a look?"

They were walking toward the terrace, and the valley was alive with light as colors blended and exploded and expired in shimmering pulsations.

"I feel rather tired," the countess said. "I really don't think I could sit through it."

Wargen nodded obediently and signaled the steward, who went to call their limousine.

He knew his mother wasn't tired. She had seen him in conversation twice with Erith Korak, and she thought three times in one evening might be dangerous. Murmuring farewells they made their way through the shifting throng and out into the clear, double-mooned Donovian night.

As they passed through the doorway, Wargen casually glanced backward at the shadowed balcony where Ronony Gynth lurked. The Mestillian agent's position was so excellent, her organization so efficient, her technique—not even Wargen knew what she looked like—so flawless, her recording microphones so cunningly placed, that he sometimes felt pained that he could not make use of her himself.

He wondered if she would find out what Jaward Jorno was up to before he did.

Some called the vast World Management Building the Cirque because it was circular; others called it that because they thought the activities there very strongly resembled a circus. The corridors were endless and ornate, the offices mammoth and opulent. Few who enjoyed a formal audience with the World Manager in his plush reception room were aware that he did his work in a small, windowless cubbyhole in the almost inaccessible upper reaches of the building. It was furnished only with an elaborate chair custom-designed to ease the shrunken contours of his aging body, and there he spent most of his working hours—sometimes in solitary thought, but more often in conversation. He could not reach decisions without information, ideas, opinions, so he waited for visitors as a hungry insect waited for prey, ready to pounce on them and suck them dry. It was no coincidence that those who knew the room best referred to it as his lair.

Because of his failing eyesight he could no longer cope with the voluminous paper work that in his younger years had held him captive at his desk. He banished the desk and delegated the work. By occupying the only chair in the room he forced his visitors to stand, which kept interviews gratifyingly to the point and shortened them by a measurable forty per cent, a priceless saving of his diminishing stores of energy.

When his superiors, the members of the World Quorum, sought to reconcile the fact of his advancing age with the phenomenon of his miraculously increasing efficiency, he smiled modestly and did not reply. He submitted his resignation annually; annually it was refused. In a changing universe, every citizen, every world, needed something of permanence. Donov had Ian Korak.

An invaluable adjunct to Korak's failing sight and mobility was the brilliant young chief of his Secret Police. Neal Wargen went everywhere, and he had a gift for observation, a positive instinct for being in places where there was something to observe, and an encyclopedic memory. Much of the information he passed to Korak had little to do with police work. He also had a philosophic turn of mind that Korak found stimulating. While Korak probed Wargen's knowledge, the younger man tested his wisdom.

The private entrance to Korak's lair was by way of an elevator from Wargen's office on the underground level, and through elaborate electronic arrangements the two were in constant communication when Wargen was at the Cirque. It was therefore commonplace for a certain light on Wargen's desk to flash, and for him to respond at once when he was alone.

Korak's dry voice said, "Last week you dictated a memo on the interesting behavior of one Jaward Jorno."

"Yes," Wargen said. "Did I include the information that he left Donov Metro the day after I saw him?"

"You did. Now he's back, and he just handed in a petition endorsed by twenty-five members of the Quorum requesting an interview. Would you like to look on?"

"Certainly."

Wargen activated the screen on the wall opposite his desk, and a moment later he saw Jorno enter the lair. Jorno wore the casual, colorful dress some of the artists affected when they came to the Metro, and he probably was unaware that both his costume and the broad smile he flashed as he bowed were wasted on the World Manager's weak eyesight.

Korak pronounced the name. "Jaward Jorno?"

Jorno bowed again. "I've never liked it, but it's the only name I have."

"One is all an honest man needs," Korak observed.

"At least I have no siblings with blighted reputations to curse my Good Works. Are you interested in Good Works, Excellency?"

Korak smiled. "My own, or other people's?"

"In this case, mine. I'm one of the idle rich, so I dedicate myself to Good Works. You won't know if you've never had the actual experience, but there is something about Good Works, something—"

"There is indeed," Korak conceded. "Which of your Good Works brings you here?"

"I caught a news item about three hundred animaloids who escaped from Mestil in a battered old ship and somehow managed to coax it across space to Tymoff, where they were refused permission to land. They're still in orbit there. Tymoff replenished their air and food—once—and there is talk of giving them a refueling so they can go away. No one on Tymoff has bothered to find a world that will accept them. That's just one ship, Excellency. There may be ten or a hundred carrying other innocent, terrified animaloids in flight

41

from human-inflicted horrors. Has there been no discussion of this problem on a world level?"

Korak shook his head slowly. "I've attempted to discuss those horrors and their causes with the ambassadors of every world concerned. All of them have informed me—quite properly—that these are internal matters not concerning my world and therefore none of my business. As for the terrified refugees, what would there be to discuss? Each world has its own admission requirements. If the Mestil refugees had met those of Tymoff they would have been permitted to land. Obviously they did not, so they'll have to try elsewhere—or return to Mestil."

Jorno said earnestly, "Are you aware, Excellency, of the intelligence, the talent, the capabilities of some of these animaloids? They would be a tremendous asset to any world. On that one ship are a philosopher whose works are in every university library in a dozen sectors, one of the greatest mathematicians in the galaxy, and an inventor whose patents have made a thousand humans wealthy and enriched the lives of uncounted millions. Naturally as animaloids they were not permitted to own their own copyrights or patents. I'd like to wipe that word 'animaloid' from human thought, because it means nothing at all except that there are intelligent creatures who look as freakish to us as we do to them. In their achievements some of them are greater human beings than either of us. I bring you a question: there have been no riots on Donov. Are the people here merely indifferent, or have they compassion for the unfortunate?"

"I've learned to speak for no man's compassion except my own," Korak said quietly.

"I'm a member of a newly formed organization. The Committee for Interplanetary Justice. Our objective is humane treatment for all life forms everywhere."

"I commend you. And I recommend that you begin your operations elsewhere. Donov is a poorly chosen place to start a program of equality among the species, because it has so few."

"We need advice, Excellency. We wish to start a refugee colony on Donov. We petition for your recommendations as to how to proceed and for your support. The committee will furnish all necessary funds and any required financial guarantee for the future."

"Forever?" Korak asked politely.

"I beg your pardon?"

"Someone in the Quorum is certain to ask the question. How many refugees did you have in mind?"

"No specific number. We have no notion as to what

42

problems we might encounter in—ah—removing them from their present worlds. Since they're being murdered on sight, one might suppose that their governments would be pleased to see them go, but we fear that this won't be the case. A hundred, a thousand, ten thousand—we'll raise whatever funds are necessary to support any number available, assuming that we can find a place for them."

"Someone in the Quorum is certain to ask if you're prepared to offer financial guarantees to support them forever. Refugees rarely return to their original homes, even if they're eventually permitted to do so. They'd have to be considered immigrants, and of course Donov's immigration laws would apply."

"We've investigated the immigration laws. They aren't much help."

"Then you should ask your friends in the Quorum to sponsor special legislation."

"That's even less help. Privately endorsing a humanitarian appeal is òne thing. Publicly supporting such a measure in the face of so much turmoil on other worlds would be a different matter. Is there no other way?"

Korak shook his head. "I know of no world manager who owns a magic wand, and if one did he'd hesitate to use it on a problem as complex and uncertain as this one. It's unfortunate."

"It's the worst tragedy in the histories of more than twenty worlds. If you should think of an alternative, Excellency, I, the committee, and humane-thinking people everywhere will thank you."

Korak said slowly, "If I think of an alternative—and it seems to be in the best interest of the people of Donov—I'll let you know."

"And in the meantime those poor creatures—" Jorno broke off and bowed deeply. "Thank you. I'm sure you'll do your best."

As Jorno departed another light flashed on Wargen's desk and he strode to the private elevator. A moment later he was in the lair.

"What do you know about him?" Korak asked.

"Millionaire," Wargen said. "Not a native of Donov."

Korak chuckled. "Do you know any who are?"

Wargen said wonderingly, "I never thought of that. It's true—all of our millionaires, or at least their immediate ancestors, are imports."

The penalty we pay for being the vacation world of the galaxy," Korak murmured. "Continue, please."

"Jorno inherited an enormous fortune. He shuns Metro

43

society, but in the resort circles he frequents he's popular. For a long time he was considered a most desirable catch on the matrimonial front, but none of the delectable baits offered were able to attract him. Some thought this reflected a fondness for bachelorhood, and others felt that since he didn't need money he could afford to hold out for a richer heiress than those available in recent years. Speaking as a wealthy bachelor, this makes no sense to me."

"Nor to me, speaking as an impoverished married man," Korak said. "His occupation? Profession?"

"His profession is law. His father kept him at it until he qualified, but he never practiced it. His occupation is spending his father's money, and all the indications are that he has a splendid talent for that."

"Which tallies with my information precisely. The one thing that does not tally is his 'Good Works.' "

"I didn't investigate that, since I didn't know he had any. Nor does anyone else; at least, no one talks about them. He does spend a great deal of time on other worlds, and it's possible—but wait. He owns an estate on the southern coast. A large chunk of the coast and a string of islands. Undeveloped, all of it, except for an elaborate winter home. Jorno's father considered it a valuable long-term investment, and it'd be excellent resort property right now if it were properly developed and promoted. It's along the eastern edge of the Rinoly Peninsula."

"I know the area."

"Jorno evidently has or had an interest in agriculture. He introduced a new fiber plant there, *tarff*, persuaded farmers to try it, and even financed a marketing organization to handle it."

"I don't recall hearing anything about that," Korak mused. "It's a poor agricultural region. How'd the fiber do?"

"Very well. It thrives in that particular rocky soil. Unfortunately, there's no market for it on Donov. Its processing requires huge amounts of cheap labor. The farmers have accepted quotas, though, and they're growing just enough to export at times of peak demand on other worlds, and it's resulted in small cash incomes for them, which they desperately needed. From their point of view that certainly was a Good Work. Jorno is very popular down there."

"Interesting. What with his importing alien plants and participating in interworld organizations, he must have far-flung contacts."

"He has his own space yacht—Donov registry."

"It's odd that the one group of refugees he mentioned

44

should be from Mestil," Korak observed. "Any new developments there?"

"No, and there won't be any."

"I'm very much afraid we'll have to do something about Ronony Gynth."

"So am I, but I keep hoping that we won't. An elaborate spy organization is amusing to watch, not to mention educational. Of course hidden microphones are one thing and outright acts of burglary are something else. I knew about the filmstrips the day Colyff received them, and I also knew that Ronony would find out that he had them. So I posted a scan on Colyff's home and office, and four of Ronony's best men were caught in the act. Neither she nor the embassy dares to show any interest in them. They think we're rather naïve, but they don't go so far as to consider us fools. As for the refugees—why not accept them on Donov?"

Korak smiled sadly. "The young really can't appreciate man's capacity for hatred."

"I still have the conviction that the riots followed—are following—a plan, but I suppose hatred is as susceptible to manipulation as any other emotion."

"The problem is difficult to comprehend on Donov, because we have no animaloids. The occasional visitor is an object of curiosity rather than animosity. Where animaloids exist in large numbers, humans come to fear them—in some instances with good reason, I might add, but that isn't true of any of the riot worlds. Obviously fear can lead to hatred for no reason at all. The Quorum would certainly refuse to admit them. Have you anything else?"

"Perhaps. According to a news item, one of the animaloids killed in the rioting on Sornor was an artist."

Korak leaned forward. "What artist?"

"He lived on Donov for many years and was quite well known here. He went by the name of Franff. I remember him myself—I saw him when I was a child. He handled the sprayers with his mouth. Attracted crowds wherever he went. He was a rather good artist."

"I missed the news item," Korak said. "Franff was more than a rather good artist—he was one of the celebrities of his day and a friend and companion of a host of immortals. He was more than that, even. He was Franff. He was unique. Several of his paintings are masterpieces. Has there been talk about this?"

"Only among the older artists. He seems to have been a popular character. Are artists more tolerant than other humans?"

"Animaloid artists are rare, and one per generation isn't a

45

fair test. I'll answer that when I've seen their reaction to a thousand. Anything else?"

"I've recently attempted an investigation among artists, and I made no headway at all because I have very few contacts. This reminded me that Eritha wants to study art."

"She merely wants to go off and live like an artist," Korak said disgustedly. "She sees something childishly romantic about it."

"Yes, sir. And because of certain developments I badly need someone who is childishly romantic enough to be willing to live like an artist."

"What sort of developments?"

"Some days ago an animaloid artist was killed in the rioting on Sornor. Yesterday Harnasharn Galleries opened a special exhibit of paintings by an anonymous artist."

"Are you suggesting that there's a connection?" Korak demanded.

"Anonymous exhibitions are extremely rare. There hasn't been one in Donov Metro for at least five years—probably much longer, but five years is as far back as I checked."

"An animaloid artist is killed on Sornor," Korak mused, "and Harnasharn opens an anonymous exhibit. Of that artist's painting?"

"I don't think so."

"Did you see the exhibit?"

"Of course. I consulted the Artists' Index both before and afterward. I'm no art expert, but it doesn't take one to see that Franff's registered work is totally different from the paintings in the special exhibit. He was a visualist, painted precisely what he saw. What an animaloid sees isn't what a human sees, but in Franff's case the differences aren't strange, they're merely charming. The Harnasharn paintings aren't of this universe."

"Indeed. What universe are they of?"

"I couldn't say. Looking at them gives one contradictory sensations—the hauntingly familiar and the completely improbable. It's like arriving in a fantastically strange place that you didn't know existed and having the feeling that you've been there before."

"They must be rather good, or Harnasharn wouldn't exhibit them."

"I'd say they're rather good. They're *finished*. When art falls short of perfection, I have the feeling that the artist either should have stopped sooner or continued until he accomplished whatever it was he was trying to do. A great painting is *finished*. Nothing that doesn't belong, nothing left out. It simply *is*. These paintings *are*. If they have a flaw it's because the paint is applied in a way I never saw before. They look as though they were woven, rather than painted. That may distract only because it takes a bit of getting used to. I rather liked the things."

"I still don't see the connection between Franff's death and this exhibit."

"Maybe there isn't any. I couldn't help wondering about it because these paintings are so different. They could represent a view of the universe never revaled to any human artist. If they *were* done by an animaloid, perhaps when Harnasharn heard about the death of Franff he was discreet enough to exhibit them anonymously."

"That doesn't sound like Harnasharn, but what if he did?"

"Wouldn't it be wise to prepare for trouble just in case the word leaks out and the people of Donov, not to mention the artists, have more animosity than we suspect?"

"Go down to the Licensing Bureau," Korak said. "Find out precisely when Harnasharn licensed this exhibit and how he described it. Then see if you can find the date that news about Franff's death first reached Donov."

Wargen did so and returned with the information that Harnasharn had posted the exhibit as that of an anonymous artist five days before Franff had been declared dead on Sornor and nine days before the news reached Donov. He said sheepishly, "I'm retiring from the field of art criticism."

"No, you're not," Korak told him. "I doubt that you understand it yourself, but you have an instinctive awareness of such things. Never hesitate to pursue it. These riots have been going on for weeks, and even without the death of Franff, an art dealer on Donov might consider them ample reason for exhibiting an animaloid's paintings anonymously. Obviously this exhibit merits our attention."

"I'll keep an eye on it."

"*Our* attention." Resignedly Korak pushed himself to his feet. "How shall we go?"

"As tourists," Wargen said. "A tourist's costume excuses anything."

"Even a blind man attending an art exhibit?" Korak asked, chuckling. "Bring the costumes."

Those who knew world government thought of Korak, not as Donov's manager, but as its creator. He had taken an impoverished, mineral-poor, backward agricultural world and made it one of the leading tourist and vacation centers of the galaxy. He had accomplished this with a stroke of genius of such breath-taking magnitude that few even comprehended how he could have thought of such a thing. Donov had nothing to offer tourists—no facilities, no attractions that were not available in better quantity and quality on dozens of competing worlds, nothing whatsoever of distinction except, in certain regions of its subtropics, a dazzling splendor of light. And what could light possibly mean to a tourist?

For that matter, what could it mean to a world manager?

Few were aware of Korak's guilty secret, that in his misspent youth he had aspired to be an artist. He had, alas, a paucity of talent, and he'd been honest enough and wise enough to recognize that fact early and turn to another profession, but he remained enough of an artist to recognize perfect light when he saw it. As a young man just out of Qwant University, he had come to Donov to be interviewed for the manager's position, and like fifty candidates before him he had been appalled by what he found there.

But he courteously took the inspection tour that had been arranged for him, and he saw that light, the wondrous, inimitable artists' light that flooded the Donovian seacoasts. He accepted a job that no one else wanted and remained a long lifetime.

He had no thought of tourists. He thought only of that glorious light being wasted, and out of his miserable budget and over the indignant protests of a grumbling, miserly World Quorum, he created a dozen fellowships, offering passage money and a starvation subsistence to promising young artists who would agree to work for a year on Donov. He established them in a picturesque old fishing village on the Zrilund cliffs and told them to paint, and when their first work was shipped off to agents on other worlds it created a sensation. The deluge of artists followed, tourists began to make pilgrimages to the scenes immortalized in paint, and from that point any shrewd world manager could have exploited the situation and Korak was shrewder than most. In a single generation Donov became one of the leading art centers of the galaxy and Korak had begun the extensive development of resort hotels and vacation centers—on beaches, in the mountains, even in Donov's diminutive deserts—that would eventually give the tourist trade a foundation solid enough for it to survive even when the tourists became jaded with the glories of Donovian art.

The world prospered on the lavish exchange provided by tourists and vacationers, millionaires came in droves to establish vacation homes, natives left their impoverished agricultural holdings and received fantastic salaries as servants, cooks, chauffeurs, and guides. Many saved their money and established their own resorts or devised a flood of novel attractions to please the tourists and enable them to spend

48

their money. To the native Donovians, the only blight on all of this prosperity was the presence of the untidy, undisciplined artists whose predecessors had started it all, but as long as Donov had perfect light and Ian Korak as world manager, it would have great art colonies.

Korak's only regrets were that the afflictions of age denied him enjoyment of the new generation of artists, and that he could no longer experience the pulse-quickening pleasure of gazing at Donov's glowing landscapes and seascapes under a perfect artists' light.

Wargen brought the costumes—hats with huge flopping brims and half-length cloaks, all in a mélange of gaudy colors. Donovian peasants had once worn hats and cloaks vaguely like them for field work on sunny days. For reasons never fathomed, the tourists made the costume their own, with the inevitable result that the peasants indignantly discarded it. Artists had satirized and caricatured cloaked and hatted tourists mercilessly, but the first act of many tourists was to envelop themselves in this monstrous clothing. It was an excellent costume for long periods of exertion in the sun— which was, of course, the last use to which any tourist would subject it.

A successful tourist trade was not without its price, and some of the expressions once applied to artists—pollution, epidemic, seizure, and so on—were now directed at tourists.

Wargen inspected Korak, gave the wide brim of his hat a crease that concealed his face, and nodded approval. Korak took his arm for support, and they moved toward the private elevator.

The exhibit, Eight Paintings by an Anonymous Artist, had received only the routine publicity announcements and as yet no critical comment, and it was attracting a very modest attendance. Korak found this disappointing. The eight widely spaced paintings held no interest at all for him—he saw them only as blurs in bright ovals of illumination. He wanted to study the reactions of those viewing them.

"Nine," Wargen whispered, looking about the room. "Hualt, the art critic, and his wife. I don't recognize any of the others."

It was a solemn, introspective group of art viewers whom they passed, one or two at a time, as they circled the room. The critic completed his own circuit and started another. Passing him, Korak remarked in subdued tremolo, "It's *something*, but surely they don't call it art!" Hualt paid no attention. They continued to circle the room, spectators came and went, and except for a newly arrived woman in tourist costume who asked her companion what possible value a painting could have if it had no people in it, Korak perceived no reaction that he could get a grip on.

"Harnasharn just looked in," Wargen whispered. "He recognized us—he winked at me."

"Let's go see him," Korak said.

Harnasharn had disappeared, but Wargen solemnly informed the receptionist that they wanted to arrange for an appraisal of an early work of Zornillo's, and a moment later the art dealer strode quickly into the room. He stopped short when he saw them, and said, a note of disappointment in his voice, "Come this way, please."

A genuine art dealer, Korak reflected. The owner of a Zornillo was more welcome in his galleries than a world manager.

He led them to his private office, placed a chair for Korak, and proffered another to Wargen, who shook his head and remained standing.

"This is an unexpected honor, Excellency," Harnasharn said.

Korak said wryly, "You mean that the blind don't often come to look at paintings. Neither did I. I came to listen to reactions to paintings, and there don't seem to be any."

"Few of our viewers know what to make of them," Harnasharn said. "Even the critics are bewildered. Hualt has been here four times, and he just left shaking his head. I wouldn't have thought, though, that any kind of public reaction to an art exhibit would be momentous enough to occasion a visit from the World Manager."

"I sincerely hope that you're right. Lester, are those paintings by any chance the work of an animaloid?"

"Do you ask out of curiosity, or is this in some way a matter of governmental concern?"

"It could be a matter of governmental concern."

"I have a solemn pledge to honor, but I'm confident that I can transfer it to the two of you. In strict confidence—yes, the artist of those paintings is animaloid."

"Did you consider that exhibiting them at this time might be risky?"

"Risky!" Harnasharn exclaimed, obviously astonished. "Why would it be risky?"

Korak leaned forward. "It it conceivable that you aren't aware of the unfortunate events on some of our neighboring worlds?"

"I never gave it a thought! Nothing like that has ever happened here."

"Violence on that scale has never happened anywhere, but

it's happening now. What I'd like to know is how you happened to stage this exhibit at this particular time."

"The paintings became available. They're great paintings. Why should I withhold them?"

"I see."

"Do you really think this exhibit could cause trouble?"

"I don't know."

"Do you want me to close it?"

"No. Thus far there hasn't been any talk or—Wargen?—even a hint of a rumor."

"None at all," Wargen said.

"If you closed it there might be. There is, or was, a woman there who made the remark that no painting was valuable if it didn't have people in it. Under the circumstances that's suggestive."

"Will you point her out to me?" Harnasharn asked Wargen. Wargen did so, and Harnasharn spoke with the attendant and then told Korak, "She entered on a second-division student card from the Institute, meaning that she's studying art history or criticism. The Institute has hundreds of such students, and I doubt that anyone takes their opinions seriously. At least, I hope not. Do you want me to find out who she is?"

"No." Korak pushed himself to his feet. "Carry on, keep your mouth shut, and if anything develops or seems to be developing, notify Wargen at once. How much longer does the exhibit have to run?"

"It's posted for a month. Then I'd planned to move the paintings into our permanent exhibit."

"Have you announced that? Don't, then."

"You don't want me to move them—"

"I don't want you to announce it. Plenty of time for that when the exhibit closes."

Harnasharn bowed them out.

"Strange," the World Manager said softly. "Your reasoning was entirely wrong, and yet you arrived at a correct conclusion."

"As I said before, I'm retiring from the business of art criticism."

"Your business is people, and you're as much an expert there as Harnasharn is with art. The question that worries me is whether anyone else is likely to incorrectly reason his way to the same correct conclusion." He paused. "I think it would be an excellent idea if Eritha were to study art. You decide where you want her to go."

clerk gripped, took the shipment order, and deactivated Milfro's turban, swiftly containerized the vast surface that the lobby behind him and then picked his way through conveyed and convectors

✷ 5 ✷

In Donov Metro, capital city of a celebrated world of art, artists in full regalia were paradoxically an uncommon sight. Gof Milfro, face bristling with black whiskers too short to be braided and too long to be curled, untidy turban on his head, a corner of his ragged cloak touching the floor, created a sensation as he marched through the customs office. Waiting claimants scrambled out of his way, clerks and crate handlers gaped, and conveyors suddenly left running without loads clanked and rattled high-pitched protests.

Milfro fixed the nearest clerk in an intense but guileless gaze. "Look, friend. I have a crate of art supplies on that Sornor liner. I have fifty artists waiting for them, and I have a hired transport waiting for me. Every minute of delay wastes fifty minutes of artists' time and costs me money. Would you kindly effect delivery before the paints coagulate?"

The clerk sniffed haughtily. Viewed closeup Milfro was threadbare and distinctly untidy, if not actually dirty, and whatever his status as an artist, it was certain that his contribution to the Central Tax Office was minuscule. The answer came in tones of measured coldness. "My good man, I'm sure that your shipment is being handled as efficiently as possible," The clerk turned away.

Milfro leaned across the narrow counter and gripped his arm. With his other hand he removed his turban. His shaven head, in juxtaposition with his thickly foliaged face, gave him an unexpectedly fierce appearance. The clerk shrank visibly.

"On this world," Milfro proclaimed oracularly, "the word 'efficiently' is used in many contexts, but in none of them does it actually mean 'efficiently.' *Someone* in this office had better understand the word the way I do, or I'm going to remove a clerk's ears and ask them why not." He released the clerk and pointed a finger. "Donov has always represented itself as being hospitable to artists. Are *you* authoring a change in world policy?"

"Why, no, but—"

Milfro leaned forward. "My shipment. *Now!*"

The clerk gulped, took the shipment order, and departed.

Milfro turned, briefly contemplated the vast silence that filled the lobby behind him, and then picked his way through the stunned and motionless claimants and workers. He entered the supervisor's office, marched past the startled receptionist before he could voice a protest, marched past two blankly staring assistant supervisors, and pointed a finger impalingly at the occupant of the large desk at the rear of the room.

"How long," he bellowed, "must an outraged public suffer these crass insults?"

The supervisor, a mild-looking, elderly man, timidly edged his chair backward, his eyes bulging with astonishment.

"I have transport waiting," Milfro continued thunderously. "Hired transport. And I must pay rent while these oafs you call customs clerks pare their nails and discuss each other's sordid domestic entanglements. Bah! Would it please your World Quorum if we artists decided to take our persons, our purchasing power—it isn't much for any one of us, but the aggregate must amount to a sizable sum for a slum world such as this one—the marketing of our paintings, and the tourist trade that depends on us, to some world capable of a grudging appreciation? Do you want to see Donov crumble in economic ruin because *your* subordinates refuse to do their work and *you* spend your days napping behind this desk?"

The supervisor said stiffly, "If you have a complaint—"

"Complaints!" Milfro roared. "Not just one. Complaints. Your clerks are guilty of stupidity, negligence, and fraud. Not to mention ignorance, incompetence, and discourtesy. Do I get my shipment while I still have enough money to pay for the transport, or don't I?"

The supervisor got to his feet. Milfro strode away quickly, making the man trot to keep up with him. They arrived at the clerk's station just as that unfortunate individual rode up with the crate. He shuttled it neatly onto the dock and hopped off the carrier, and Milfro said sarcastically, "My apologies. I thought it arrived on the Sornor liner. I didn't know you'd have to go to Sornor after it."

The supervisor protested, "But the Sornor liner only arrived—"

"I came for my shipment, not a debate." Milfro slammed down the invoice. "Tear it apart and do your dirty work. But I'm warning you—if you ding one capsule of paint or tear one piece of fabric or knock one sprayer out of adjustment—"

The clerk circled the huge crate, broke the seal with trembling fingers, and carefully pried open the inspection

53

panel. Milfro bent over his shoulder breathing disdainful snorts. The supervisor hovered nearby, uncertain as to why he was there and equally uncertain as to whether he should leave. His presence did not soothe the clerk's nervousness.

The shipment consisted of an enormous bale of art fabric with small cases of art supplies packed at one end. The clerk performed the most perfunctory of examinations and snapped the inspection panel into place.

He stamped the invoice. "Your fee—"

"Fee!" Milfro screamed. "The Metro Artists are a registered nonprofit association—you can't imagine how non-profit they are!" He turned on the supervisor. "Don't *any* of your clerks know the regulations? Don't *you* know the regulations? For your information, article seven, paragraph four, under the heading, 'Special Exemptions,' explicitly states—"

The supervisor himself, with hands trembling as violently as those of the clerk, stamped FEE WAIVED on Milfro's invoice and handed it to him. "Sorry to have inconvenienced you," he muttered. The panic-stricken clerk somehow managed to shuttle the crate onto a conveyor. When he finished the supervisor was waiting for him. Milfro calmly turned his back on them and violated a clearly posted regulation by riding the conveyor with his crate.

At the call dock he intimidated a lift operator into depositing the crate gently—*very* gently—into his waiting transport. He climbed in beside the driver, who nodded his red beard approvingly and grinned at him. The driver touched a button, the motor hummed, and they lifted six inches and floated away.

"How'd it go?" Arnen Brance asked.

"Easy. A touch of luck all the way, no mislaid papers, they didn't even have trouble finding the thing, and the clerk gave us a big assist by trying to collect a fee. The supervisor was preparing to dissect him as I left. If he'll just stay out of his office long enough to—what are you dawdling for?"

"This is Donov Metro," Brance announced dryly. "A city. All traffic is patroled, and if one does not observe certain categorical and arbitrary regulations and follow traffic lanes, a referee swoops down from up yonder and asks why not."

"I see. Slowest is quickest."

"Something like that."

"Either way I don't like it. The moment that pup from the Sornorian embassy decides to admit that he's been had, it becomes a question of simple addition and not enough time. I don't suppose the referees pay much attention to those categorical and arbitrary regulations when they pursue customs violators. Do we dare to open it?"

Brance took a deep breath and shook his head.

"Do you realize—"

"Of course!" Brance snapped.

They floated low over the short grass of the throughway, with Milfro turning from time to time for an anxious look behind them.

"If it's referees you're expecting," Brance said finally, "try looking straight up."

"They'll figure we're heading for the city. If we'd found a hangout in the opposite direction we might have gained some time."

"We would have found the police there waiting for us. Wild-looking artists don't normally congregate in quiet suburbs. Those who do can expect to be spied on. Didn't you know Donov has a secret police?"

"No! Donov? What would Donov want with a secret police? If it's ever operated in my neighborhood, it's been invisible."

"Of course it has. If everyone knew when it operated, it wouldn't be secret. The likes of us aren't safe unless we go where everyone else is at least as disreputable as we are."

"We also aren't safe until we get there. There's a bright yellow flier overhead."

"It's a dirty shame," Brance said resignedly. "Just a little longer—"

"*Now* can I open it?"

Brance shook his head. "Even if they catch us we may be able to bluff our way out."

"Then let's get moving."

"Not until we're challenged. There's a chance they won't be able to identify us, and until they do we've got to be the most law-abiding transport in Donov Metro."

"You're sure the com equipment is properly bollixed?"

"The first referee that tries to signal is going to think he needs a refresher course."

A light flashed; a buzzer rasped. Milfro said tensely, "It's your show," and climbed into the rear compartment where he began removing seals and labels. Brance shot the transport into a turning lane and an instant later settled it at street level. He turned, turned again, and they gained a residential section and followed a narrow, winding local service way. Glancing upward, he swore softly. The referee hovered above him, much lower than before.

The light flashed; the buzzer rasped.

Milfro shouted, "Head for the tunnel!"

Brance shook his head. "Our only chance is to play innocent. That will—maybe—keep them uncertain about us and they just might wait long enough. The moment we try to get away, they'll nab us."

"How much longer?" Milfro demanded.

"I don't even know where we are."

They were somewhere in New City, a vast, conglomeratic community of residences for the lower orders. Dreary, multistoried brick buildings lined the street, each huddled against its neighbors in neat, angular dullness. Each had its gleaming power mast and—apparently—its hoards of children, who scattered as Brance approached, mouthing shrill taunts. Milfro snarled back at them from the cargo opening.

The street curved, and an intersection loomed directly ahead. Brance breathed a sigh of relief and humped up to a turning level. For a long moment they floated in a swarm of traffic, Brance anxiously nudging his way from lane to lane to put himself beside, or under, or over, vehicles similar enough to their transport to confuse the referee.

And now he knew where he was. Again he humped up to a turning level and drifted under a large transport traveling the intercity altitude. He made his turn and floated clear, and instantly the light flashed, the buzzer rasped.

"Now there's three of the miscreants," Milfro growled.

"If they'll let us have another five minutes—"

"Do they know we're not receiving their stop signal?"

"Yes, but they may not know what we are receiving."

The flashing and buzzing continued. A yellow flier sank to the level above; Brance calmly slipped under it and matched its speed. Another two minutes passed. Then Milfro swore, and Brance knew without looking that he was boxed. A yellow flier settled in just ahead of him, and behind him another was locked in at the level above waiting for an opening. As the referee ahead of him turned to hand-signal, Brance abruptly shot to a lower turning level and slipped into a side street.

For precious seconds he lost them completely. Now they had a choice between maneuvering to a turning level and following him or returning to patrol altitude and starting over again. Either would take time. He turned, turned again, hoping that none of the referees would make a lucky guess and cut him off. Milfro was purring, "Slick! Slick!" Brance silenced him and told him to keep watch.

Now they were in Old City. In a rural setting, any of these venerable picturesque buildings, with their steep, tiled roofs, leering gables, and gaping courtyards, would have been a charming art subject, but an entire street lined with such edifices overpowered the imagination. Brance had never heard of any artist attempting to paint it.

They turned in at a courtyard, and as Brance maneuvered the transport's cargo door against a building entrance, Milfro sighted a referee drifting overhead.

He swore, and Brance shouted, "Everyone out! We have thirty seconds!"

The courtyard quickly filled with artists. Eager hands lifted the crate onto a weight frame and rolled it away. Another, identical-looking crate was pushed into position behind the transport, and Milfro began attaching labels and seals to it.

A yellow flier settled into the courtyard. Milfro, his task completed, strode forward protestingly. An angry argument ensued, and finally he gestured to Brance.

"This miscreant," he said scornfully, "claims he can make this illegal and outrageous invasion of private property on the basis of Code 21—he claims to have witnessed a violation of the law. Did you break traffic regulations on the way back?"

"Not to my knowledge," Brance said.

"Why didn't you stop on order?" the referee demanded.

"I received no such order."

"Orders were transmitted repeatedly."

"None were received and you know that. Better go home and check your com equipment."

The referee was a young man, obviously uncertain of himself, and as a circle of scowling artists closed in on him, he sought to prop up his waning confidence with bluster. He said stubbornly, "I'm citing you for operating a vehicle without properly functioning communications."

"Just in case you aren't aware of it," Brance said, "regulations make the proprietor of a rented vehicle responsible for its communications. Write that citation on the transport company. All I received was a command to clear for emergency traffic, which I obeyed."

The referee pocketed his citation.

"What violation did you witness?" Brance demanded.

"You were ordered to stop repeatedly."

"No such order was received, and you had no business transmitting one without a violation. What was it?"

"Smuggling."

Brance said incredulously, "You're claiming to have witnessed an act of smuggling?"

"On the basis of information received—"

"You're violating the law, fellow. You've landed that crate illegally on private property. Bust off, or we'll have you at the Hall of Justice in the morning."

"You picked up a customs package on the basis of a false declaration," the referee persisted.

"Let's see your writ."

"One is on the way."

"Glad to hear that—I've always wanted to see one," Brance said with a grin. "Now tell me what law lets you camp on private property because there is, you think, a writ somewhere else."

"I'm guarding that shipment until the writ arrives," the referee said stubbornly.

Brance turned to Milfro. "He's made his accusation before a dozen witnesses. Take his identification and send someone to the district arbiter to file a complaint. In the meantime, we're going to have to open that crate, or some of the boys will miss their Port Ornal connections. If there's anything wrong with the shipment, I'd like to know about it myself. Why don't we let him check the invoice as we unpack—under protest, of course. If he finds anything that isn't listed he can have it."

Milfro turned to the referee. "Is that satisfactory?"

The referee nodded.

Milfro chased a messenger off to the arbiter's office, and then he led the referee to the substitute crate and opened the inspection panel. "Here, you lazy oafs, come and help out!" he called. "His honor will check the invoice, and when we've finished he'll offer to eat it. This box—" He lifted a carton through the panel. "This box is supposed to contain a gross of paint sprayers, sixteen-head size, medium-pressure capacity."

The referee ran a finger down the invoice. "Paint sprayers, sixteen-head size, medium-pressure capacity," he acknowledged. Milfro opened the carton and began to count.

Brance quietly edged away.

He moved along a hallway, took a quick look behind him to make certain that he hadn't been followed, entered a room, looked behind him again, and then pushed aside a wall panel.

He stepped through, and the panel swung shut behind him. In the center of a small, windowless room stood the crate from customs. It had been opened with frantic haste, the sides ripped away, the delicate paint containers and sprayers kicked aside, the bale of fabric slit open.

It was hollow. In the center an animal huddled—seated, after a fashion, on an oxygen tank, its forelegs extended stiffly, its eyes closed, its ears drooping lifelessly, its lustrous fur ruffled and matted. The oxygen mask hung limply over its frothing snout.

"Dead?" Brance demanded hoarsely.

The eyes opened. The creature shook the mask off, took a great, shuddering breath. Its ears jerked, it lurched forward onto its four hoofs and struggled upright. The long neck slowly uncoiled. A husky, whispering, blurred voice asked, "Whose funeral is this? Not mine, I hope."

Brance flung himself forward and embraced the long, silken neck. "Franff!" he sobbed.

Ian Korak assumed the management of a world that had no capital city. The meeting place of the World Quorum shifted according to legislative whim or political manipulation. Shifted along with it were files containing twenty-four expensive surveys of sites that urban engineers had recommended for a world capital, minutes of twenty-four lengthy hearings during which politicians had rejected the sites proposed by the engineers, thirty-seven legislative reports advocating other sites, and thirty-seven expensive engineering surveys proving that any of these would be a disastrous choice.

"Gentlemen," Korak told the Quorum, "the engineers are searching for an ideal location. Donov doesn't have one. You politicians are searching for a location that will please everyone. Donov doesn't have one of those, either. Let me make the choice. It won't be ideal, and it won't please everyone, but at least other worlds will stop referring to Donov as a world where the Quorum stands because there is no seat of government."

The Quorum incautiously gave him the authority that he wanted. He selected and acquired the site for a capital city, and the engineers and politicians immediately stopped arguing among themselves and began raging at Ian Korak. Predictably, the Quorum attempted to veto the choice by withholding funds.

Korak thought the site delightful. There was a broad river with a vast sweep of rolling plain on one side and encroaching, steep hills on the other. There was a deep bay and stretches of contrasting seashore. There was even a freakish little desert in one of the converging valleys. Korak prevented its being irrigated out of existence, and eventually it found owners who liked it the way it was.

Before the first plans were drawn, land values had inflated beyond Korak's most sanguine expectations and almost beyond his belief. Millionaires from neighboring worlds were delighted with the astonishing diversity the site provided and pleased at the prospect of a vacation estate on the doorstep, as it were, of a glittering new world capital. They bid fantastic prices for the hills and valleys across the river, or for choice seashore estates. Korak judiciously sold other parcels only when necessary, taking full advantage of the rampantly inflating values, and he presented the Quorum with a complex of governmental buildings already paid for and retired Donov's longstanding indebtedness as well.

There was a native style of architecture, appropriate to an impoverished world of farmers and ranchers: sturdy, frugal, and uncomplicated; and the first millionaires found it charming and managed to incorporate it into vast mansions. Their followers allowed pride in the worlds of their origins to expand beyond rational limits, and they gathered together into neighborhoods where their new homes flaunted the more objectionable features of the dwellings of their native worlds.

Millionaires from Wrytho, a world of vast, shallow seas and lush, flat islands, settled on the bay, laced their little community with a network of canals, and built their homes on ornate stilts to guard against the floods that had never occurred in all of Donov's recorded history. Those from the mountainous worlds of Skuron and Qwant took to the steep hills with glad cries of recognition and built homes in their native tradition, which seemed to insist that a building with fewer than five steeply ascending levels was best reserved as a stable for servants. Along the seashore the natives of Adjus, a world of raging oceans, ornamented their homes with complicated launching ramps capable of putting a ship safely afloat in the wildest seas, and they actually used these to launch pleasure craft in Donov's quiet waters. Those from the desert world of Minoff claimed Donov Metro's diminutive desert as their own, built stubby towers of cast silicons, imported varieties of desert blooms and killed them off with the lavish amounts of water available from the surrounding hills, and sometimes actually constructed and used their own recycling systems to convert wastes to fresh water.

The millionaires occupied an inordinate amount of space and not infrequently behaved as though their investments in Donovian real estate also gave them a controlling interest in the government, but no one resented them. The lavish homes gave employment to thousands.

The remainder of Donov Metro was a complex of cities separated by belts and chains of parks and throughways: Government City, at the center, was surrounded by Commercial City, with its stores and offices and vast blocks of hostels for visitors and tourists. Old City was made up of buildings Korak had insisted on preserving from the original provincial town on that site, and they contributed a priceless flavor and heritage of the past. Port City included Donov Metro's seaports and spaceports, along with a sprawling complex of service facilities, customs warehouses, and homes for vast numbers of its employees. The seaport was another project Korak brought into being over the protests of the politicians—he thought it silly for an impoverished world to be indulging in the more expensive forms of transportation when money was so much more important than time. There was New City, a regimented arrangement of dwellings where the lower-paid government workers lived, and other cities for other classes, from the moderately well-off to those nabobs who were too snobbish to associate with their fellow millionaires, whom they claimed were snobbish.

This was Donov Metro, which would be Korak Metro the moment Ian Korak was no longer in office to prevent it. Visitors invariably thought it the most unusual city they had ever seen, but it was also the most memorable, with its wild vistas and sea views, its strangely structured mansions perched atop steep hills, its magnificent government buildings in pastel-tinted Donovian marble, its stunning sea cruises and languid river-boat rides, its unequaled art collections. Few who saw it were satisfied to see it only once.

Neal Wargen knew Donov Metro as he knew the top of his own desk—in a sense it *was* his desk top—and he loved all of it and all of the world of Donov. He considered himself the most fortunate of mortals, because he had youth, health, and wealth, and his work permitted him to do the things he most enjoyed, in the places he most loved.

But he did not entirely escape frustrations. M'Don had supplied reports on the rioting and all the supplementary information Wargen requested. Whenever one of his agents returned from a riot world, M'Don sent him to Wargen to deliver an eyewitness report. Wargen posted a large star chart upon one wall of his office, and on this he traced the course of the riots with a color scheme of his own devising, and what emerged was a sinister, coiling star monster that seemed to be positioning itself to strangle the world of Donov.

It was as though a freakish spacial wind had spiraled through that sector of the galaxy, tossing the bitter flame of hatred from world to world. The wind had died down; the rioting was continuing sporadically but was no longer spreading. The pattern that Wargen discerned was the path of the wind, but he was utterly unable to say why, or whence, or how.

In the meantime he had a job to perform, and therein lay his frustration. Instead of pondering cosmic causes and effects, he was forced to devote his full attention to a developing scandal concerning the Sornorian embassy and two obscure and apparently inconsequential artists.

For some days members of the embassy staff had been scanning the artists' activities. An embassy clerk in a small staff van with diplomatic markings followed the artists: a large rented transport crammed with embassy guards followed the clerk. The operation was about as subtle as a tidal wave and flagrantly violated both law and ethics of interplanetary diplomacy.

Wargen never willingly credited anyone with stupidity. He had to assume that the two virtually anonymous artists had somehow achieved, on the peaceful world of Donov, an involvement of such crucial concern to the interests of another world that they had to be interfered with even at the risk of a colossal diplomatic scandal.

Both artists had long-established reputations for impecuniosity, but recently they'd been spending money with reckless indulgence. They traveled, they rented vehicles, they stayed at one of the Metro's more expensive hostels, they sent substantial sums to Sornor to a person who proved to be, on discreet inquiry, nonexistent, and they ordered large quantities of art supplies.

The purchase of art supplies by artists seemed unremarkable until Wargen reflected that the shipment came from Sornor, a most unlikely source. Further, the artists took shipment of the supplies at Port Ornal and immediately transshipped them to Donov Metro, where they were picked up by local artists and taken to a communal artists' dwelling in Old City. Considerable of both time and money could have been saved in buying from a different source and having the supplies shipped directly to Donov Metro.

The shipment had passed customs properly, and the invoice showed nothing remotely suspicious. It was possible that the pair had devised a new smuggling technique, but the world of Sornor would not prod its embassy into frenzied activity because of smuggling on Donov. If it were a question of merchandise *leaving* Sornor illegally, Sornor could have placed a hold through proper channels and requested legal arbitration. It had not done so.

As a final fillip to Wargen's frustration, the artists affected an unsuspecting naïveté that defied comprehension. They seemed to extend themselves to avoid causing the van driver strain or inconvenience. At the same time the thugs in the transport went to ludicrous lengths to simulate an innocent crowd of tourists enjoying the thrilling view of various inconsequential byways through which the artists led them.

Wargen's men followed the transport, the transport followed the van, the van followed the artists, and the artists seemed to be enjoying themselves immensely. If Wargen had been less perplexed about the situation he could have found it hilarious.

That changed in an instant. The artists and their rented transport vanished, having set the van driver up for it so beautifully that he continued straight ahead for a full mile before he realized that he was scanning an empty street. The Sornorians had a dozen vehicles on the scene almost at once, and all of them performed reckless gyrations through an entire quadrant of Donov Metro in search of the artists.

Finally they admitted failure, and a short time later there came an electrifying report from General Police Headquarters. The Sornorian embassy had furnished information on a smuggling conspiracy and provided a detailed description of the artists and their transport. Customs immediately affirmed that one of the described men had claimed a crate of art supplies a short time before, a traffic referee identified the artists' transport on a Metro throughway, and the chase was on.

Wargen requested a copy of the invoice on the art supplies, and while he monitored the pursuit he compared it with the invoice on the previous shipment. The two were identical. He was still pondering this when he received word that all of the Sornorians were headed for Old City at somewhat faster speeds than the law permitted. This meant that the Sornorian embassy was also monitoring the pursuit, which was not illegal but immensely interesting.

By the time the referee had completed the protested inventory of the artists' shipment and flashed a negative report, Wargen had added up his meager accumulation of facts and was grimly contemplating the result. He still had no notion of what Sornor thought the artists were doing, but at least he understood how they had done it.

A short time later Wargen had a visitor—Bron Demron, the portly, graying superintendent of Donov's police. The two men were immensely fond of each other, and because Wargen was generous with the information at his disposal and gave advice only when asked, they got along well. The fiasco Demron's traffic referee had blundered into could have humiliating consequences, and he was asking for advice.

"Referees don't often have to function as police," he said, "but they know the law, and they were told to locate the suspected vehicle and report. One of them thought he'd be a hero, and now I'll have to support him. The fool!"

"It's a problem in depth," Wargen said.

"Ah!" Demron pulled up a chair and waited expectantly.

Wargen described the week-long behavior of the Sornorians. "They expected the artists to lead them to whatever it is they want, and they intended to take it from them by force. When the artists gave them the slip, they filed the smuggling complaint and let your referees find them again."

"Then why didn't my man find whatever it is the Sornorians are after?" Demron demanded.

"Because these particular artists could give lessons to your man *and* the Sornorians. In fact, they just have." He told him about the duplicate shipments.

"So which one contained the contraband?" Demron asked.

"The second. Obviously. If it'd been the first, they'd have it thoroughly hidden by now, and this farce they've just enacted wouldn't have been necessary. The second shipment contained the contraband, and they had just enough time to whisk it out of the way and transfer the labels and seals to the first crate—which they'd never opened—before your referee landed."

"We'll go back and look again. I still have a writ of search."

Wargen shook his head. "The arbiter has voided it because of the artists' complaint of a prior illegal search."

Demron groaned. "I should have posted a watch. By this time the contraband is scattered all over Donov Metro."

"I doubt it. All of the artists are still there. The street outside is rather crowded, though—in addition to my men, there are two dozen Sornorians on watch. Obviously they're convinced that the artists still have what they want. Can you have fifty uniformed men there before dark? My men will show them where to go."

"What's the plan?"

"After dark the Sornorians will storm the place and try to take whatever it is they're after."

"I'll have them picked up now," Demron said.

"Since you man couldn't find the contraband, let's let the Sornorians try."

"No." Demron shook his head emphatically. "They'd claim diplomatic immunity, and we wouldn't even be able to search them unless we caught them committing a felony."

"But you will. You'll catch them breaking into a private residence and also taking part in the brawl that's certain to follow. The last I heard there were twenty-five artists living in that dwelling, and they always have a crowd of visitors. A number of them are the kind of people I'd rather have on my side in any kind of a fracas. The Sornorians are badly underestimating what's required to take something away from a houseful of artists."

Demron said indignantly, "What do you want me to do? Just stand there and watch them fight?"

"Only until one side is obviously getting the better of it," Wargen said, grinning.

"So what does that accomplish?"

"Surely your police don't need a writ to enter a dwelling where an outrageous violation of the peace is occurring."

"Ah!"

"And once they've entered, they'll have the right and the duty to search the premises thoroughly for violators and weapons. Naturally your men won't take sides—they'll arrest everyone in sight and let the arbiter sort things out in the morning. After a night in confinement the artists may decide to cancel their complaint about today's illegal search in return for a dismissal of charges about disturbing the peace, but that's merely a deserved windfall for your hard-working police."

For a moment Demron stared at him. Then he leaned back and wheezed and gasped for breath as his huge body shook with laughter.

Demron and Wargen watched from across the street while cameras recorded the stealthy approach of the Sornorian thugs. A short time later a dozen shoulders hit the gate leading into the artists' courtyard, and battle was joined.

The artists hadn't imagined such an open flaunting of the law. The Sornorians were inside the building before they could react, which satisfied Wargen—the police would have had difficulty in justifying a search of the house had the fighting taken place in the street. When the artists did react it was with an awesome ferocity. One after another the Sornorians were tossed back into the street. When the fifth landed there, Wargen signaled the police into action.

The fracas was under control before neighboring Donovians had sufficiently aroused themselves from their postrepastal lethargy to wonder what was happening. Police treated both the artists' complaints and the Sornorians' bleated claims of diplomatic immunity with splendid impartiality and told both sides to tell it to the arbiter in the morning. Demron's detective squad went to work and a few minutes later Demron summoned Wargen. "Want to see something?" he demanded, his eyes shining with excitement.

"Did you find it?"

"Everyone who occupies one of these dwellings," Demron said, "thinks that the concealed room is his own personal secret. The fact is that every dwelling in Old City has one, in exactly the same place. Look here!"

Wargen stared. Several highly dejected artists were being led out, and with them came one of the galaxy's most beautiful creations, a *nonor,* of gleaming fur, graceful proportions, long neck, and high, noble forehead above a long, tapering snout. Some scientists claimed that it was also one of the galaxy's most intelligent creations.

"No wonder the Sornorians were in a stew!" Wargen exclaimed. "But wait—surely they wouldn't make all that fuss over just any nonor. It must be one of the leaders."

"It's more than that," Demron said. "It's Franff."

"Franff is dead!" Wargen protested.

"Maybe that's why the Sornorians were in such a stew."

to bring Anna to see you before you leave. As for
Zrilund, you might not like it. It's showing its age, and the
rest have ruined it. You shouldn't believe the paintings on
the Florentine exhibit

★ *7* ★

The next morning Wargen visited the Hall of Justice disguised as a tourist. Only the charges against Franff and the
artists Brance and Milfro were filed for arbitration. The
other artists had been released in exchange for a withdrawal
of the illegal search and trespassing complaints. The diplomatic immunity of the Sornorians had been conceded, but
orders had been issued expelling the ambassador and the
entire embassy staff. Sornor's application for Franff's extradition would be heard along with the police charges—illegal
entry against Franff, and conspiracy against the two artists
for their role in smuggling Franff onto Donov.

Wargen seated himself at the rear of the arbitration room,
arranged himself with the flopping tourist's hat covering his
face, aimed its pointed brim at the artists and Franff—who
sat together in the conference area talking in low voices—
and pretended to take a nap. A directional detector picked
up their words clearly. Thus far they had no attorney to
confer with, and the government's protagonist had tired of
waiting and left, placing himself on call.

"We shouldn't have brought Franff to Donov Metro,"
Milfro said.

Brance said tiredly, "The way the Sornorians were
snooping around, this would have happened anywhere we
took him. What we should have done was get an attorney
before we started."

"They won't participate in illegal activities."

"Of course they will. All they ask is some advance notice
so they can figure out ways of doing illegal things legally."

"None of that is any help to us now. Let's start thinking
about what we're going to do."

Franff's whispering voice reached Wargen faintly. "If you'll
get me out of here, I'll go to Zrilund and disguise myself as a
wrranel. A talking wrranel ought to be a splendid tourist
attraction, and I'd like to see Zrilund again. I'd also like to
see Anna."

Brance reached over and caressed the long, silken neck.
"Even if they send you back, old fellow, we'll somehow

68

manage to bring Anna to see you before you leave. As for Zrilund, you might not like it. It's showing its age, and the tourists have ruined it. You wouldn't believe the paintings on sale there."

"Anna's showing her age, too," Milfro said.

"Is the fountain showing its age?" Franff whispered.

"No, the fountain hasn't changed, except that it's hard to see it for fake artists and tourists."

"I would like to try to see it. I was the only artist who never painted it—I loved it too much. And I would like to see Anna. I painted her when she was young—did you know that? One of the paintings hung in the Sornorian National Gallery until someone decided that paintings by animaloids are not art. Anna the good. Anna the beautiful. Anna the bright and wonderful."

"She's an old woman, Franff," Milfro said. "Better you should remember her the way she was in that painting."

"Nonsense," Franff whispered. "I knew her for thirty years. Age does not corrupt the spirit, and Anna was as good and beautiful at fifty as she was at twenty. I will see her if I can and thank her for my memories."

"If we don't find an attorney, you may be on your way back to Sornor on today's ship. What *is* holding up those dunces?"

"What's that tourist doing?" Milfro asked.

"Resting his feet," Brance said. "Halls of Justice are the only places in Donov Metro where tourists can sit down. What if we can't get an attorney?"

"I suppose the arbiter will give us a list of available hacks, but in that case we'd be better off without one."

An artist hurried in. They jumped up to greet him, and he raised his hands forlornly and announced that they'd already been turned down by half the attorneys in Donov Metro. Wargen was wondering how much longer he could safely feign a napping tourist when a familiar figure entered the room and strode scornfully past the guards: Jaward Jorno.

He paused, bowed deeply, and introduced himself. "I happened to overhear some friends of yours discussing your problem. Perhaps I can help you."

Brance regarded him suspiciously. "I've never heard any-one discussing you. Who are you?"

Jorno said good-naturedly, "Listen. The idea of even one nonor escaping the Sornor carnage is offensive to certain interplanetary interests, and those interests have power and money and frequently hire attorneys. Even on Donov they frequently hire attorneys. No attorney who thinks he has a chance at any of that money, now or in the future, will consent to represent you. I also have money and such power as money brings me, and I frequently hire attorneys. I've sent for one, and he'll come as soon as he's able and do what he can for you—not from humanitarian impulses, but because he's collected large sums from me in the past and has every expectation of continuing to do so. While we're waiting, I'd like to hear more about your problem. I devoted much of my youth to the study of law—my father was determined to make an attorney of me, and it's the only one of his fancies that I no longer resent. Knowledge of the law has unexpected uses and applications throughout one's life."

"How do we know you're not a police spy?" Brance demanded.

"Why would they bother?" Milfro asked. "They have their case, and they already know what our problem is."

"There's a lot they don't know."

"We don't have to tell him that. If we try to handle this ourselves, Franff is certain to be sent back to Sornor and you know what'll happen to him there. Mr. Jorno has offered to help us, and we can't afford to turn down anybody's help. We'll have to trust him."

"Yes. Well—" Brance was still eyeing Jorno suspiciously. "We'll have to trust you, but we won't trust you more than we have to. You know about the rioting on Sornor. We had to get Franff off—the Sornorian government announced that he was dead, but it went right on looking for him, and if it'd found him he would have been dead a moment later and never seen again. We have friends there, never mind whom, and we made arrangements, never mind how. We got him off, and we got him through the port here, and we would have got away with it cleanly if it hadn't been for those dratted Sornorians from the embassy. I don't know how they got wind of it, but they kept a watch on us, and after dark last night they tried to break in and grab Franff. They didn't find him, but they raised such a ruckus they brought the police down on us, and the police arrested Franff and all of us, and here we are."

"What did you plan to do with Franff?" Jorno asked.

"Does that matter?" Brance asked politely.

"It might matter a great deal. I'm looking for something to build a case on. Can we claim that he's an innocent tourist who's mislaid his papers, or do we present him as a fugitive from injustice, knowing full well that the Sornorians will have forged a damning case against him, or could he be a well-intentioned immigrant who didn't know the proper procedures, or what *is* he?"

"We had so many problems in getting him here that we didn't make plans beyond that."

"No plans at all? How many other nonors are there on Donov?"

"As far as I know, none."

"That makes him rather conspicuous—the only one of his kind on an entire world. Did you think no one would notice?"

"Look," Brance said hotly. "The urgent thing was to get him off Sornor. On Donov he's been arrested, but he's still alive and he'll have a hearing. That's a substantial improvement over Sornor. As for what we planned to do with him, he's an artist. All of us are artists or ex-artists. We got him his permit, which is the usual procedure, and we thought he could—well—make like an artist."

"How many animaloid artists are there on Donov right now?"

"Except for Franff, none."

"I suppose you assumed that if he worked energetically enough making like an artist, no one would notice that he's a nonor. What kind of permit?"

"Just a permit. Every alien artist has one. It's only a formality, or so the Donovian government has always maintained. Donov welcomes artists."

"I never thought about it, but I suppose it must. It has so many of them. May I see the permit?"

Brance handed it over, and Jorno studied it silently, his dark, intense face twisted by a faint scowl. "This," he announced finally, "gives Franff permission to remain on Donov for a period of three years while engaged in the study or practice of art, renewable on application subject to provisions of Code 129. What code is that?"

"One that says artists have to behave themselves and not become public charges. I've heard that Donov can require an artist to furnish bond as a guarantee that he has sufficient money for living expenses and his return passage, but I've never heard of it being done. The Artists' Council assumes responsibility for indigent artists."

Jorno tapped the paper with one finger. "How'd you get this?"

"By asking for it."

"Franff didn't have to apply in person?"

"No. I'm listed as his sponsor, you see. The artist can apply himself, but the government prefers that application be made by an artist already in residence, or by a citizen of Donov—someone who agrees to assume responsibility for the newcomer."

71

"I had no notion that the regulations were so lenient. Did you show this permit to the police?"

"We haven't had a chance."

Jorno tapped the paper with one finger. "Franff is on Donov legally. This is his permission to be here. You openly applied for this and received it prior to his arrival. Therefore you are accused of crimes that never happened—there was no conspiracy and no illegal entry."

"That's nice to know," Brance said, "but it doesn't help us with our worst problem. Sornor has charged Franff with being a fugitive from justice. If Sornor's application for extradition is successful, it won't matter whether Franff is here legally or not. He'll be sent back."

"Do you have a statement of charges?"

Brance produced another paper. "It's quite a statement. If we knew how, we could prove that none of these things happened. If they did happen, we could prove it was while Franff was in hiding after the government announced his death or while he was in space on the way here—if we knew how."

Jorno glanced at the paper and whistled softly. "Was Franff the leader of the animaloids on Sornor?"

"No. The nonors didn't have a leader, because it wasn't an uprising. It was simply a case of an entire population of animaloids running for its life and only too often unsuccessfully."

Jorno said impatiently, "I know. I know better than you realize."

"The Sornorians don't want any witnesses at large telling other worlds what they've done, and especially they don't want Franff at large because he has a certain fame as an artist and for that reason people might pay attention to him."

"Listen," Jorno said. "You may not be aware that extradition is an extremely serious matter. When a government files such a request, it places its full integrity behind the charges, and the request is either without fault or it's worthless. This request is worthless. I think we won't wait for my attorney. I can settle the Donovian charges myself in two minutes. The extradition proceedings will probably drag on for months, but there's no chance at all that Franff will be extradited. All we'll do today is ask for time to prepare a reply. I'll get all of you released, and then I'd like to ask a favor."

"If it's anything we can possibly do, we'll do it," Brance said fervently.

"I think it is. I'd like to hire some artists."

Milfro laughed heartily. "If you offer an artist money, he

72

doesn't consider that he's doing you a favor. What do you want painted?"

"Nothing," Jorno said. "I want some art lessons."

"Have you studied my report?" Neal Wargen asked the World Manager.

Ian Korak nodded. "I've listened to it twice. We'd already requested the recall of the entire embassy staff."

"What about the transparently false extradition charges? Among other things, Franff is accused of complicity in the murder of more than twenty humans, and official government releases as well as the reports of all alien observers stress that no humans were killed on Sornor. It's doubtful that any were even injured."

"Arbiter Garf is no fool. He'll investigate the charges thoroughly, and Franff is free to remain here while he's investigating. If Sornor is wise it'll withdraw the request. It might have made a case with just one charge, but the ambassador stupidly thought the more iniquity the better. It's in the arbiter's hands, though, and as far as we're concerned the case is closed. What did you want to see me about?"

"Jaward Jorno."

"His appearance as Franff's attorney? Another of his Good Works, I suppose."

"He just left Donov Metro with either thirty-seven or thirty-nine artists. The two men I had scanning him counted differently."

"Is that supposed to be interesting?"

"I find it fascinating."

"Your report mentions his interest in hiring artists. That isn't an uncommon thing on Donov, you know. I've had occasion to hire artists myself."

"These particular artists are no longer on Donov," Wargen said. "They left today on Jorno's space yacht. Let me change the question. Do you remember Jorno mentioning a battered old ship containing three hundred animaloid refugees from Mestil?"

"Certainly. That was why he came to see me. It was in orbit somewhere—Tymoff, wasn't it?—and not permitted to land."

"I just thought you'd like to know that those refugees are coming to Donov."

Korak smiled. "Indeed. To go into orbit?"

"No, sir. To land. They'll have proper clearance from all relevant authorities."

"There's no possible way they could obtain it."

"Ah, but there is. Have you read Code 129 lately?"

73

Korak was silent for a full minute. Finally he asked, "Three hundred animaloids claiming that they're artists? Surely no port or customs or immigration official would swallow that!"

"They'll swallow it because it'll be true. These animaloids will of course not claim to be *good* artists, but if we amend Code 129 so as to make it applicable only to good artists, we'll lose nine-tenths of our artist population and that'll include a lot of bad artists who'll later become good. The other tenth would probably leave too, in protest. The point I'm trying to make is this. These thirty-seven or thirty-nine artists aren't going to paint anything for Jorno, and they aren't going to instruct *him*. They're going to teach three hundred animaloids how to paint. As soon as they have done so, at least adequately enough so that the animaloids can handle sprayers without dropping them and produce paintings that are recognizable as such even if deplorably bad, that ship will land on Donov."

"You say the artists have already left?"

"They left today," Wargen said. "Were you thinking of stopping them?"

"Of course not. I was wondering how much time we have. I'll speak with Immigration in the morning. If need be, I'll ask the Quorum to devise special legislation. I'd like to wind up this diplomatic crisis with Sornor before I commence one with Mestil."

"It's too late to do anything at all about these particular animaloids. Before Jorno left he took out three hundred three-year artist permits."

Some days later the animaloids arrived—not one ship, but ten; and not three hundred, but three thousand. Jaward Jorno had cannily taken out artist permits for the entire three thousand, three hundred in Donov Metro and the remainder a few at a time from every tax office on Donov.

⋆ 8 ⋆

Harnasharn's anonymous paintings remained on display for the scheduled month, attracting an increasing amount of attention and even cautious critical approval, and then Harnasharn quietly moved them to his permanent exhibit. There had been no hint of a rumor as to the artist's identity, but Wargen remained concerned.

He decided to send Eritha Korak to Zrilund. Harnasharn's assistant had made an inexplicable visit there shortly before Harnasharn had posted his anonymous exhibit, and Wargen drew the inevitable conclusion, even though a discreet investigation turned up no trace of an animaloid artist on Zrilund.

He didn't mention the paintings to Eritha because there was no need for her to track down their source—Harnasharn would tell them that if they asked. Wargen's concern was that there might be an undercurrent of talk that could result in dangerous rumors. He also wanted to know if Donov's artists had anything else on their minds that might properly be the concern of the government, and for that Zrilund was as good a place to start as any.

He saw Eritha off to Zrilund, telling her only that he wanted regular reports on what the artists were talking about. Then he gave himself the luxury of an entire morning devoted to meditating the paradoxes of coincidence that he found in M'Don's riot reports.

There was the utterly commonplace world of Cuque. Not even its own scientists had evidenced much interest in the fact that at irregular intervals, and for unknown reasons, an alga of its tropical oceans proliferated monstrously. Neither was it thought unusual that during its period of uncontrolled growth the alga became poisonous. Such outbursts had been occurring throughout man's long history on Cuque without occasioning reaction other than mild expressions of scientific curiosity.

The coincidence arose from the fact that the most recent outburst came immediately after the world's animaloids, the *llorms,* had their fishing rights curtailed. The alga was a staple food of many minute forms of sea life, and whenever

75

it became poisonous those life forms died, and so did predators and scavengers that fed on them in a chain of death that littered the seas with corpses. Thus it had always happened, but this time Cuque was swept with rumors that the llorms had poisoned the ocean to retaliate for their loss of fishing rights. Before the authorities were aware of what was happening, the world was torn by rioting.

There was a second coincidence. The riots occurred almost precisely when that spiraling galactic wind of hatred would have touched Cuque. The Cuque riots happened in exact sequence with those of twenty-three other worlds.

Wargen pushed the Cuque file aside and took up that of Franff's world of Sornor. A fungus occasionally damaged native grasses. This year it suddenly raged out of control and laid waste to vast tracts of choice grassland. By coincidence the nonors, a grazing animaloid, had just petitioned unsuccessfully for an extension of their reservation pasturage. The populace instantly assumed that the nonors were poisoning the grazing land that had been denied to them. By further coincidence, the resulting riots occurred in sequence with those of twenty-three other worlds.

The apparent cause of rioting on each world was an accident or a natural phenomenon that had happened frequently in the past. By coincidence this most recent occurrence came immediately after a dispute or altercation between humans and animaloids, which as usual the animaloids had lost. Incredibly, the humans blamed the animaloids and attempted to destroy them.

Wargen could have accepted such a coincidence on one world, or perhaps several. There were twenty-four.

The outbreaks of rioting could be charted on a star map as a time sequence.

Shaking his head he leafed through the other files. On the world of Bbrona, where most buildings were of wood, there had been an outbreak of fires. Such had happened often enough before; such would continue to happen as long as Bbrona's buildings were constructed of flammable materials. This one occurred immediately after a human-animaloid confrontation, and the humans called it arson.

And rioted. Precisely on schedule.

On Proplif, where a certain insect sporadically destroyed grain crops, it had done so again and the animaloids were blamed.

On K-Dwlla ...

On Pfordaan ...

On Laffitraum ...

On twenty-four worlds: A confrontation, followed by some

form of familiar local affliction, followed by rioting. That series of events could not have occurred in sequence on twenty-four worlds without planning, and planning required that such natural phenomena as the proliferation of an alga or a grass fungus happen on schedule, which was impossible.

The spiraling wind of hatred had dissipated, and the rioting had almost run its course. Massive cleanups were in progress on most of the worlds, and both governments and individuals were interring their guilt with the bodies of their victims. Wargen's official requests for information were ignored, which worried him. M'Don had done his best, but too often his reports were based upon rumor and hearsay.

A messenger arrived with a memo from Demron. The Superintendent of Police was perplexed about a series of petty thefts in a northern precinct. Wargen reluctantly pushed his files aside and went to see him.

"What's being stolen?" he asked.

"Nothing of special value. He picks up whatever he gets his hands on, but no one has lost anything worth more than half a don. The puzzling thing is that in every instance someone saw him making his escape."

"He sounds like a notably inept thief."

"Then why haven't we caught him?"

"Description?"

"He's an artist."

Wargen whistled softly. "Ah! What does the Artists' Council have to say about this?"

"It's alarmed. We've processed data on every registered artist on Donov, and on all of the thefts, and the computer says the thief couldn't be a known artist."

"Of course not. I can't remember the last time Donov had a police problem with artists, but if it does happen I'm positive the artist won't be so naïve as to attract attention to himself by wearing his work clothing. For a non-artist, an artist's costume would be a rather good disguise. The fact that he let himself be seen merely means that he wanted it thought that he's an artist."

"A non-artist disguised as an artist could be anyone," Demron grumbled.

"True. You're likely to have a long investigation on your hands."

"Since he's got all of us bamboozled, why doesn't he steal something of value?"

"Ask him that when you catch him," Wargen said with a grin.

When he returned to his office, a bright young agent named Karlus Gair was waiting for him.

"I called you in to give you a vacation," Wargen said. "Go down to the Rinoly Peninsula and relax for a week. It's really a splendid place."

"To do what?" Gair demanded. "There's nothing there."

"That's the advantage. You'll be the only tourist in the entire precinct."

"Sure. What's so important in the wilds of Rinoly?"

"Three thousand animaloids. Those refugees from Mestil have literally vanished from human ken, and no one I've talked with from that area knows anything about them. We have no contacts there—we've never needed any. I think we'd better find out what Jorno is doing with his animaloids."

Gair went to Rinoly for a week and returned three days later. The natives wouldn't talk with strangers—he hadn't even been able to rent a bed—and as for Jorno's estate, it was formidably fenced and the gates were guarded. He thought that an approach from the sea might be possible, and he wanted to know if he should try it.

Wargen told him not to bother, and the following week he went to Rinoly himself.

It was a humped and rocky land and one of the most impoverished agricultural regions on Donov. Wrranel carts were still the chief mode of transportation. The unimproved roads were deplorable in good weather and impassable during the spring and fall rains.

Rinoly's young people left for the cities and the resort areas as soon as they came of age, and many of the elderly farmers who stubbornly clung to their holdings were surviving on handouts from their children who worked in the service trade. Abandoned farms were a blight on an already blighted land, for few of the young people cared to inherit the laborious poverty of their parents.

The closest community to Jorno's estate was Ruil, a grubby little crossroads village, and Wargen could not find a decent house there in which to rent a room. He had exercised his influence with a horticultural firm and brought with him a bag of seed samples, and that was sufficient credential to make him welcome in the home of a neighboring farmer. He spent several days in calling on farmers in the area to offer free seeds in return for a report on comparative yields. His generosity with the samples loosened tongues, and Wargen quickly learned that Jaward Jorno was the one authentic hero these surly farmers had.

"Just sold him five load of stone," one would say. Or, "My boy works on his dock. Good pay." Or, "He started the tarff co-op. More'n the government ever did for us." The few merchants in the area were even more voluble in their praise. Jorno was, without exception, everyone's best customer.

But though Wargen listened carefully everywhere he went, he heard no mention of the animaloids. None of the farmers had seen them—most did not know that they existed—and the occasional person he encountered who worked for Jorno was invariably closemouthed and deserving of any confidence Jorno placed in him.

Wargen returned to the precinct capital and arranged for a tourist flight along the coast. Passing over Jorno's estate, he saw a newly cut road leading to the shore, where a pier and a large warehouse had been built. The string of islands followed the curving coast line, the most distant no more than a mile offshore, and on the largest of them a village had been laid out. The island had its own pier and waterside warehouse, and he was able to identify the ship docked there. Back in the precinct capital, he checked the ship's registry and left the same day for Port Ornal.

But at Port Ornal he could only learn that Jorno had bought supplies in shipload quantities and saved money taking delivery by water. Reluctantly he decided to return home and try again when he'd thought of an approach that promised better results.

At the Port Ornal Space Terminal he spent an hour eavesdropping on departing tourists. The sturdy Donovians tended to be scrupulously honest, but a thriving tourist world attracted operators dedicated to instant profits, and if not promptly detected and put out of business, these were a threat to Donov's reputation.

Wargen and his men regularly made the rounds of the resorts and scanned the terminals to learn what tourists were complaining about. It not infrequently happened that a departing visitor who had been grumbling about a strangely multiplying hostel bill, or a guided tour that skipped half the advertised attractions, or a lavish restaurant with expensive but inedible food, was approached by a friendly young man who invited him to furnish details and sign a complaint; and after his return home the tourist would be utterly astonished to receive a refund.

Wargen circled the terminal with apparent aimlessness until he chanced to hear the name, "Harnasharn." The two elderly men who were conversing belonged to that rarest type of tourist, the vacationing art connoisseur, who came to study Donov's permanent collections and also to gamble— there was no better investment in the galaxy than a painting by a young artist who would become great. The problem was to select the right young artist—as the Donovian saying went, to find the one gray hair on a white wrranel.

"I didn't get up to the Metro," one of the men said.

"You should have. Those eight anonymous paintings in Harnasharn's permanent exhibit are worth the trip."

"Anonymous? That's an oddity."

"So are the paintings. Strangest things I've ever seen, but for that kind of thing they're simply magnificent. I might have bought one if they'd been priced reasonably, but they weren't for sale."

"That's odd, too."

"Harnasharn was accepting registered bids, but you know how that goes. He expects the price to keep going up, and he'll hang onto them for years. Anyway—just to show you how odd they are—a tourist told me with a perfectly straight face that they'd been painted by a Zrilund swamp slug."

Their laughter chased Wargen all the way to the exit.

At Port Metro he commandeered one of Demron's patrol vehicles, and they careered through Donov Metro on the emergency altitude. When they reached the Harnasharn Galleries, Wargen leaped out and stared at the building in foolish uncertainty. He did not know what he expected to find—radicals haranguing an enraged populace, perhaps, or anti-animaloid fanaticists pulverizing the pavement to manufacture missiles, or a mob threatening to storm the place.

Confronted by the establishment's usual quiet and dignified mien and the sedateness of the few viewers who leisurely paced their ways through the exhibits, Wargen had embarrassed second thoughts.

But he dismissed the driver and went to see Harnasharn.

"I've just come from Port Ornal," he told him. "A couple of tourists departing the space terminal were discussing your permanent exhibit, and one of them said that a tourist had told him the eight anonymous paintings you're displaying are the work of a Zrilund swamp slug."

Harnasharn turned on him aghast.

"What sort of animaloid did paint them?" Wargen asked.

"A Zrilund swamp slug."

"I see. Blabby sort of creature that couldn't resist bragging to its friends?"

"Mr. Wargen. This is extremely serious. There should be only three people on Donov who know that—my assistant, myself, and the slug's owner. I'm pledged on my word of honor not to divulge the origin of those paintings to anyone, and I have not and will not except to yourself and the World Manager and that only because your positions entitle the two of you to share a confidence of this order. I know my assistant has not told anyone. Having observed how concerned the slug's owner was to preserve his secret, I feel certain that he wouldn't tell anyone. Otherwise, why the fuss about extracting pledges from us and having them written into contracts? You say a *tourist* said that?"

"Actually it was a visiting art connoisseur who said he'd heard it from a tourist. Neither he nor the person he was talking with believed it. What the tourist thought about it I couldn't say."

"Had they been to Zrilund?"

"I don't know."

"I'm wondering if others may have known about the slug—friends or neighbors of the owner, for example. I'll have to investigate this for my own protection. I don't want a situation where the owner starts a rumor and then attempts to cancel his contract by blaming me for it."

"It seems to be a singularly unsuccessful rumor," Wargen observed. "Our only source is a man who was leaving Donov and anyway didn't believe it. We may be making a fuss about nothing."

"I'll investigate just the same," Harnasharn said. "I'm very glad you told me about this."

Wargen returned to his office and longingly contemplated his riot files: Cuque, Sornor, Mestil, Bbrona, Proplif, K-Dwlla, Pfordaan . . .

Also on his desk was a red memo, the form used by Wargen and Demron for confidential reports to each other. This one reported more than one hundred thefts by persons in artist clothing in four adjoining precincts. Demron was becoming desperate.

Disgustedly Wargen turned the memo over and wrote on the back, "I'll find your thieves if you'll find me a Zrilund swamp slug."

Eritha Korak arrived in Zrilund Town with a ferryboat load of tourists and checked in at the Zrilund Town Hostel. "Just call me Ritha," she said brightly, as Rearm Hylat, the hostel's tall, gaunt proprietor, squinted uncertainly at her signature. "I'll pay in advance."

The granddaughter of Donov's World Manager possessed a legion of friends, and an encounter with one of them while using an alias could have been embarrassing. She had decided to use her own name but not to flaunt it.

Hylat accepted a week's rent with alacrity, and Eritha did not comment when he wrote, "Erita Karol," on her receipt. She took possession of her room, deposited her personal effects and bundle of artist's equipment, and went to have a leisurely look at Zrilund Town.

A lavishly printed guidebook contained stunning reproductions of Zrilund masterpieces and very little information about the island's history. The fact was that outsiders didn't know and natives didn't care. Fishermen and farmers had inhabited the island for as long as anyone remembered. The fishermen operated smoking and drying sheds on a small bay where there was an excellent harbor and a sloping sandy shore upon which they could beach their ships. They built their homes on the tall cliffs, in a village satisfactorily remote from the offensive sights and smells of fish processing. The village quickly became a small commercial center for the fishermen and for Zrilund's farmers. Shops lined the oval, and as the fisheries thrived and drainage claimed more land for agriculture, the village grew into a town and the tidy, narrow streets of sturdy stone buildings lengthened.

Then came the deluge of artists, and when this was followed by the deluge of tourists, the fishermen moved away in disgust. They established Fish Town, a new village on the north shore, and they updated their processing to modern methods involving refrigeration and radiation and delivered their catches directly to mainland markets and processors. Their old stone houses were bought by people interested in exploiting the tourist trade, and for a time virtually every building in Zrilund Town had some commercial use, if only in the form of a front room that served as a souvenir shop.

Those were the great days of Zrilund, when enormous throngs of tourists filled the town, sunned themselves on the pier or on the cliffs, climbed down to the beaches to swim, took long walks along the shore, occupied every room in the hostels and all available space in private households, and bought paintings by the hundred, many of which later became museum masterpieces.

Those great days were now mocking memories. Buildings on the side streets were vacant and could be, as the Zrilund saying went, rented for an excuse or bought for an alibi. The town died ten times daily—when the ferries took away their loads of tourists—and overnight guests were a rarity. Hostels in Nor Harbor, on the mainland, were more modern, more convenient, and close to an expanding group of non-art tourist attractions.

As the island's prosperity diminished, so did its civic harmony and pride. The townspeople bickered among themselves and squabbled with the artists. A proposal to require a license of artists selling paintings directly to the tourists had recently failed only because the artists threatened to move en masse to Nor Harbor.

Eritha had garnered this background before leaving Donov Metro, but she detected no signs of disharmony in her first view of the splendid old town. She covered it from one end to the other and climbed the highest of the gleaming chalk cliffs to watch the departure of the ferry. When she returned to the center of the town, she found the oval deserted.

Easels stood in place, palettes and sprayers were racked ready for use, but at first glance the artists seemed to have vanished along with the tourists. At second glance Eritha accounted for six of them, all relaxing over mugs of adde in the Philpp House. The Chalk Cliffs had another ten and the Swamp Hut, obviously an artists' hangout, more than she could count. Each eating or drinking place had its scattering of custom, even the dining room of the Zrilund Town Hostel, though its prices and gourmet dishes were aimed at the better class of tourist.

Tired and hot from her long walk, she sat down on the far side of the hostel's dining room, ordered a mug of adde for herself, and sipped it while eavesdropping on the artists. Suddenly a shout rang out, and the artists drained their mugs and rushed for the door. Eritha stepped to the window and saw artists erupting from doors all around the oval, and when the first ferry passengers arrived they were at work again.

She asked Rearm Hylat, "Why do the artists stop work when the tourists leave?"

"Because they aren't artists," he answered sourly. When he saw that she was genuinely interested, he sat down to talk with her. "Many tourists who buy paintings seem to do so because they actually see the artists painting them. So the artists try to get a number of paintings almost finished, and then when they have a prospective customer they can finish one while he watches. I said 'paintings,' but I should have said 'souvenirs.' No real artist would work that way."

"I see. But there are some real artists here, aren't there?"

Hylat shook his head.

"I came here to study art. If there aren't any artists—"

"There are some very competent painters here," Hylat said slowly. "There are some excellent craftsmen. They ought to be, they don't do anything but paint. Being an artist is something else. It's kind of like a state of mind. The moment an artist stops trying to do his best work in every painting, the moment he takes a shortcut because the painting is only going to be sold to a tourist who doesn't know any better, he stops being an artist. The moment he tries to please his customers instead of himself, he starts being a fraud. There are a lot of non-artist frauds here. Some of them earn a pretty good living and own property and have bank accounts. Maybe all of them could be competent artists if they wanted to, but they find it easier to paint souvenirs. There is one serious artist here, name of Todd W'iil, but he doesn't paint anything. Besides, he's crazy."

That night Eritha went to the Swamp Hut for dinner, hoping to scrape up a few artist acquaintances. While she ate she listened to the conversation about her.

". . . it's the reds and yellows that attract attention. I sold two today, and they didn't argue about the price, either."

". . . offered me a contract. The other dealer said there was no way I could guarantee quality, and I told him my reputation as an artist was more a guarantee of quality than his reputation as a dealer was a guarantee of sales, so even though he was paying me two dons more . . ."

"It's a mistake to dicker. Set your price, I say, and if one tourist won't pay it . . ."

"The tourist who's just wandering around, he isn't expecting to buy a painting, and what decides him is first that it attracts his attention, and second that he likes it, and third that it's cheap. As for me . . ."

That night Eritha wrote to Wargen. "You wanted to know what the Zrilund artists are talking about. They talk all the time, and it's always about the same thing: money."

Todd W'iil had been underage when he came to Donov. He ran away from home, and his parents, resigned to the inevitable, sent him as much money as they could manage, as long as they could manage. Years passed, his father died, his mother despaired of ever seeing him again, and finally the money stopped.

W'iil survived somehow and painted. He was the only artist on Zrilund who *practiced* at painting, who deliberately attempted to perfect his technique. He worked on a single problem, over and over, tirelessly: exercises in color harmonies and contrasts, in textures, in perspectives, in backgrounds, in sunlights and shadows, in human figures, in animals. When he became satisfied that he had learned as much as he could from one of these rigorous disciplines, he destroyed it. At the age of forty he looked like a shrunken old man, gaunt, ragged, wild in appearance, perpetually undernourished, and he survived only on the bounty of those almost as badly off as himself. He never sold a painting; he never finished one. He painted only to prepare himself for the brilliant execution of the unborn masterpieces that he held within him, and he anticipated their birth with the same attitude of certainty with which a pregnant woman assembled a layette for her unborn child. W'iil's faith in his artistic pregnancy was a pure, brightly burning flame.

Eritha Korak found him the only artist on Zrilund willing to talk with her about how to paint. He was painfully shy, and her fumbling artistic efforts must have horrified him, but he respected her sincerity and they became friends. When, after a week at the Zrilund Town Hostel, she rented a vacant house that once belonged to an artist and had a well-lighted studio, she invited W'iil to work with her.

He preferred to paint out of doors. Inside light, even the light through the studio's huge, slanting skylight, seemed artificial to him. He came to see her at the end of every day, and whatever task she had set for herself he demonstrated for her in an unfinished corner of a fabric before destroying it. Sometimes he took her with him to show her how to study a masterpiece: he would position himself in the precise spot from which Zornillo painted the philpp trees or Ghord the fountain, and he would paint the same scene with a small copy of the painting before him for reference. He painted only until his failure became evident to him, and then he shrugged cheerfully, filled the blank spaces with whatever interested him, and carried the fabric off to destroy it.

Once he asked Eritha to model for him, and he took her out on the chalk cliffs to a place where Etesff had posed a beautiful young woman in tourist costume. W'iil had found a gaudy tourist's hat that he wanted to contrast with the white cliff, and he perched it atop Eritha's turban and told her to lean against the cliff, and stand still. She soon tired of modeling and withdrew from the picture, and he painted on without her while she sat nearby watching him.

She was puzzled. She'd had several queries from Wargen as to whether there'd been any evidence of artists stealing from Zrilunders. She took the problem to Rearm Hylat, who chuckled and said a large number of artists would borrow a man's toenails right off his feet if they thought of a use for them. They owed everyone in Zrilund, including each other, twice over, but he'd never heard of any of them taking anything without asking.

"Todd," she called, "did you ever hear of an artist stealing?"

"Every day," he answered absently. "Taking money for those things they paint is the worst kind of stealing."

Eritha had been fingering a fragment of chalk. "Isn't it funny the way things look different from what they really are?" she remarked.

W'iil paused and absently fidgeted with the trigger of his sprayer. He said slowly, "Things look different from—what was that again?"

"Look at the cliffs," Eritha said. "They look like stone. They even feel like stone, but actually they're like a soft powder pressed together. If you separated the chalk into what it really is, it'd be soft and clinging. It doesn't look like what it is."

"It doesn't look like what it is," W'iil echoed, in a puzzled voice that seemed to originate light-years away. After a long silence he asked, "What would it look like if it did look like what it is?"

Eritha did not answer. W'iil sat down and lost himself in thought, as he so frequently did, and after a time Eritha stole away and went down to the Swamp Hut, where a chunky artist named Wes Alof sometimes presided over a clique of hangers-on. He claimed to be a successful painter of portraits and human figures and had a full purse to prove it, and an artist with a full purse invariably attracted satellites who were willing to help him spend his money whenever he was willing to let them.

"Wes," she said, "have you ever heard of anything being stolen on Zrilund?"

"Sure. Some of those tourists will take anything that isn't fastened down. What'd you lose?"

"A sprayer. But there weren't any tourists around. Did you ever hear of an artist stealing anything?"

"Never," Alof said flatly. "One might have picked it up by

mistake, but I'll guarantee that no artist stole it. Artists beg and borrow, but no matter how broke they are, they don't steal. Look at this prize collection." He swept the table with a gesture. "Not one of them has a don to his name, and if I was to walk out and leave my purse on the table, there isn't a one but would chase me clear across the Big Zrilund Swamp to return it. No, I've never heard of an artist stealing anything, anywhere on this crummy world of Donov."

On her way home Eritha met Todd W'iil, and he looked directly at her without a sign of recognition. She turned and stared after him. "What'll it be now?" she wondered aloud.

Her casual remark had jolted W'iil like an electric shock. The morning after their conversation his mind was still numb with the wonder of it. He walked about slowly, speaking to no one, and he stopped frequently to ask himself, "What would *this* look like if it really looked like what it is?" It was a difficult theory to get a grip on, because it seemed to him that a great many things *did* look like what they were. Finally he took his bundle and went to the cliffs, and he sat for a long time seeing the looming white rock as soft, powdery, and caressing to the touch.

He searched for lights and shadows that would set off the mystical texture that he sought, and he found what he wanted where an enormous hump of chalk thrust out five spurs of contrasting rock that had somehow become embedded there.

He set up his easel and began to paint, and under the skillful touches of his sprayers the hump of rock took on a velvety sheen and a supple, furry texture. W'iil worked with increasing excitement. The five spurs, thrusting up into the hard, chalk-reflected light, formed a brittle, almost translucent contrast. The shadowed chalk in the foreground had softened, purpling overtones. He had filled his fabric with rock textures, leaving only the background blank, before he suddenly realized that he had failed utterly. He stepped aside, sank dejectedly to the ground, and stared at the looming spurs of rock.

Two tourists, a man and a woman, had climbed quietly to the top of the cliff for a view of the sea, and as they turned away they looked at W'iil's painting. "Now ain't that something!" the man said.

The woman turned and spoke to W'iil reproachfully. "It isn't finished."

"Finished?" W'iil echoed. It had never occurred to him that anyone might care if he left part of the fabric blank. He stepped to the easel and eyed the painting critically, wondering if the application of a background might bring out the elusive quality of texture that he had failed to achieve. Quickly he adjusted a sprayer, found the hues he wanted, and filled in the pale sky and deep blue sea and blended them at a shimmering, watery horizon.

But that, too, was a failure. He shook his head resignedly and began to gather his equipment.

The man and woman stepped forward for another look. "Darned if it doesn't look like an animal's paw," the man said. "A furry paw sticking up out of the rock with long claws. Think of imagining a thing like that!"

"But if you look at the cliff just right, that's sort of what it looks like—a paw with claws."

"Darned if it doesn't."

"I like it," the woman said. "It's unusual."

"At least it isn't like those gaudy things in the shops, or the messy things the other artists were painting. It's restful."

"Let's buy it."

The man nodded and turned to W'iil. "How much? Will you take twenty dons for it?"

W'iil gazed at him blankly.

The woman nudged her husband. "Like you said, it ain't one of them shop paintings. It's more like the things we saw in the museum. Or in that big picture gallery in Donov Metro. And he's a real artist, you can tell by looking at him. He don't sell no pictures for twenty dons."

"Those things at Donov Metro were *expensive*," the man protested.

"We were going to buy one, only we didn't find any we liked. Maybe he'd let us have this for a little less, being as he won't have to pay the gallery to sell it for him."

The man shrugged. "All right. But the cheapest paintings in the gallery were a thousand dons." He sighed. "Would you take five hundred for it, fellow?"

Comprehension came slowly to W'iil. "You want to buy—"

"Oh, all right. Six hundred."

W'iil hadn't believed the first figure. It was an unheard of sum, no Zrilund painting had brought anything like it since the days of the masters, and this painting was a failure. He was going to say no, to explain that he never sold his paintings, never even finished them, had finished this one only by accident—but the man was counting money into his hand.

The woman said, "We'll have to handle it carefully. It may not be dry yet."

"It doesn't have his name on it," the man said. "Shouldn't a painting have an artist's name on it?"

The woman giggled. "We bought it before he finished it."

W'iil took a needle spray and wrote, "W'iil," at the bottom of the fabric. The couple hurried away, the man carrying his prize with exaggerated care.

W'iil stared after them, hypnotically watching his painting until it disappeared from sight. The money he clutched in his perspiring hand felt warm to his touch; inwardly it was searing his soul. He turned toward the sea, meaning to fling it—to fling himself—from the cliff.

He was hungry. He could not remember the last time he had eaten a substantial meal. The girl Ritha kept inviting him to eat with her, but he had learned long before that poverty was tolerable only when one was unaccustomed to anything else.

He had no pocket, so he tucked the money into his sprayer box and again gathered his equipment. As he started down the path he turned to look back at the multiple-spurred rock. He had a feeling of loss, of shame, of betrayal, of having sold something of himself, which he had to admit was silly. If he hadn't sold the painting he would have burned it. He had betrayed nothing but the fire, and yet—

He *was* hungry.

The ferry had left; the artists were thronging the more popular hangouts, and W'iil wanted a quiet place in which to think. He went to the Zrilund Town Hostel, and when he got himself settled in the most remote corner and asked the scowling Rearm Hylat for food, Hylat asked to see his money.

W'iil fumbled in his sprayer box and handed over a coin. Hylat blinked at it. "Where'd you get this?"

"Sold a painting."

Hylat stared at him. "When did you eat last?" he asked finally.

W'iil couldn't remember.

Hylat brought him a handful of change. "You've paid for a meal," he said, "but you'd better have it in installments, or you'll kill yourself. I'll start you off with some soup. Stop in again whenever you feel hungry, and I'll give you another course."

The thick soup, with a biscuit, tasted as good as W'iil remembered, but his shrunken stomach's capacity was reached with a few mouthfuls. He gazed regretfully at the half-filled bowl—the waste horrified him—but he could eat no more.

He hurried to Ritha's house. She was in her studio, and he panted up the stairs and dropped his bundle. Before he could speak she poured him a mug of adde, nodded at her easel, and asked, "What'd I do wrong?"

W'iil glanced at the painting, took up a sprayer, and neatly incised two lines of perspective to show that they did not meet properly. "The money you loaned to me," he said. "I'll pay you back."

"It wasn't a loan," Eritha said. "I paid you for lessons. Remember?"

He did remember, vaguely, but he had made so many excuses for the small handouts that kept him in art supplies that it never occurred to him that anyone might take one of them seriously. "Oh, lessons." He shrugged. "I'll give you lessons. But the money—I'll pay that back."

"You've already given me lessons. You're giving me a lesson now. You don't owe any money. I won't take it back."

"Oh," he said. He opened his hand and stared dumbly at the heavy fistful of change that Hylat had given to him.

"Where'd you get all that money?" Eritha exclaimed.

"I—I sold a painting."

"Really? You actually finished a painting? And sold it? Todd! That's wonderful!"

He nodded glumly. "For six hundred dons."

Eritha backed over to a chair and collapsed into it. "Who—I mean, what—" W'iil held the open sprayer box under her nose. "Todd!" she whispered breathlessly. "You're rich!"

"You see? I'll pay you back."

"You don't owe me anything, Todd."

"Then what am I going to do with it?" he asked bewilderedly.

"The money you got from me wasn't a loan, but I know some of the artists have loaned you money, and every artist in Zrilund has given you art supplies when you needed them. You ought to pay back something."

Todd nodded excitedly. "I'll do that."

"Why don't you buy some new clothes and go to a hostel for a few days? You should give yourself a good rest."

"I'll do that!"

It was a different Todd W'iil who climbed the cliffs the next morning. Well rested, bathed, immaculately clothed in the best-styled artist's garb, he set up his easel in the same place as the day before and painted the same rock formation. He worked just as carefully at capturing the essential texture of the rock as it would look if it looked the way it really was, and just as unsuccessfully, but this time he completed the picture. He seated himself on a nearby rock and waited. A crowd of tourists came by, glanced at the painting, halted, and stared. One of them said, "Darned if it doesn't look like a furry animal's paw coming up out of the rock." Another said, "You know, the rock really looks like that, sort of."

The first turned to W'iil. "How much?"

"Six hundred dons," W'iil said.

"Ridiculous! Why, the shops are full of paintings that don't cost more than twenty!"

W'iil said complacently, "What would you rather do—spend twenty dons for a painting that's worthless, or spend six hundred for a painting that's worth a thousand?"

"Six hundred dons is a lot of money," the tourist said. The crowd moved on; W'iil was unperturbed. He knew what his work was worth. When the ferry left he strolled back to town, leaving his easel in place, and he joined the other artists in the Swamp Hut and shyly bought everyone a mug of adde. Then he went to the com center and sent a message. Suddenly he wanted to know if his mother was still living.

The next ferry arrived, and he sold his painting almost at once, for six hundred dons. He started another. When Eritha came up the cliff lugging her bundle and asked him something about mixing colors, he snapped, "Can't talk now. Got to get this done before the next tourists get here."

★ 10 ★

"Rumors can start about anything," Neal Wargen told the
World Manager, "but this one started about nothing. There is
no such thing as a swamp slug."

Korak turned quickly. "Indeed? I thought you said Harnasharn told you—"

"He did. Immediately after that I spent several days
looking for a photograph or even a description of a Zrilund
swamp slug—the notion of a slug painting pictures of any
kind, not to mention good pictures, intrigued me. I wanted to
know how it would go about it. I examined every reference
book I could find, I queried several professors at the
university, and finally I put a referencer at the Quorum
Library to work on the problem. I just received the results. If
Zrilund has swamp slugs no authority on slugs has ever heard
of them. So I went back to Harnasharn and accused him of
perpetrating a joke at his government's expense, and he
indignantly informed me that there was so a Zrilund swamp
slug, and he not only had seen one, but he'd seen that particular one, and he'd seen it painting."

"Interesting," Korak murmured.

"He says it only appears at night, at which time it looks
like an enormous dark blob of slime with a million legs or
filaments. Which makes me half suspect that someone has
perpetrated a joke on Harnasharn."

"No," Korak said firmly. "Harnasharn may not know
much about slugs, but this world has no greater expert on
art. Anyone perpetrating a joke involving a swamp slug artist
wouldn't allow Harnasharn in the same precinct with it.
Anyway, the paintings are real enough, and paintings that are
possible masterpieces normally don't get used in jokes."

"All right. Just put it that a Zrilund swamp slug is a very
rare creature. To the tourist, Zrilund is synonymous with art.
A picture-painting *Zrilund* swamp slug is evidently believable
while any other kind of picture-painting slug would receive
the derision it deserves. Do you want me to track down the
rumor?"

"It would be interesting to know where that tourist came from. Mestil resents Jaward Jorno's refugees. Sornor is resentful about Franff. Other worlds that have had riots resent the fact that Donov hasn't. Rumors are usually slanted to someone's disadvantage, and the reverse of the slant will point unerringly at the author. A rumor that's true, though, is a rumor with a devilishly awkward kink in it. It points everywhere and nowhere. Even if some world *is* plotting against Donov, the question remains of where it picked up that remarkable item of true information. Has Demron given you the latest report on the thefts?"

Wargen nodded. "He's perplexed, and so am I. They occur on a vast scale, and yet they're so trivial—a few pieces of a housewife's laundry, a small amount of fruit from an orchard, a tool that a worker has laid aside for a moment. Nothing of value is taken, but a tremendous number of people have been inconvenienced, and those people are angry. Fortunately we know how he's doing it, or we think we do. We're working up a plan to catch him."

"I'm glad to hear that."

"I've sent for Eritha."

"To ask about the swamp slug?"

"Yes," Wargen said. "I'd also like to know if Zrilund is hatching any more true rumors."

He was chagrined that he had wasted so much time by not taking the thefts seriously, and more concerned about them than he cared to admit; and the immediate cause of his worry was a report he had just received from M'Don about the world of Tworth, one of seven riot worlds concerning which he'd had no detailed information. Tworth showed a long history of bad feeling between humans and animaloids, and in this instance the animaloids seemed to have occasioned most of it—they were a thoroughly untrustworthy lot.

What interested Wargen was that the Tworth riots had been touched off by a rash of thefts committed, or apparently committed, by animaloids.

If thefts allegedly by animaloids could cause a rioting on Tworth, could thefts allegedly by artists cause rioting on Donov? People were becoming angry, and already there had been incidents where artists were ordered out of towns and villages. The people knew that genuine artists weren't responsible for the thefts, but when they encountered a man in artist's clothing they had no way of knowing whether he was genuine or a fake artist ready to steal and run at the first opportunity.

In the absence of a human-animaloid relationship to

exploit, was it possible that someone was attempting to turn the people of Donov against the artists?

Something had to be done, and quickly.

Eritha arrived in Wargen's office like a spritely breeze from the Zrilund chalk cliffs, jaunty in turban and cloak, making the artist costume look—almost—respectable, and she instantly spoiled the effect by saying accusingly, "What a place to send a person to learn to paint!"

"What better place is there?" Wargen asked innocently as he escorted her to the elevator. "The works of all those masters to emulate, great traditions to inspire you—"

"There's more mold than greatness in Zrilund's traditions. It's an awful place. The townspeople are embittered beyond redemption. The tourists aren't believable even after you've seen them. Most of the painters could do really good work if they wanted to, but they'd rather paint souvenirs. The only person on Zrilund who had the makings of a real artist went commercial overnight. Now he does the same painting over and over, and sells it for an appalling price, and it's such a startlingly strange thing that any tourist who can afford it seems to think he's getting a great bargain. It's all my fault. I had to go and suggest that things don't look like they are."

Wargen was regarding her strangely. "What do they look like?"

But they had reached the lair, and Eritha was advancing on her grandfather. "Shame on you for blighting Donov with tourists! They've made Zrilund a dreadful place."

"There's always the fountain," Wargen suggested.

"True, but I'm not going to try to paint that. It's the one beautiful and interesting thing Zrilund has left, except for Franff."

"I forgot to mention that," Wargen told Korak. "Franff has returned to Zrilund."

"He arrived day before yesterday," Eritha said. "He brought an extremely old woman named Anna with him, she used to be some kind of model."

"Some kind of model!" the World Manager exclaimed. "You, a student of art, think Anna Lango was 'some kind of model?' When you leave here you're to go directly to the Institute's Zrilund Collection and spend the day studying paintings that Anna Lango modeled for. There are at least two dozen in the collection, and all of them are masterpieces—as was she. She was the most beautiful young woman I've ever seen. Franff painted her several times, and one of those paintings was a masterpiece, too, and he refused to let Donov have it because he was patriotic. He let it go to Sornor, and I heard that Sornor has burned it."

"Burned it!" Eritha exclaimed. "The poor fellow."

"In the current madness, great art painted by an animaloid gets burned. Animals can't paint, and therefore—but to continue with Anna Lango. She'd had an unhappy love affair and swore off romance for the rest of her life. She and Franff shared a dwelling for years, and it was a social center for all the prominent artists on Donov. Then Franff went home to help his species in what he rightly predicted would be a grim struggle for survival. Does he still paint?"

Eritha shook her head sadly. "He only just arrived, but I don't think he'll ever paint again. His eyes are failing, and he wouldn't be able to hold the sprayers, he's lost so many teeth. And his spirit is utterly shattered. One of his friends from happier days is letting him and Anna stay in a little house that has a spectacular view of the cliffs. Anna is almost blind herself, so neither of them can admire it, but they seem awfully happy in just knowing that it's there. They're dreadfully old and so very tired—they sit together in the sun, and she braids his mane as she used to do, and they invoke the ghosts of their departed friends with soft whispers."

"And Sornor is still trying to extradite him," Korak said angrily. "Fortunately there's no chance at all that it'll succeed. Arbiter Garf keeps asking for more evidence, and Sornor keeps supplying it, and every bit of it is transparently fraudulent. When Garf is ready he'll file a complete report with the Interplanetary Tribunal, after which Sornor will have grave difficulty in extraditing anyone, human or animaloid, from anywhere, or even in placing its bonds and contracts. Sornor must be aware of that danger, but it's determined to pursue Franff until it destroys itself."

"We've taken the necessary steps to protect Franff," Wargen said. "Aside from that, is there anything you want me to do about him—or for him?"

"Yes. Take the new Sornorian ambassador to see him."

"What would that accomplish?"

Korak gestured tiredly. "Nothing, I suppose. I thought perhaps if His Excellency could have a glimpse of that noble old artist and his friend reminiscing together he might experience a flash of insight into what life is about, but you're right. It would only disgust him." He turned to his granddaughter. "Do any of the Zrilund artists keep pets?"

"Of course."

"What sort of pets?"

"All sorts."

"Do any of them keep Zrilund swamp slugs as pets?"

Eritha stared at him. "That sounds like a strange sort of thing to make a pet of!"

"Ever see one?" Wargen asked.

"A Zrilund swamp slug? I've never even heard of such a thing!"

"It's extremely rare," Wargen said. "There may not even be such a thing. Were you serious about wanting to leave Zrilund?"

She nodded. "Now that Todd W'iil has gone commercial, there isn't a person on the entire island who'll even talk about art, and no one takes a Zrilund artist seriously. Gerald Gwyll—that's Harnasharn's assistant—was in Zrilund recently, and he—"

"If no one takes Zrilund artists seriously, what was Harnasharn's man doing there?"

"He has an old friend there, someone who runs a farm back in the island. On his way to visit his friend he did a quick turn through the oval looking at all the paintings, including mine, and he left shaking his head. If I associate with those non-artists much longer, my reputation will become blighted. Can't I go down to Garffi for a few months? The tourists haven't discovered Garffi, and there are real artists working there."

Korak turned questioningly to Wargen.

"She's probably right," Wargen said. "If we want her to find out what the artists are talking about, Zrilund's the wrong place for her. Let her go to Garffi."

"Very well. But first she goes to the Institute and learns something about Anna Lango."

"I think I do remember her," Eritha said. "Todd W'iil had a copy of something or other by Etesff showing a young girl in tourist costume posed against the chalk. I think the model—"

"Something or other by Etesff!" Korak exclaimed. "Does she have a letter in her hand?"

"Letter? I think maybe—"

"Etesff's 'The Assignation!' Something or other by Etesff, indeed. It's one of his most famous works, and you, a student of art—"

Eritha fled.

Wargen said thoughtfully, "I'll have a talk with Harnasharn about sending his assistant to Zrilund. Since there are no artists there, it makes people wonder. Gwyll probably went to investigate the tourist rumor about the swamp slug, and by the time he tracks it down, if he ever does, he'll have started a dozen worse rumors. If we can keep Gwyll away from Zrilund, I think we can forget the slug. It's got to be a very unsubstantial bogy if Eritha never heard of it."

"I agree. Tell her why you asked, though, just in case she does hear it mentioned. Right now we have another kind of bogy that's worrying me, and this one has substance. Since you're unable to learn anything at all about Jorno's animaloids, I want you to call on him in your offical capacity as my First Secretary. You'll be preparing a report for the Quorum, and you'll need complete information about the refugees. Naturally you'll insist on seeing everything for yourself."

"Certainly," Wargen agreed. "But before I go, would you mind if I took the time to catch a thief or two?"

"Please do," Korak said.

Reasoning that the thief could not vanish so efficiently without an accessory in a vehicle, Wargen arranged with Demron to seal off an area completely the moment a theft was reported. After three failures, in which Demron got his men onto the scene too late, they captured a small van complete with thief, artist's clothing, accessory, and stolen property. The two men were from the world of Rubron, which was not a riot world. They refused to answer questions, and the arbiter fined them and ordered them expelled from Donov. Wargen left for Rinoly in a vastly relaxed mood.

Jaward Jorno himself met Wargen at the precinct capital and drove him through the bleak Rinoly countryside. This was a different Jorno from the elegantly turned-out fop of Ronony Gynth's rev. He looked thin rather than slender, and his dark face bore a darker overlay that bespoke hours in the sun. He wore work clothing and a tastefully sedate version of the tourist's cloak.

As he drove, he talked about his animaloids. "The *meszs*," he said. "The original inhabitants of Mestil. Have you met them?"

"Only in pictures," Wargen said.

"They suffer the misfortune of looking almost human. They're highly intelligent, they're talented in the arts, and they make brilliant scientists, mathematicians, and philosophers. They're also competent technologists and engineers, even without training. Any one of them can build anything. Unfortunately, they're much too gentle and trusting to survive in this harsh universe. Until humanity arrived on Mestil their language had no words for 'war' or 'fight' or even 'quarrel.' They had a splendid civilization—in my opinion one vastly superior to what Mestil has now. The mesz tragedy is that they are similar enough to man to arouse his animosity and dissimilar enough so that he feels no obligation to treat them humanely. You want to know about their potential contribution to Donov, I suppose."

"If they have one, I'll be very interested to hear about it, but that isn't why I'm here. Whenever possible our World Manager solves his problems by anticipating them and taking action before they happen. Sooner or later someone will stand up in the Quorum and ask questions about these refugees of yours. Are they healthy? Do they have decent shelter and a proper diet? Are they well-treated? Is their morale good? What do they do with their time? Is there any likelihood of trouble between them and the citizens of Donov? What is the potential impact of three thousand meszs on the economy of this region, on the tourist trade, on our diplomatic relations with Mestil, and so on. When the questions are asked, we want to have the answers ready."

"You didn't have to come all the way down here for that," Jorno protested. "If you'd asked me—"

"Excuse me, but I did have to come. When those questions are asked in the Quorum, it wouldn't do to answer them by saying, 'Jaward Jorno, the man who brought these animaloids to Donov, *says* their diet is adequate. Jorno *says* there is no likelihood of trouble. Jorno *says*—"

"You're quite right. And you're welcome here any time, with or without advance notice. If you think it advisable I'll also extend an invitation to the Quorum to send a committee or come en masse."

"Thank you. Perhaps at the time that questions are raised, such an invitation—"

"Whenever the World Manager thinks best."

They turned off before they reached the lavish old buildings of Jorno's estate and followed the new road to the shore. Jorno halted on a rise of ground overlooking the pier. "Out there—" He pointed at the long, dim smudge of land beyond the gently swelling waves. "Mestil Island. I asked them what they wanted it named, and they wanted some remembrance of their native world, so I had the name changed officially."

"Do you own all of the islands?" Wargen asked.

Jorno nodded. "Only two are large enough for development. The other is Virrab Island—up that way. It doesn't belong to the chain, it's a geological freak. It's as lovely as Zrilund was before tourists and artists ruined it. Someday I may promote a resort there."

"How many of the meszs are staying on the mainland?"

"None at all. These are queer times, and I want no trouble between humans and animaloids on Donov, it's the one thing that would ruin my plans. The local people are profiting hugely from the meszs—I buy materials and supplies locally whenever possible, and it's created a business boom in these parts—and one would think that those profiting would be the last to cause trouble, but after what I've seen on other worlds I'm taking no chances. The meszs will remain on their island."

Jorno handed Wargen into a cavernous flat-bottomed scow. It was already loaded and rode deeply in the water—the center compartment was filled with round building stone, and at either end, bags were carelessly intermixed with unmarked metal containers. Jorno said with engaging apology, "It's not exactly a plush ride, but there's no passenger craft available—I have no need for one—and you'll have to ride with the freight because we're too pressed for time to let the boat waste a trip."

"Three thousand mouths," Wargen murmured, "require a lot of feeding."

When they stepped onto the Mestil Island pier, Jorno was instantly surrounded by meszs. Some bowed jerkily, some touched wrists with him, and some even tried, in a pathetic expression of devotion, merely to touch his garments. All greeted him with broad smiles.

Jorno had been right—they suffered the misfortune of looking almost human. They were shorter than humans, slighter in stature, and they had long body hair on their arms but none at all on their heads. They seemed to have a profusion of fingers at the end of each arm and no hands at all. Their earless skulls were short and narrow and grotesquely elongated to a cranial capacity exceeding that of humans. Their eyes were wide set, their noses a smear of tissue with wide nostril gaps, and their mouths a repulsive, circular sucking device. Some animaloids possessed their own intrinsic beauty—Franff's species, for example, which was also different enough from humanity to be judged on its own merits. The meszs, at the same time startlingly similar and distortedly different, revolted and repelled. They were simply hideous. Wargen found himself wondering what further absurdities were concealed by their baggy clothing.

He followed Jorno up the gently sloping road. A short distance inland a village was taking shape, with neat stone houses arranged in tight squares, eight to the square, and broad avenues of packed white stone.

"There isn't much to see," Jorno said. "They've been working awfully hard—how they are working! The first thing they did was plant gardens, and fortunately they're now able to have their own kinds of food. They're strict vegetarians and very selective, and they have to liquefy everything they eat."

Wargen was counting the houses—there seemed very few of them for three thousand meszs—and puzzling at the odd architecture. The buildings were oval in shape, with rippled walls and elongated, vaulted roofs. "They must be rather crowded," he observed.

"The village is only about one-third completed."

"Has the population grown any since they arrived?"

Jorno shook his head. "They've been restricting births for a long, long time—they didn't want their children born into the slavery they were reduced to on Mestil. If they're happy here, and if they think their children would be happy, they may reproduce again." He smiled. "You can tell the Quorum that they will voluntarily stabilize their population at whatever figure this small island will support."

"Will they grow crops commercially?"

"They'll grow only their own special foodstuffs—which can't be obtained on Donov and for which there would be no market except for themselves. They will not compete with the natives in agriculture or in anything else. It would arouse resentment, and these poor creatures have had enough trouble. There's a businessman in Donov Metro who has film-strips of the Mestil massacres—you'll notice I don't call them riots. I think you should see them."

"I already have. And I have one misgiving about your project. What will the meszs do when their village is completed? This level and fertile land should be easy to cultivate. Surely a few meszs with proper equipment could take care of the entire island. What will the others do?"

"Whatever they like," Jorno said. "That's an aspect of mesz character that infuriated their human masters on Mestil. A mesz does what he wants to do when he wants to do it. In the crisis of becoming established on a strange world the entire community is working furiously, but later they'll revert to doing precisely as they please. The mathematicians will follow their mathematical research, the philosophers will devote themselves to meditation, the poets will poetize. Some of the meszs were much taken with painting, which is a new art to them, so we may have a few mesz artists. And so on."

"Just in case none of them feel like farming, I hope you're prepared to continue feeding them."

"I will if it's necessary," Jorno said. "But it won't be. Things always work out with a mesz community. Even a great mathematician feels the need of some physical labor for his health's sake, and he goes to the fields in the evening if there are tasks to be done there. If he doesn't feel the

100

need, others will. Essentials are always taken care of It's a charming society. It's even worth one's study."

"I gather," Wargen said politely, "that it's been worth yours."

His one misgiving remained. There could be no doubt that Jorno had planned his project astutely and well, but Wargen had little faith in things working out merely because the meszs were creatures of sterling character. When they reverted to doing as they pleased, Jorno might find that ten random shiploads of refugees could contain some appalling duplications. What if they were *all* mathematicians, willing to perform a few evening tasks when they felt like it? Wargen hoped that Jorno's finances were as sound as appearances indicated. As he'd recently observed, three thousand mouths required a lot of feeding.

It was dusk when they returned to the mainland. As they stepped off the pier, a waiting shadow uncoiled, a husky, whispering voice pleaded, "Mr. Jorno, I beg of you, at least hear what I have to say." It was Franff, his fur lustrous and beautiful even in the dim glow of the pier lights. At his side stood a bent human figure, an aged woman: Anna Lango.

"The Island of Virrab is ideal for my people," Franff pleaded. "Can you not extend your mercy to them also?"

"You picked a bad time to come here, Franff," Jorno said, a note of amusement in his voice. "This is Neal Wargen, the World Manager's First Secretary. His job is to prevent such an unauthorized invasion of Donov."

"I know of Count Wargen," Franff whispered. "And while he is pledged to enforce his world's laws, I cannot think that he would create obstacles where none exist when it is a question of alleviating the misery of his fellow creatures. I beg of you—bring some of us here, let us have Virrab Island. We will trouble you no further, and my species will survive."

Jorno spoke an order to one of the men on the boat. "Go with him, Franff. He'll take you up to the house, and the two of you can make yourselves comfortable there. Mr. Wargen has to make a connection to the Metro. After I've delivered him I'll talk with you."

Franff and Anna followed the worker into the gathering darkness.

Jorno heaved a sigh. "I'm Franff's attorney of record, did you know that? When I first met him, he and his artist friends were in a jam and couldn't find a legal advisor, so I helped them out. My own attorney, Medil Favic, is representing Franff in his extradition hearings. Whatever we do, we can't begin to grasp the full dimensions of this tragedy. Three

101

thousand refugees are so few, and Mestil is one world of many. I suppose the nonors could survive on Virrab. It's a rugged place, but they're grazing creatures and they'd certainly be able to graze there the year around. It's a temptation, but there's a limit to what one man can do. I'd rather have a limited success with the meszs than a vast poorly planned failure with every deserving type of animaloid available."

"I take it that you haven't heard of the new regulations."

"New regulations?" Jorno said quickly. "Don't tell me Donov is putting restrictions on artists!"

"Hardly. The new regulations are to make certain that artists applying for permits are in fact artists. We leave the certification to the Artists' Council, and since the artists are appreciative of their freedom here, they aren't likely to abuse our confidence by approving permits for refugees masquerading as artists."

"I see. Then the new regulations will have no effect on those artists already in residence."

"None at all. It does mean that there'll be no more animaloids entering on artist permits unless the Artists' Council is willing to certify them as *bona fide* artists. I'd suggest, though, that you see that your meszs renew their permits properly. We'd all be embarrassed if we had to expel them."

"I'll see that it's taken care of at the proper time." Jorno promised. "Thank you."

The next morning Wargen found himself reading the police report on Franff's sudden journey to Rinoly. Since Jorno was Franff's attorney of record, it seemed odd that Franff had to travel halfway across a continent for answers to a few questions. Had Jorno been avoiding him?

"On the other hand," Wargen mused, "if an animaloid were begging for my help, I'm afraid I'd start avoiding him, too. What, really, can one do?"

Sifting through his mail rapidly, he picked out another red memo from Demron, read it, and swore. More than fifty thefts had been reported in a single precinct of the southern continent.

As Neal Wargen moved about both continents on official business, he began to see harbingers of the changing year: The peregrinating artists were moving south—toward the warmer regions of the northern continent and toward the cooler regions of the southern. Such wanderers could be found anywhere on Donov in season, and their movements heralded an approaching winter or summer.

Many went on foot, with bulky packs or rolls of possessions on their backs and the inevitable artists' bundles under their arms. The more affluent traveled by wrranel and cart, with the cart modified to serve as living quarters. All of them drifted about leisurely in search of interesting scenes to paint, of picturesque old buildings, of quaint, isolated villages. Some of their treks lasted for years and covered an entire continent. Occasionally one would even emulate the great naturalist painter Ebbel Throy and dedicate a brief northern summer to travel by boat among the polar islands, climbing ice cliffs to paint the snowbirds and frost lizards in their natural habitat. Most artists were less venturesome; as one of them once remarked to Wargen, there was hardship enough just in wandering about rural Donov.

Their dress varied from full artist regalia to ordinary work clothing, but all wore the artist's turban. No one knew why this colorful headpiece had become the profession's official insignia, but the fad began on Donov and spread so quickly that from the tall grasses of Dworn, at one end of the galaxy, to the clotted vines of Nimfra, at the other, these bobbing, colorful folds of cloth meant *artist at work*.

Wargen contemplated these wandering artists and worried. This year he fancied that there were fewer of them, and he wondered if they would be the first casualties of the distrust maliciously sowed by the masquerading thieves. Demron had caught and deported more than a dozen, and the thefts continued and threatened to destroy something priceless.

Unlike almost any other world similarly situated, Donov had fostered no folk tales of fowls, fruit, and vegetables vanishing in the wake of a passing artist. The fact was that no rural Donovian would withhold food from anyone asking for it, and the artists were neither thieves nor beggars. They offered a fair exchange for what they ate, and the marks of their passing were not thefts, but paintings.

A meal bought a carefully executed drawing of a farmer's homestead. Sometimes an artist would do an elaborate painting for no payment other than food and lodging while he worked. The most remote and isolated Donovian farmhouse had original paintings and drawings on display, and some of these were genuine treasures. An art dealer, acting on a none too credible rumor, called at a shabby farm near Vaszlin and found early works by Ghord, Morvert, and Vasque, all executed on long-forgotten walking tours and all worth substantial sums at any art auction.

This brought a plague of art dealers to rural Donov, but those who thought to swindle ignorant peasants were foredoomed to failure. The thrifty Donovians were not selling their paintings. To them, an object with a demonstrated cash value was worth keeping!

And the unknown, solitary, impoverished artist wandered, turned south or north as the seasons changed, tarried briefly at an art colony, took to the road again, working, working, and now and then offered paintings to one of Donov's serious art dealers. They received in return, along with the inevitable rejections, a few words of encouragement and sometimes even small sums of money fictitiously labeled advances on future work—for all of Donov's art dealers were aware, along with Gerald Gwyll, that there could be no great art without the striving of a great many artists to become great.

Winter arrived at Donov Metro in an unseasonable burst of rain. In the midst of it Lilya Vaan announced a huge garden rev and everyone went, because if the guests got soaked none of Lilya's friends wanted to miss her embarrassment. But Lilya had converted her endless, cascading rev rooms into a vast indoor garden; the laughter was on the guests, and a splendid time was had by all.

To Neal Wargen the winter was a dismal period of accumulating theft reports, and his rare success was as frustrating as his failures. The captured thieves said nothing at all, and the arbiter fined and deported them.

Spring rains arrived on schedule, and in the midst of them an unexpected splash of sunshine struck Wargen's office in the form of a dripping Eritha Korak. She breathlessly removed wrappings and held up a painting. "Look!"

Wargen regarded it critically. "What do you want—an expert opinion?"

"Certainly not, silly. Just your opinion."

Wargen stared at it, stared down from the top of a steep cliff into one of nature's most savage moods. The bristling outcrops of jagged rock were profane parodies of familiar shapes, and far below the sea rushed through a narrow opening into a circular basin where it formed a churning caldron of frothing water and violent whirlpools.

"It's gloomy, but in an exaggerated sort of way it's rather good," Wargen pronounced.

"Is that the best you can do? 'Rather good?' The crinking thing is a masterpiece. I've just come from Harnasharn's. Old Lester flipped when he saw it."

Wargen scrambled to his feet, overturning his chair. He said incredulously, "Do you mean to tell me that *you* painted?"

"Posh, no! I had a friend buy it for me, and it cost every bit of an entire quarter's allowance. I don't think Grandpapa will mind, since Harnasharn just offered me twice what I paid."

"I never suspected that you were making an art dealer of yourself. Let Harnasharn have it. Then you can buy two paintings, and then four, and then—"

"Posh! I didn't even know it was worth anything. I just bought it because I liked it, and I want to keep it."

"If I were you I wouldn't tell my grandfather that. I'd tell him I'd made an astute business investment that's already appreciated a hundred per cent. If he suspects you bought it on a whim, you may find yourself eating whim for the next quarter. Why'd you waste time and money coming to Donov Metro? You're supposed to be spying on artists."

"My time," Eritha said. "Your money. I'm turning in an expense voucher. I came because I have something to report."

Wargen seated himself. "Report, then."

Eritha patted the painting. "I've been reporting ever since I walked in. You'd never guess whom my friend bought this from, so I won't ask you to. It was Jaward Jorno."

"Are you suggesting that Jorno is broke and has to sell—"

"For an improverished millionaire he certainly does things in style. No, Mr. Jorno shows no overt signs of being broke. The contrary—he's expanding his business interests. That's how he happens to be selling paintings."

"Sit down. Start at the beginning."

"Right," Eritha said, perching on the edge of a chair. "The beginning was when Jorno invited fifty artists to be his overnight guests. Fifty *established* artists, that was his word, and the Artists' Council helped him select them. He paid all of their expenses."

Wargen grinned at her. "The Artists' Council didn't help him select you."

"I wasn't selected. A friend of mine was, and she got sick, and I went on her invitation. Since Jorno met me once—at Ronony Gynth's rev, remember?—I had to disguise myself and perform all kinds of contortions to keep out of his way. I don't think he noticed me."

"Then you were fortunate. A person who performs all kinds of contortions is highly conspicuous."

"He had other things on his mind. He owns this island—"

"I've been there. Mestil Island."

"Not that one. Another one—Virrab Island."

"Jorno mentioned it to me. It's the island Franff wanted for his people."

"It has the most magnificently wild scenery." Eritha patted the painting again. "There are hundreds of views as good as this one or better, so Jorno has this notion of establishing an art colony there. He's trying to arrange things so the artists can live and work without disturbing the natural beauty of the island, and so the tourists can visit the scenes the artists are going to make famous without disturbing either nature or the artists."

"Poor Franff!" Wargen said softly. "Think how much more beautiful that scene would be with a nonor standing by the pool."

"Anyway, the artists' village is in a valley in the center of the island, and it's lovely. Each artist will have nice living quarters with an upstairs studio. The tourists' village is on the shore, and the roads and walks and lookouts are arranged perfectly. The whole scheme is absolutely magnificent."

"What does Jorno get out of it—or is this another of his Good Works?"

"As far as the artists are concerned, it's a Good Work. Accommodations are free, the food is at cost, and no souvenir painters need apply—the artists themselves will decide who is allowed to live and work there. Jorno is gambling that he can make the island as popular as Zrilund, and if he does that he'll own the boat service and accommodations both on the island and on the mainland—he's built another tourists' village there. Also, he'll control the sales of souvenirs and paintings, which is how he happened to be selling this one."

"What do the artists think of that?"

"They like the idea. An artists' committee decides what will be sold and sets the price. No artist has to offer anything, and if an artist doesn't like the price the committee puts on his painting, he can recall it and offer it elsewhere. Jorno's shops will display and sell the paintings for a small service

106

charge. Each painting will have a certified, appraised value. The tourists can buy with confidence, and the artists will receive a fair price. The most important thing is that the serious artists won't be competing with the painters of cheap souvenirs, which is partly what ruined Zrilund. Everyone is enthused."

"It proves that Jorno is a first-class promoter, but I never doubted that," Wargen said. "A new resort will be a splendid thing for the economy of that area, but it's nothing you couldn't have put in your next report. Why the trip back here to tell me about it?"

She held up the painting. "Guess who the artist is."

"Should I be able to?"

"Not too long ago you and Grandpapa were wound up about some paintings allegedly done by a Zrilund swamp slug. Remember?"

"Vividly. Don't tell me Virrab Island has swamp slugs."

"Nope. At least, I didn't hear of any, and it doesn't have a swamp. But it does have animaloid artists."

"Jorno's meszs!" Wargen exclaimed.

"Three of them are temporarily in residence in the new artists' village, and their paintings are *good!*"

Wargen said slowly, "Take three thousand highly intelligent creatures, all of whom have strong individual talents, and teach them to paint, and some are likely to be very good at it. I should have expected this. Anyway, Jorno mentioned that some of the meszs were enthused about painting."

"I thought you'd like to know right away, since you were so wound up about that swamp slug. Now you can get wound up about the meszs. Come along and help me talk Grandpapa out of another quarter's allowance."

Wargen shook his head. "I have to clear my desk, because I have to be ready to leave as soon as you finish your talk."

"Where are you going?"

"To Rinoly. When I was there last fall the Virrab resort was mentioned as a possible project for the remote future. I want to know how it got completed so suddenly, and I want to see it for myself."

Jorno was not at home, but an assistant had instructions as to what to do with government officials, especially one named Wargen. He was received cordially and asked what he wanted to see, and when he answered, "Everything," the young man neither winced nor looked surprised. He proceeded to show Wargen everything.

The mesz village was still unfinished, but the strange houses floated in a sea of early-blooming flowers. Clusters of young trees heralded another generation's stately groves. It was already beautiful, and it would become more so.

There were few meszs about. Wargen strolled up the slope to the end of the gleaming white avenue, much farther into the island than he had gone before, and he was startled to see looming in the distance a long, white, moundlike building. "What's that?" he asked.

"The factory."

Wargen turned quickly. "Mr. Jorno assured me that the meszs would not complete with native labor."

"That's correct. This is a textile factory. As you know, Donov has no textile industry. Some years ago Mr. Jorno chanced to find a fiber plant that was excellently suited to this land and climate—it's very poor agricultural land, you know, but this one plant thrives here."

"I remember hearing the fiber mentioned."

"It's worked out well for the local farmers, even though they can't compete with growers on worlds where the fiber is processed except at times of peak demand. Shipping charges are too high."

"I heard that, too."

"Our problem has been to find a way in which the meszs can support themselves without competing with natives, and Mr. Jorno suggested that we investigate this fiber. If the meszs are able to use it, it will provide a handsome market for the one product that thrives in Rinoly, and it will also provide inexpensive textiles for all of Donov. So we've put up an experimental factory and thus far the operation seems to be a success. Next winter we'll triple the size of the factory, and by harvest time the following year we'll be ready to take as much fiber as the farmers can grow. It's work the meszs can do profitably, the Rinoly farmers will have an important cash crop for the first time in history, and the people of Donov will no longer have to pay import prices on textiles and textile goods."

"It sounds like a magnificent arrangement," Wargen murmured.

"We think so, too."

"I'm wondering why someone didn't try it sooner."

"Mr. Jorno sees potentialities where no one else sees them, and he has the courage to invest large sums in what really is a frightful gamble. The worlds where this fiber is being processed aren't about to send us free technical assistance. They won't even sell machines to us. The meszs had to formulate their own manufacturing procedures and design and build their own machines. Would you like to visit the factory?"

Wargen shook his head. "Several governmental departments will be immensely interested. I'll inform them, and doubtless they'll send competent people to see what you're doing. I wouldn't understand it. Tell me about the art colony and tourist resort."

"Ah!" the assistant said brightly. "We'll have to go back to the mainland, then."

"Certainly. I take it that the art colony is your own special project."

"Mr. Jorno has entrusted me—" He paused. "How did you know that?"

"Sometimes I have flashes. Carry on."

They stood on one of Virrab Island's steep bluffs with the tourist village spread out below them in the jewel-like precision of a masterfully crafted miniature. It was completed; the tourist village on the mainland was also completed, as was the artists' village. It had been a crash building project for three thousand meszs, and they had performed brilliantly. They were now partners with Jorno in the resort business—they had furnished the labor, he the land and capital.

"Will the meszs work in the resorts?" Wargen asked.

The assistant was shocked. The meszs had no contact at all with any humans except Jorno's employees. Not only would the resorts' workers be people, but they would be local people. Jorno insisted on that. They would have to be trained, a few at a time, which meant that the resorts could not operate at capacity for at least a year.

"What about the mesz artists?"

"That's different," the assistant said. "That's entirely up to the artists. Serious artists judge other artists only on the basis of how well they paint, and if they choose to work with meszs, or nonors, or whatever, that's their affair." He encompassed the wild landscape with a gesture. "It's a new and superlative art subject, and we'll have a new kind of resort. Beaches, sea cruises, and spectacular vistas of unspoiled nature with only Donov's greatest artists at work painting them. We'll have the unique architecture of the meszs—and that's only the beginning. In less than a year Zrilund will be forgotten."

"I suppose all those great paintings of Zrilund will be forgotten, too," Wargen murmured politely. He thought untamed nature a rather gloomy art subject, but he could understand the artists' enthusiasm over such striking new scenes to paint.

Back at the mainland tourists' village, the assistant took Wargen to see a seaside park that the meszs had laid out and

109

shaped with loving care. "Deeded and dedicated to the public," the assistant said with a smile.

And so it was. The low hill at the center of the park was dominated by a massive sculpture of a mesz and a human touching wrists. The plaque read, "This park was created for the people of Donov and their visitors by Donov's guests, the meszs. In friendship and gratitude."

"Perfect!" Wargen exclaimed.

Everything was perfect, and to a skeptical Chief of Secret Police, that could only mean that something was very, very wrong.

He wished he knew what it was.

★ 12 ★

M'Don sent a new report to Wargen. On the world of Skuron, malfunctioning control devices had permitted tons of poisonous industrial wastes to pollute the drinking water of a major city. Several hundred thousand people became ill, several hundred died, and the world's animaloids were virtually exterminated. Wargen consulted his chart and was not surprised to find that the rioting had occurred on schedule.

He was searching for patterns within patterns, but poisoned drinking water on Skuron was not the same thing as Cuque's poison alga; nor did Skuron's tragedy with a contaminated reservoir show any similarity to the reservoir tragedy on Mestil, where almost one hundred thousand people had drowned.

The meszs had opposed this reclamation project because they thought the dam site and the terrain surrounding it geologically unstable. Unfortunately, their acknowledged scientific brilliance weighed less than their misfortune of looking almost human and the fact that the proposed new lake would inundate half of their largest reservation. The Mestillians ignored them.

It happened precisely as the meszs had predicted. Seismic tremors dumped tons of rock and soil into the reservoir, and the huge waves that resulted smashed the dam, perhaps weakened by those same tremors. It was the worst tragedy in Mestillian history, and through some perversion of reasoning the meszs were blamed for it because they had said it could happen. The rioting started immediately.

Precisely on schedule.

Wargen reluctantly pushed the files aside. One of his agents was waiting to see him.

Sarmin Lezt was a brilliant young investigator with a flair for disguises. For months he had been attempting, unsuccessfully, to link Ronoly Gynth's employees to the thefts by phony artists.

"I'm giving you a change of scene," Wargen told him. "Of the thieves we've caught, natives of Rubron outnumber those

111

of any other world five to one. All of them have come to Donov by way of Rubron. Obviously they're being hired there. The inducement is a well-paid vacation on a vacation world and virtually no risk, since the articles they steal have so little value that a small fine and expulsion is the worst penalty an arbiter could impose."

"Someone is in charge here on Donov," Lezt observed. "They work one area just long enough to stir things up, and then they switch operations across the continent. Someone is telling them when to switch and where."

"True. But we don't know who the thieves are until we catch them, and the one thing we can absolutely count on is that they'll have no further contact with that local control once they're caught."

"You're sending me to Rubron?"

Wargen nodded. "Demron just caught four more. They'll be returned to the world they came from, which is Rubron. Pick as many men as you think you'll need, travel on the same ship, and once you reach Rubron keep a scan on them just in case they report back to their employer."

"I'd rather not take everyone on the same ship. I'd rather have someone there waiting for them."

"Make your own plans and let me know what you'll need. You may be there for a long time. If the thieves don't lead you to the person responsible, I want you to try to find him yourself."

Lezt departed, and Wargen turned over his mail and found a note from Eritha Korak. Artists at Garffi had been solicited for contributions to a fund for Franff. The old nonor and Anna were in acute financial need. Eritha made a donation, and a short time later it had been returned to her. Franff had refused to accept the artists' money.

"Can't you do something?" Eritha asked.

Wargen spoke with the World Manager, who suggested use of an obscure loophole in the administrative regulations for a supplemental retirement fund for elderly citizens. Wargen had no difficulty in arranging a small pension for Franff, and then he had to return to Korak a few days later with the news that Franff had declined it.

"He'll accept hospitality," Wargen said. "He's grateful for Donov's hospitality and for that of the friend who loaned him the house in Zrilund. Charity he doesn't want."

"Did we find out for certain whether he can paint? I'd be glad to commission a painting."

"It's certain that he hasn't painted for years. If he's not able to, a commission would do more harm than good."

112

"I'm afraid there's nothing more that we can do."

Wargen smiled mischievously. "Fortunately there's more than one loophole in those administrative regulations. Since Anna now has an old friend to look after, I figured that made her 'head of a household.' The director agreed not to look too closely at the application when I explained the circumstances, so Anna will receive a modest increase in her pension. Franff won't be able to decline that."

The World Manager nodded his approval.

"It only amounts to token assistance, though. The proper solution would be to find a way for Franff to earn money. I have this friend who gives revs. Lilya Vaan, her name is, and Lilya is always on the prowl for unusual entertainment for her guests. She pays extremely well, and if she were to hire Franff—"

"To do what?" Korak demanded. "Franff is no entertainer. He wouldn't accept payment unless he believed he could give full value for it, and what could he possibly do to entertain guests at a rev?"

"Talk," Wargen said.

"About what?"

"Art. Except for the present generation of younger artists, Franff has been a personal friend of virtually every great artist who's ever worked on Donov. He's painted and played and exchanged advice with a host of immortals. I've heard that Ghord wiped out half of his 'Fountain Lights' and repainted it because Franff told him he had the perspective wrong. Any art historian in the galaxy would place his filmstrip collection in hock for a few hours of the anecdotes Franff could tell about the great artists and the origins of some of their great paintings. In addition to his remarkable experiences, he has a really quaint sense of humor. He should make a wonderful lecturer and earn a good income from it. What do you think?"

"There can't be any harm in giving him an opportunity, I suppose. All the same—" Korak chuckled dryly. "I don't think I'd care to attend that rev."

For the tenth time in an hour Lilya Vaan listened to Neal Wargen's reassurances and remained unassured. The rev was going well in spite of the odd guest list, and the motley crowd of art critics and scholars at least had the good sense not to mingle too familiarly with the other guests; but Lilya had never before offered a *speaker* as her featured entertainment, and this speaker was a remarkably dubious choice for such a risky experiment. For one thing, Franff's voice was a croaking whisper. The amplification system would carry his words perfectly to all parts of the room, but Franff's voice amplified could be nothing more than a *loud* croaking whisper. Even though her guests might find the notion of a talking beast amusing, this would be unlikely to sustain their interest through the hour lecture that she had paid for.

And then there was this human relic who accompanied Franff and who seemed every bit as peculiar as the animaloid. Wargen claimed that her portraits hung in every worthwhile art collection in the galaxy, and that she had known the greatest artists of the past century and had been the mistress of several, and this weighed not at all with Lilya Vaan. She was not a moralist, she didn't care how many lovers a woman had as long as none of them ranked lower than baron. A nobleman was, after all, a nobleman, but an artist was only a decorator. What particularly outraged Lilya was that this dubious female had appeared uninvited and could not be summarily evicted because she accompanied the guest speaker.

The two of them remained together at the far end of the room: Anna, clothed in a drab, shapeless wrapper, sat on a low chair with one hand resting caressingly on Franff's gleaming shoulder, and Franff perched on his haunches with forelegs stiff in front of him, eyes closed, and seemed to sleep. Guests normally gathered about Lilya's entertainers and familiarly asked questions, but they avoided this pair as though the end of the room were under quarantine.

Finally Lilya sought out Wargen. "I'd rather not," she said. "I've already paid him, so he shouldn't mind if I just let the rev run until it's too late for entertainment."

Wargen smiled. "Lilya, I never thought *you* would take a coward's leap. Do you want me to announce him?"

"I don't want anyone to announce him. I just want him to go away. All right, you do it. Then maybe they'll blame you for what happens."

Wargen stepped to the center of the room and said loudly and firmly, "May I have your attention . . . ?"

The guests found chairs; the servants withdrew except for one charged with the manipulation of lighting effects. As Franff waited for the room to become silent, this servant slowly moved a lever, and Franff's fur changed from gleaming gold to emerald green. Part of the audience—Lilya's part—burst into applause, but Wargen's stormy scowl quite spoiled her elation. Regretfully she signaled the servant to desist and thereby abandoned her only opportunity to add something of interest to this alleged entertainment.

Then Franff spoke, and the amplifier *did* carry his whis-

114

pered words perfectly to all parts of the room. He said, "We are all guilty."

Lilya turned blankly to Wargen, but Wargen was gazing just as blankly at Franff, as were the other guests.

"Every life is a monument to all life," Franff continued slowly. "Every life is a destroyer of life. Each race, each species, must answer to those it has tormented before it accuses its own tormentors. Look about you, see the manifold miraculous forms and guises assumed by that malleable stuff you call humanity. And yet you had, somewhere, a common ancestor. The differences between your species and mine are only in degree more striking than the ways in which you differ from one another. If, as the saying suggests, all men are brothers, are not men and nonors at least cousins? The more so because they hold their one priceless quality in common: Life. Each of their lives is a monument to all lives, and all are guilty because all have destroyed life. How many priceless sparks were extinguished to place before this gathering the servings of meat that I saw you eating? How many priceless sparks destroyed along the way when your relentless vehicles brought you to this place? And afterward, when you leave, will it be possible to step on the grass without crushing the countless lives the night conceals there, will it be possible to discourage the biting night insect without committing murder, without destroying the irreplaceable? For every life, no matter how minute, how humble, how loathsome in appearance or habits, every life is a monument to all life."

Wargen nudged Lilya. "What'd you ask him to talk about?" he muttered.

"A subject of his own choice."

"Damnation!"

The guests, all of them, were still stranded in the backwash of the stunned silence that had greeted Franff's first pronouncement. Franff had paused briefly to ruminate, and before he could speak again, Wargen leaped to his feet.

"Franff," he called desperately, "why is it that artists achieve more of this cousinhood of life, this brotherhood, than do other people?"

Franff weighed the question and responded with whispered deliberation. "Artists create, and those who devote their lives to creation are slower to destroy."

Wargen had remained on his feet. "Between the really great artists, was there much of enmity or jealousy?"

"The most generous, selfless men I have ever known have been artists," Franff said slowly, "but not all of them were great or even good artists. Not all of the great artists I have known were generous and selfless. I was guilty of a danger-

115

ous generalization and I apologize. Surely there are generous and selfless men in all professions and occupations, and if those I have known have been artists, that is only because most of the men I have known well have been artists."

One of the art critics had caught Wargen's game and was ready with a question of his own. "You were a close friend of Ghord's. Is it true that he achieved his unique texture with a secret formula for mixing oils with vegetable colors?"

"I saw Ghord paint many pictures," Franff said. "I never saw him use oil paints in any form."

Anna spoke up. "He never used anything but vegetable paints. It wasn't oils that made the texture, it was how much he spit into each color while he was mixing it."

Lilya had too much presence of mind, was too poised, to reveal her horror, but she was not too horrified to act. Her every instinct as a hostess told her that this had continued long enough. She got to her feet and politely thanked her guest speaker. The audience applauded generously, and Wargen, watching Franff's courteous acknowledgment, thought it just as well that the old honor would never realize that the appreciation was not for what he'd said but because it seemed likely that he had stopped.

"It was a peculiar experience," Wargen told Korak later. "I've never had an idea that failed so utterly, in every respect. Even the moralizing effect of Franff's lecture failed. In spite of his talk about the brotherhood of man and every life being a monument to all life, Lilya was ready to exterminate me with no more compunction than she'd use on those biting insects that Franff mentioned. However, I made a little speech, explaining that the old artist refused to accept charity and their kind and generous hostess had hit upon this ingenious scheme as an excuse to let him earn money for his simple living expenses, and I thanked them for their most kind cooperation and their patient indulgence of a great creative spirit who had suffered more than his share of the evil in the universe. The guests gave Lilya a standing ovation, and eventually she forgave me, or at least she said she did. Are you listening?"

"Oh, I'm listening," Korak said.

"I came away with the feeling that I'd spent the evening suspended over an exploding catastrophe, but as long as no harm was done to anyone I'll have to confess that I'm satisfied with the way things turned out. It's unfortunate that Franff isn't interested in giving art lectures, he really could make a unique contribution, but at least his first and last speaking engagement was a financial success. Lilya paid him well, and he seemed to have no qualms about keeping the whole fee even though he didn't speak for anything like the agreed hour. He and Anna will be able to live in good style for a year, or in reasonable comfort for perhaps as long as five years."

"Would he give an art lecture if he were hired for that specific purpose?"

"I don't know. I don't know how long nonors live, but he must be extremely old, and his experiences on Sonor took an inevitable toll. Artists who know him say that sometimes he's perfectly lucid, and other times his memory fails him or he has difficulty in concentrating."

"We might try him with an audience limited to understanding people interested in art, just to see what happens."

"We might," Wargen said, "but I'm satisfied to leave things as they are. He no longer has financial worries, and according to the art critic Hualt, Anna's casual remark was worth every bit of the money Lilya paid. The paint-mixing habits of artists of Ghord's generation were considered so commonplace that no one thought to describe them for posterity. Then artists' habits changed, and posterity was left flapping about how Ghord and his contemporaries achieved their effects. Now Anna has revealed all, or at least Hualt thinks she has, he'll know for certain after he does some experimenting. Are you listening?"

"I'm listening," the World Manager said. "And thinking. You aren't enthused about the chances of persuading Franff to lecture on art subjects?"

"I'm afraid not. It'd be a risky thing."

Korak sighed. "He took out a license this morning."

"Franff?"

"A license as a public lecturer. Did Lilya's money corrupt him, or did he just find out that he likes talking about every life being a monument to all life?"

"He certainly enjoyed delivering his message."

"That's what I was afraid of."

Three days later Bron Demron came to Wargen with a strange, incoherent report that had reached him from a small rural village sixty miles north of Donov Metro. "I've been in this business for forty years," he said bewilderedly, "and I've never encountered anything like this. It makes no sense at all."

It made too much sense to Wargen. He left immediately and traveled north through a prosperous agricultural region, enjoying the touch of spring that lay on the land until he remembered that the wandering artists should have been on the move and he had seen none. That afternoon he overtook a large, slow-moving cart that was enclosed in the fashion of carts used by artists and drawn by two lumbering wrranels.

Anna rode in the cart; Franff walked leisurely at her side and from time to time moved forward and seemed to commune in some silent language with the ungainly wrranels. They halted wherever they found an audience. Anna's gentle fingers placed the microphone fabric around Franff's throat, and he talked. Field workers pausing for a few gulps of adde froze where they stood and listened in astonishment. On the oval of a village, curious shop owners and housewives gathered about the cart.

The message was brief. Franff stated his thesis, expanded it clumsily for a few minutes, and fell silent. Then Anna would remove the microphone fabric, and the wrranels, without any spoken command, would nudge the cart forward. The reaction of the audiences varied from dumfoundedness to frank puzzlement.

But Wargen could detect no hostility. A Donovian farmer suddenly confronted with an animaloidal apparition inform-him that the bugs eating his front plants were his cousins reacted with bewilderment but showed no inclination to stone the speaker.

Further, most of these rural Donovians had never seen an animaloid. Obviously Franff was doing no harm and should be permitted to keep his license, and by showing the Donovians what a peaceful harmless creature an animaloid could be, he probably was contributing more than any governmental policy to the prevention of riots on Donov. In the ultimate scheme of things, the old nonor's message might weigh as a more potent Good Work than the elaborate promotions of Jaward Jorno.

Wargen turned back, and Franff's whispered, amplified voice drifted after him. "Life is life's greatest gift. Guard the life of another creature as you would your own, because it is your own. On life's scale of values, the smallest is no less precious to the creature who owns it than the largest. Every life is a monument . . ."

Thoughtfully Wargen drove away.

13

Only those few tourists who took their sight-seeing with fanatical seriousness got up in time for the morning boat to Zrilund. There were rarely any artists on hand to perform for them, and few townspeople about, and they could ponder the famous scenes in uninterrupted solitude until the first ferry arrived and artists and tourists met in the town oval like two converging plagues.

By that time the early tourists had worked up an appetite or at least a thirst. They circled the oval in search of a decent place to eat or drink, and most of them selected the Zrilund Town Hostel.

When the ferry left and the early tourists moved on, the hostel's dining room was all but deserted. Arnen Brance and Gof Milfro, who had eaten a late breakfast in silence while wincing at the gay patter of the tourists, now ordered adde and settled back in the relaxed manner of old friends who meet rarely and have much to talk about.

"I hadn't an inkling that you were in town until I looked out the window and saw your ugly face strutting past," Milfro said. "What *is* going on here?"

Brance interrupted a leisurely draught of spiced adde to ask with a grin, "How would I know?"

"I came out for a visit with Franff," Milfro said. "Franff and Anna are gone. One of the artists claims they went to a rev in Donov Metro and never came back. I think he was drunk. I think everyone in Zrilund is drunk. When was the last time the old Zrilund Theater was used?"

"I don't remember. Years ago."

"Last night it was packed like a swarm of gulper fish, and there were people outside who wanted to get in but couldn't. I tried to find out what was happening, but all the artists I know are members of secret committees. They talk in conspiratorial whispers until an old friend happens by, and then they look embarrassed and say nothing at all. I didn't even hear any gossip about you until I saw you this morning, and then my landlord told me with a perfectly straight face that

119

you'd bought a house in town and were no longer an impoverished, web-footed kruckul farmer. I wouldn't have believed him, but there was an irrational tone of respect in his voice when he pronounced your name, as though on some occasion within his memory you'd patronized his establishment and paid cash. Why didn't you let me know? I could have looked you up last night and saved the price of my room."

"I should have let you know," Brance agreed. "It happened rather suddenly, you see, and I haven't decided yet whether I should believe it myself."

"Then it *is* true. Where'd you manage to steal enough money to buy a house?"

Brance told him.

Harnasharn's generous advance on the paintings had been invested in Franff's flight to freedom, every don of it, and in addition Brance and Milfro had been forced to solicit contributions and to borrow. The money Jorno had paid them for the mesz's art lessons had gone to repay some of the loans. Brance returned to his hovel more impoverished than ever but immensely satisfied.

Then one of the slug's paintings caught the fancy of a multimillionaire's wife. She had remodeled her rev room, and she was searching for paintings to match the new decor. She registered a bid, raised it twice, and finally demanded to see the artist so she could negotiate a price. Harnasharn did not have to inquire to know Brance's probable reaction, and he refused. Grimly the woman kept entering higher bids, and these eventually reached a figure more appropriate to a mature work of a long-deceased master than a new painting by an unknown living artist. Finally the woman stormed into Harnasharn's office, told him curtly that she wanted this nonsense halted, and doubled her most recent offer.

Harnasharn made the damp pilgrimage to Bottom Farm. "I think she'll raise her bid one more time," he told Brance. "If she doesn't, I think I could negotiate a somewhat higher price. Frankly, I wouldn't have expected an offer like this during my lifetime—or yours. I recommend that you accept."

"Decorating rev rooms," Brance said scornfully, "is an appropriate activity for *my* talent, but the slug is an artist."

"True, but the disgrace—if you want to call it that—is temporary. It'll last only until the next time she remodels her rev room. Eventually her art collection will pass to an important institution, which will be delighted to receive it. Even in disgrace the slug's painting will have excellent company. She's also decorating her rev room with two Etesffs and a Ghord, not to mention a number of artists who were highly talented but less famous. There's no possible way for an artist to keep

120

his paintings out of millionaires' rev rooms. The only question to decide is whether you'll sell now, when you can enjoy all that money, or whether you'll die broke and let your heirs get rich placing the paintings in millionaires' rev rooms."

Brance decided to sell. He repaid the money Harnasharn had advanced to him, and he loaned his kruckul farm to his nearest swamp neighbor, who didn't want it. On a small court off the Street of Artisans in Zrilund Town, he found a house that suited him. Its half-dozen rooms gave him a feeling of triumphant luxury after the harsh years at Bottom Farm.

The house had a garden surrounded by a high wall, and there Brance built a stone enclosure. He brought in genuine Zrilund swamp mud in small quantities until the pen was filled, and then he put his slug in residence. Around the edges of the enclosure he planted a putrid blooming swamp plant, so that any neighbor who looked down from a distant upper-story window would direct his suspicious thoughts, if he had any, at Brance's preferences in flowers. The nearby houses had no upper stories. As for the fetid swamp odor that inevitably accompanied a slug, its potency was blanketed, in that particular location, by emanations from adjoining gardens. All of Brance's neighbors kept wrranels.

Brance's tastes were simple and he wanted for nothing. He had no ambition. He was immensely happy where he was, he had ample money to last him a long lifetime, and—Rearm Hylat had a widowed daughter—he even toyed with the idea of marrying. Of all the satisfactions that money brought to him, none equaled those he experienced when he was able to extend hospitality to an old friend or carry home a keg of adde without first negotiating credit or a loan.

The few close friends Brance had in Zrilund took to referring to him as Poofz Paafz, after a celebrated character of Donovian folklore. Paafz was a cowardly little thief, filthy in person and morals, and so stupid that he was invariably caught within minutes, severely beaten, and booted into the world to steal again because no jailer would accept such a scruffy client. Then, according to the legend, a miracle occurred: Paafz was instantaneously transformed into a pillar of civic respectability and a man of substance because he managed to steal something successfully.

"Delighted to hear that, old man," Milfro said. "Now I know where I'll borrow my fare back to the Plai. You still haven't told me why the mob at the theater, or what's going on around here."

121

"No one bothers to consult me about it. My neighbors know I wouldn't care."

"Either that, or they're innately suspicious of men who wear beards and keep pet swamp slugs."

Brance scowled. "My neighbors don't know about the slug, and they won't if my alleged friends will stop running off at the mouth in public places. As for what's going on, here's Hylat. Why don't you ask him—he knows everything." He waved a hand. "Join us, Hylat, and have an adde on the house."

The lanky landlord drew himself a mug of adde and came to their table, his long face veneered in its usual layers of gloom.

"What was going on at the theater?" Brance asked him.

"Town meeting," Hylat said.

Brance regarded him incredulously. "Really? An official gathering of the good citizens of this decaying community? That's hard to believe. Years ago, when *you* tried to get up a town meeting about some petty crisis or other, no one came. What were they meeting about?"

"Some petty crisis or other," Hylat said bitterly. "I didn't go. If I have time to waste, I can find more pleasant ways of doing it." He raised his mug, lowered it without drinking. "Do you remember the old Zrilund Merchants' Association?"

Brance shook his head.

"Well, there was one. Had a high-sounding motto about the preservation of the island and courtesy and fair value to visitors and what not, but too many Zrilund merchants wanted to use it to keep prices high and value negligible. They figured the tourist boom wouldn't last anyway, and they might as well milk it while they could. Which they did, and a lot of them got rich and got out. Some of those who stayed are still trying to milk it, only now they think they have an inalienable right to every tourist who comes to Donov."

"So why the meeting?"

"They're considering what to do about Jorno's new resort."

Brance set his mug down with a thump. "What to *do* about it? Just how do you mean that?"

"A lot of people think Jorno aims to put Zrilund out of the tourist business. One of his assistants said publicly that Zrilund wouldn't last a year after Jorno's resort opened. Well, Virrab has been open for months and my business is about the same as usual—meaning that it's bad, but at least it isn't getting any worse."

"If Zrilund had one thing that Virrab has, it could put Virrab out of business," Brance said.

122

"What's that?"

"A far-sighted millionaire like Jaward Jorno."

Hylat said scornfully, "There's enough tourist trade on Donov to keep a hundred Zrilunds and Virrabs operating at capacity, but more and more of it goes to the fun resorts, with one-day side trips to art colonies for people who want to brag about how culturally uplifting their vacations were. What we need to do is improve this place so people will want to come here for more than a wrranel cart ride and a few souvenir stops. If we do that we'll have good business regardless of what Jorno does."

"Is that what the meeting was about? Improving Zrilund?"

Hylat snorted. "The fools are muttering about putting Jorno out of business—getting his license revoked, getting him blacklisted by the resort associations, and what not." He drained his mug and got to his feet. "The fools! If Jorno wanted to, he could buy this island and push it overboard. Years ago I suggested that each hostel put up a few artists without charge and give them special rates on food. We rarely have overnight guests anyway, so we could attract first-rate artists to Zrilund at no cost to anyone. No one would go along with me. Now Jorno has some of the best artists on Donov staying at his resort just because he gives them free quarters and food at cost. And these fools are holding meetings to protest about Jorno taking away the artists—who weren't at Zrilund anyway." He shook his head mournfully and strode away.

"Hylat is out of place on Zrilund," Brance observed.

"An honest man among thieves," Milfro agreed.

Brance chuckled. "I appreciate the insult, but you're wrong. I'm Poofz Paafz."

"Thieves or no, Hylat is a few light-years behind the times. The days are gone forever when free lodging and low-priced meals would bring serious artists to Zrilund."

"I'm not so sure. Lay out a few new ways and line them with interesting imported trees and shrubs. Put up a few buildings in strikingly different architectural styles. Make a new road along the cliffs—there are fantastic views that only the birds can appreciate now. If there were fresh subjects to paint under Zrilund's light, you couldn't keep artists away. As for the tourists, Zrilund has the climate and beaches and natural beauty to be the finest resort on Donov, and what are the Zrilunders doing with that? One boat a day plus the underwater ferries, and when a tourist arrives the first thing he has to do is climb a dozen flights of steps, after which he enjoys that wonderful sea only if he can think like a bird. As for accommodations, Hylat offers the best, and what Hylat offers would be third rate anywhere else. It's a shame."

"I agree. All Zrilund needs is a far-sighted millionaire. Stupid townspeople and lousy artists aren't likely to solve its problems, even if one of the artists does own a slug that—" Milfro broke off as Brance's scowl deepened.

"I don't like this development," Brance said. "Zrilunders always have complained, but in the past they didn't have anyone to blame for their troubles but themselves."

An artist looked into the room, saw them, and called out, "You're artists, aren't you? Coming to the meeting tonight?"

Brance and Milfro exchanged glances. "What meeting?" Brance asked.

"Artists' meeting. Zrilund theater. Right after the last ferry leaves. We'd like to have everyone there."

"What's the meeting about?"

"The new artists' colony. Virrab Island."

"What about it?"

"Haven't you heard about Jorno's restrictions? He's spending lots of money to develop and publicize the place, and paintings of it will be popular—and profitable—and no one can work there unless he's on Jorno's special list." His voice hardened. "Meszs can work there—animaloids—but we can't. We're going to do something about that."

"What have you got against animaloids?" Brance asked.

"When I was three years old I watched one eat my mother and two sisters. Donov doesn't know animaloids, because none of them are native here, but I could tell you a few things about them. Come to the meeting, and I will."

"Sure," Brance said. "We'll be there."

The artist hurried away. Milfro asked, "Who's he?"

"Wes Alof. Native of Xenoil."

"Any good?"

"I haven't seen his work. He has a wealthy patron, or so they say—he's never short of money."

"What kind of animaloids do they have on Xeniol?"

"No idea. Animaloids come in all shapes, sizes, and dispositions, just like humans, and no doubt Xeniol drew a rather vicious sort."

"Will anyone pay attention to him?"

"Half the artists on Zrilund owe him money and have every expectation of owing more. Of course they'll pay attention. Whether they'll do anything is another question."

"Are you actually going to the meeting?"

"I'm curious," Brance said. "And I'm liking this situation less and less."

They presented themselves at the theater door that evening, and the two artists in attendance there eyed them suspiciously. "You're no artist," one of them told Brance. "You're a lousy towny." He turned to Milfro. "This is for Zrilund artists. You don't qualify."

"Nonsense," Brance said. "We were invited."

"By whom?"

"Wes Alof."

"He hasn't been on Donov long enough to know all the spies and deadbeats. Both of you are on the list of artists that gave lessons to the meszs. Fine favor you did for Donov's artists. Bust off."

Brance and Milfro exchanged glances, shrugged, and turned away. As they walked back to the oval Milfro said, "First the townspeople and now the artists. I'm beginning not to like this myself. Do you suppose we ought to warn Jorno about what's happening up here?"

"I was wondering about that. In a sense we're just as responsible for bringing the meszs here as he is, and I've never met anyone who was such a joy to work with. The question is what we'd warn him about. Right now all we could tell him is that some people on Zrilund don't like him, and he'd probably answer that the whole world of Mestil doesn't care for him either, and so what? All of this may be nothing but a loud noise in a small adde keg. If necessary, we'll make a couple of artists drunk tomorrow and find out what went on at the meeting. Let's go see Hylat."

They stayed late with Rearm Hylat, talking and sampling different kinds of adde, and when Brance boasted that a new keg he had from Nor Harbor was the best of the lot, Hylat decided to come along with them and have a mug. Along the way they encountered a group of artists.

Brance halted them. "What happened at the meeting?"

"They took up a collection," one of the artists said. "Alof and some others are going to raid Jorno's resort."

"Are you sober?" Brance demanded.

"No, but I'm telling the truth. I don't think the collection brought them much, but Alof wouldn't need money anyway."

Brance exchanged worried looks with Milfro and Hylat. "What does Alof think a few artists could accomplish trying a foolish stunt like that?"

"He knows someone who has access to explosives. They're going to blow up Jorno's resort and maybe the meszs along with it. At least, that's the way they talked. There was a vote, but I don't think anyone bothered to make a tally. They just thanked us for our overwhelming support."

"The fools!" Brance muttered.

"When are they going?" Milfro asked.

"Tonight. Alof hired a fishing boat to take them to the mainland, and they had their connections all worked out. They expected to have the job done before morning."

Hylat said disgustedly, "I've seen artists do a lot of stupid things, but I can't believe they'd be so stupid as to vote support for anything as stupid as that."

"The vote didn't matter anyway," the artist said. "Alof already had the plans made. I didn't think much of the idea myself, but it was none of my business."

"How many artists did Alof take with him?"

"I dunno. At least a dozen."

The artists moved on. Brance said, "If there's no warning, a dozen men with explosives could do a horrible amount of damage. We'd better get a message to Jorno, and fast."

They hurried to the com center, where they found the fat com agent hopping about in a frenzy of excitement. "Some artist I never saw before," he blurted. "Walked in—just like that—and started cutting wires. Opened the cases and kicked and stomped. Then he walked out. The damage is terrible."

"You mean there's no communications with the mainland?"

The com agent raised both hands forlornly.

"When will you have them fixed?" Brance demanded.

"When the boat comes tomorrow morning, I'll send a report to Nor Harbor, and then—"

Brance turned to the others. "We've *got* to get a message to Jorno tonight."

"Alof hired a fishing boat," Milfro said. "You're the millionaire—why don't you hire a fishing boat?"

"I've already sent to Fish Town," the com agent said. "The fleet is out, and there aren't any boats available. If there were, I'd report this outrage tonight. How am I going to print the morning mail?"

"Alof made his arrangements before the fleet left," Brance said. "He planned this real well."

"That artist didn't say what time they were leaving, did he?" Hylat asked. He went on apologetically, "Alof probably arranged for the boat to meet them at the ferry pier, and if they haven't left yet—"

Brance turned and ran. He heard footsteps pounding behind him, but he did not look back. He rushed up the path and past the wrranel-cart pavilion and halted at the top of the steps that led down to the ferry pier.

The pier was deserted, and the gently heaving sea was empty to the horizon under the double light of Donov's moons.

14

Brance took the morning boat to Nor Harbor and placed a call to Jaward Jorno. After an interminable wait Jorno's face appeared, and Brance blurted, "Did anything happen last night?"

Jorno eyed him perplexedly. "What was supposed to happen?"

Brance explained. "It seemed too idiotic to be believed," he said, "but I was afraid it might succeed for just that reason."

"No, nothing happened. We'll be watching for them. Thanks." Jorno paused. "Have you told anyone about this? Has there been a police report?"

"There aren't any police on Zrilund. I'm on my way to see the Nor Harbor commander, but I wanted to check with you first."

"I have a suggestion. Let me handle it from here. If word gets around Zrilund that you took this tale to the police, your popularity might suffer. Your life might be in danger. Equally serious, the next time those idiots plot something you'll be the last to know about it. I'd rather you knew it first and told me."

"I hadn't thought of that. All right, I'll leave the police to you."

"Splendid. I think it might be a good idea to put you on my payroll."

"I'd rather you didn't. Several of us—well, we got rather fond of your meszs, and we're pleased to do what we can for them."

Jorno smiled. "I like it that way even better. I'll send money for your expenses and keep in touch with you. If you have anything at all that you want me to know, place a call. If I'm not here, leave the message and your name with anyone who answers. Whatever action seems called for will be taken."

His image faded. Brance returned to Zrilund on the underwater ferry and cautioned Milfro and Hylat about speaking to the police.

The police were already on the scene, along with com repairmen from Nor Harbor, and they were making fumbling efforts to identify the artist who assaulted the com equipment. Late that afternoon they came to see Brance. He told them he knew nothing about it except that he'd gone to the com center to make a call and hadn't been able to.

Wes Alof and all but one of the artists who had accompanied him returned that day on the last ferry. They tread a tight-lipped path to their quarters, not even speaking to artists they met along the way, and it wasn't until several days later that Brance found out what had happened.

"It's just that we got to thinking," one of the conspirators told him. "We really couldn't see that blowing up Virrab would help us. We weren't complaining because Jorno started ed a new resort—the more resorts Donov has the better. We were complaining because there'd be a demand for Virrab paintings and we'd be shut out. Blowing the place up would spoil it for all the artists, including us. So we pooled all the money and bought the best camera we could find, and we sent Ezer Molm to Virrab for a week as a tourist. He's taking all the Virrab Island walking tours, over and over, and he's photographing every scenic view from every possible angle. When he gets back we'll rent the theater and set up enlargements of his photographs, and anyone who wants to can paint Virrab scenes."

Brance reported this development to Jaward Jorno, and Jorno all but laughed himself off the screen. "You mean you don't care?" Brance demanded.

"Why should I care? Souvenirs on sale at Zrilund can't hurt the market for genuine art, and every painting they turn out will publicize my resort! But they do have a valid complaint. I only wish they'd come to me with it in the first place. We'll have to set up accommodations for visiting artists."

Brance strolled back to his house and told Gof Milfro that Jaward Jorno was an immensely wise man.

Milfro remained with Brance long enough to see the Virrab painting factory in operation, and then he left for Verna Plai shaking his head in disgust. The novelty of the new scenes produced a temporary rush of sales for all except the small coterie of artists led by Wes Alof, who refused to participate.

Alof sought out Brance at the Zrilund Town Hostel one day and joined him uninvited. "I heard they wouldn't let you in at the meeting, that night," he said in a low voice.

Brance shrugged. "They said I wasn't an artist. I'm not."

Alof eyed him narrowly. He was a small man, and he had

an unusual girth for an artist—the measure of a patron's generosity was the artist's waistline—and his round face carried a perennially angry flush. "One of the boys told you about the meeting," he said.

Brance shrugged again.

"Everyone was sworn to secrecy," Alof said bitterly, "but there's always one who'll blab. Point is, *you* weren't sworn to secrecy, you weren't even at the meeting. The police talked with you the next day and you didn't tell them a thing."

"Why should I? I don't owe the police anything."

"I think you got the wrong idea about us. We weren't going to harm anyone, or even do any damage except what we couldn't help. The object was to make a big enough bang to draw people's attention to the menace of animaloids on Donov. Very few people even know that they're here."

"That's true," Brance agreed. "There's been remarkably little public mention of them."

"That's the whole point." Alof pointed a finger scornfully. "*You* know, because you're one of the artists that gave them art lessons. Does your conscience bother you?"

"Why should it? Jorno isn't the kind who'd tell his plans to a bunch of artists. He hired us to do a job, and paid us, and we earned our money. How were we to know why he wanted the meszs to have art lessons?"

"I hadn't thought of that," Alof said. He got to his feet. "I'm glad I talked with you. We're having a meeting tonight. Private room at the Swamp Hut. Will you come?"

"What's the meeting about?"

"We want the Artists' Council to blacklist the artists at Virrab Island."

"What do you have against the Virrab artists?"

Alof's flush deepened. "Working with animaloids. Helping Jorno put over this new resort that was built from top to bottom by animaloids."

"I see. When I accepted your other invitation, they wouldn't let me in."

"They'll let you in this time. There's work to be done, and a hefty specimen like yourself will be useful. Also, you've proved you can keep your mouth shut."

"I'll think about it," Brance said.

Alof left, and Rearm Hylat gloomily strolled over and took his place. "What are they plotting now?" he asked.

"More of the same, only they're trying to do it legally. They want the Artists' Council to expel the Virrab artists."

Hylat said disgustedly, "Zrilund's merchants are paying an attorney good money to look for an excuse to challenge Jorno's resort licenses, and they've succeeded in holding up his application for membership in the League of Resort Operators. That kind of piddling harassment can't hurt Jorno, and it won't help them a bit. Any tourist they keep away from Virrab won't necessarily come here.

"So I wrote to Jorno. I told him maybe he wasn't aware that his assistant was going about saying that Virrab would put Zrilund out of business, which has deeply disturbed people hereabouts. I told him the two resorts ought to be working together instead of knocking each other. They should be displaying each other's brochures and pushing the fact that two art resorts are a better reason for visiting Donov than one would be."

"Very well put. Did he answer you?"

"Of course. Like you once said, he's an uncommonly wise man. He agreed with everything I said, and he apologized for his assistant's excessive enthusiasm. He even offered to finance a joint advertising venture, and he suggested a new association for resorts connected with art colonies. It's a wonderful idea, it would help everyone, but do you think I can convince these idiots to co-operate? I get hooted down, and they go right ahead with their silly little harassments. None of this matters to you, I suppose. You're neither an artist nor a businessman."

"I'm a resident of this lousy town, and I own a farm on this swampy island, and though I consider all tourists a damned nuisance, I have to admit that they're essential to my comfort. I enjoy dropping in at a comfortable hostel for a good meal, and if it weren't for the tourists this would be a ghost town. I wouldn't even be able to laugh at these alleged artists."

"All right. You come to the meetings with me, and then there'll be two votes for common sense—though I still can't see that it makes any difference to you personally."

"You businessmen are too accustomed to measuring things with account books. The reason I want Zrilund to thrive is because I love the old place."

Arnen Brance had a caller, a neat, friendly-looking young man who handed him a note from Lester Harnasharn and said nothing at all.

"Dear Arnen," Brance read. "This introduces Karlus Gair. I assure you that he is completely trustworthy, and I have assured him that you are the same. Sincerely, Lester."

"Odd sort of communication," Brance remarked. "Come in and sit down. Have some adde."

Gair accepted the chair but politely declined the adde. "I haven't much time," he said. "I *think* I got here without

130

being seen, and I'd like to leave the same way. I'm connected with a special branch of the police. Certain things are happening here that have us highly concerned. We have no local agent, and if we were to send a professional to a place like this he'd be much too conspicuous to do us any good. We need a reliable local person who'll keep us informed."

Brance kept a firm leash on his anger. "You want me to be a police spy. Sorry. I'm not against spying in a good cause, but I'm against police spying."

"Do you know an artist named Wes Alof?"

"In Zrilund Town, everyone knows everyone."

"We have good reason to think that Wes Alof is a professional espionage agent of an alien power. Does your aversion to police spying include spying on spies?"

Brance did not answer. Gair took a folder from an inside pocket and began passing photographs to Brance. Brance scrutinized each one and shook his head. "Who are they?" he asked finally.

"Employees of a woman named Ronony Gynth, who is in charge of espionage on Donov for the world of Mestil."

"And—you let her?"

"Of course. We'd rather have spies who are old friends, they're much easier to keep track of, and unless they do something flagrantly illegal we merely watch them carefully. This Mestil group may now be involved in something flagrantly illegal. You don't recognize any of them?"

Brance shook his head. "Of course if they came here as tourists—I never pay attention to tourists."

Gair nodded. "It also could be that they have nothing to do with it. Or it could be that Ronony Gynth has a large staff of people we don't know and is clever enough to keep it that way. Have there been any rumors on Zrilund concerning artists stealing from townspeople?"

"Certainly not! Nothing like that has ever happened here."

"Then you didn't know that all over Donov there's been a plague of thefts by people wearing artist clothing?"

"No, and I don't believe it. Artists aren't thieves."

"No, but there's nothing to prevent thieves from dressing like artists—which is what these thieves have been doing. We've caught a number of them, we know they aren't artists. We also know that someone has sent them here to impersonate artists and cause trouble between artists and the citizens of Donov, and they've managed to make much of the rural population of Donov angry with our artists. Naturally we'd like to know what world is responsible. Mestil and Sornor are obvious possibilities, but Donov may have enemies it isn't aware of—worlds whose resorts compete with ours, for

131

example. There's another factor. There were riots between humans and animaloids on twenty-four worlds. They followed a time sequence, and if you study a star chart you'll see that Donov should have been the twenty-fifth world, except that Donov has no native animaloids. Donov does have artists. Frankly, these efforts to turn our citizens against the artists worry us."

Brance said slowly, "None of that fits what's happening here. Wes Alof is agitating against Jorno because Jorno brought animaloids to Donov. Alof may be a paid agent, but he's also from the world of Xeniol, he saw an animaloid eat his mother and two sisters, or so he says, and he acts as though he came by all that hatred honestly."

"We didn't know that," Gair said.

"Most of the artists have been making money painting Virrab scenes, and Jorno has put up a new lodge so artists can visit Virrab, and except for a few of Alof's cronies the artists are out of this. They like Jorno. The townspeople don't— Jorno has a loudmouthed assistant who went around proclaiming that Virrab would put Zrilund out of business, and the Zrilunders took that seriously. So they're trying to get Jorno's resort license canceled, and they've held up his application for membership in the league of resort owners, and if they can think of any other petty harassment they'll try it. What is it you want me to do?"

"Keep your mouth shut about all of this, and keep your eyes and ears open. If you notice anything that seems connected with it, let me know at once. Will you do that?"

"I can't think of any reason why not. I recently gave a friend of mine a lecture about how I love this old island, and the island won't amount to much if the world it's on is smashed."

15

Bron Demron brought a distinguished visitor to Wargen's office. He said, "This is Jaward Jorno—oh, you know each other."

"But certainly," Jorno said, and Wargen politely touched wrists with him.

"Mr. Jorno has handed me a police problem that's slightly outside my jurisdiction," Demron said. "I suppose I should give it to the Minister of External Affairs, but it's such a strange thing—here, have a look."

Jorno silently passed a box to Wargen, and when Wargen finally managed to speak he was amazed that his voice sounded so calm. "Where'd you get it?" he asked.

"It was displayed at Mestil Space Central," Jorno said. "The departure terminal."

It was a common type of merchandise display, a countertop automatic dispenser. It contained tubes of a white powder. The display was labeled, "DONOV TRAVELERS: Virrab Island water is unsafe. Avoid illness, take your own water purifier with you."

"Were there others?" Wargen asked.

"This is the only one I know about," Jorno said. "There's a kind of fiendish cleverness in that, too. If whoever did it had placed a lot of them in the terminal, someone would have brought it to my attention at once. Just the one was overlooked until finally one of my own men chanced to see it."

"We'll have to have the stuff analyzed," Wargen said.

"I already have. It *is* a water purifier, a well-known brand on Mestil and a rather good product. It's potent against a shocking number of diseases, all of which are enumerated on the label—implying that they are endemic on Virrab. The manufacturer denies any knowledge of the display—truthfully, I believe—and there is no other identification."

"Do you have any idea as to who could have done it?"

"If it'd happened a month ago, I'd have said Zrilund—the townspeople or the artists or both. They had this foolish notion that Virrab Island posed some kind of threat to them, and unfortunately my assistant made some silly remarks that

133

were easy to misinterpret. We now have this straightened out. Zrilund and Virrab have established a new resort association to publicize art colony vacations, and I've made the Zrilund artists happy by constructing facilities for guest artists at Virrab. No, I have no idea at all, except that if my resort were to fail, no one on Mestil would grieve."

"It's the obvious conclusion, but I'm suspicious of obvious conclusions. As for your differences with Zrilund, this display could have been placed there before they were resolved."

"True," Jorno agreed.

"I'll take charge of this, if you don't mind. I'll see that the Minister of External Affairs lodges an immediate protest, and we'll alert our diplomatic staffs everywhere to be on the lookout for similar material. Without a definite clue as to the source, that's the only action possible."

Wargen took the display to the Department of External Affairs, and after a brief conversation with the minister he went to see the World Manager.

Korak heard him out in silence.

"I never realized how vulnerable Donov is," Wargen said. "Our enemies on other worlds can spread the most outrageously libelous material, and if those worlds choose not to co-operate, there's nothing we can do."

"That's one of the reasons why Donov was so reluctant to make itself a haven for refugees," Korak said. "Fortunately there is an Interworld Tribunal, and worlds that don't co-operate can be called to account. Unfortunately, stopping this kind of thing won't eradicate its effects. Those who read the message remember it long after the display has been removed."

Wargen nodded. "Just as exposing those responsible for sending thieves to Donov won't restore the former good relations between our rural population and the artists. That'll take time."

"Ah! You think there's a similarity?"

"Only in that both are malicious and both are clumsy—childishly clumsy. I've wondered if what we're experiencing isn't the result of someone's fumbling attempt to emulate what happened on the riot worlds. Some of the things that caused the riots could have been done deliberately—the thefts on Tworth, for example, or the arson on Bbrona, or perhaps even the landslides on Mestil. If so, they were done with a fiendish efficiency of an entirely different order than the one that sends us thieves disguised as artists and sets up libelous merchandise displays. If that master touch ever appears on Donov, I'm sure we'll recognize it."

"Very well. As for the display of water purifier, at least we're alerted. We know what to look for."

Wargen shook his head. "Being alerted doesn't help much when we've no idea who's responsible, or what they'll try next, or where."

The flashing night signal awakened Wargen. Bron Demron's scowling face announced, "Jorno. Asked me to come to Rinoly at once. Want to come along?"

"Did he say why?"

"No, and I didn't ask. From what I've seen of the man, he wouldn't summon a world superintendent of police at this hour if it were merely a question of another merchandise display."

Wargen squinted at his clock. "It's already daylight at Rinoly. Shall we meet at the port?"

"Right. Police office. I'll arrange a special flight."

Two hours later, with Jorno beside them, they stared down at an undulating, blood-red sea. White blobs dotted it—the bloating bellies of dead fish—and here and there could be seen the iridescent plumage of giant sea birds floating limply with vast wings extended.

Jorno spoke hoarsely. "There's much less damage out here."

Demron's voice was a stunned whisper. "Why? Why would anyone—?"

Wargen did not speak at all. Like Demron, he did not want to believe, but he had seen the filmstrips of the Mestil riots and read M'Don's reports. The correct question was why men hate, because someone assuredly had hated enough to wantonly destroy, but the answer to that lay in the provinces of medicine and philosophy. The police question was not why, but who.

"Any idea what the stuff is?" he asked finally.

"A mesz chemist is analyzing it now," Jorno said. "It's an oil, it's a dye, and it's a poison. He's trying to find out which of each, and in what combination. As you saw, it was much more deadly inshore. The current and wave action may have reduced its potency, or maybe the kinds of fish out here are less affected by it."

"When did you discover it?"

"At dawn the meszs found the seaward beaches of Mestil Island stained and littered with dead fish. The stuff is especially deadly on the gulpers. They breathe air, you know, and they seem to take in a little surface water with each breath. Meaning a little poison, probably one breath finished them. The entire population along this shore may be wiped out.

Then the scavenger fish were poisoned when they ate dead gulpers, and the birds were killed the same way. The chain of life along the Rinoly coast will be altered for generations if not forever." He spoke to the pilot who made a long banking turn. "Now we'll land and have a look from Virrab."

Jorno's calm seemed monumental and ominous. Demron was muttering half-audible plaints about such things not happening on Donov. Wargen reserved his anger for later; he had more pressing uses for his energy. He needed to know which members of the Mestillian embassy had been absent from Donov Metro the previous night, and whether any of Ronony Gynth's group of congenial henchmen had slipped the scan his men were maintaining. He needed to know whether anyone on Zrilund was not happy about the agreement with Jorno and whether any of the Zrilund fishing fleet could not be accounted for. The moment they landed, he insisted on dispatching a stack of messages.

He also informed the World Manager that the master touch had come to Donov.

They stood at the northern tip of Virrab Island looking across at the mainland, and Jorno said, "My guess is that they made two dumpings. They were expecting the stuff to drift south along both shores and ruin the resort beaches, but they didn't know the currents. There's a strong southern current that follows the mainland close inshore and then veers around the islands and heads out to sea. Then there's a weak northern countercurrent between the islands and the mainland. As a result the poison was carried past the islands on the seaward side. When you start looking for the person responsible, you can take it that he's no native of Rinoly. A native would have known the currents."

Wargen turned and walked along the rocky northern shore of the island. The cliffs towered abruptly over the narrow beach, and he had to press close to them to avoid a drenching from the occasional heavy surf. The standing pools of water were stained red, as was the base of the cliffs, and a few dead gulpers floated in the pools. The next high tide would probably obliterate the damage.

On Mestil and the smaller islands, where the land sloped away in lovely beaches, the once gleaming white sand was a filthy red. The meszs had cleared only a short stretch of their seaward beach, and already their pile of dead fish was mountainous.

"We can't dispose of them until we find out what the poison is," Jorno said. "If they can be used for fertilizer, that'll solve the problem—every farmer in Rinoly needs some—but we'll have to be certain that the poison wouldn't affect the soil or seep into water supplies. I don't know what to do about the beaches. We may have to remove the sand and replace it."

"Are you certain that your differences with Zrilund were resolved?" Wargen asked.

"Positive. I went there myself and had a very amicable meeting with everyone concerned. Anyway, I'd hardly expect the people of Zrilund to be ruining their own island, and the same thing has happened there."

"You mean—poison dye—"

Jorno nodded. "Early this morning I was willing to suspect anyone, so while I was waiting for you I called a friend of mine in Zrilund. Rearm Hylat is his name, he's the landlord of the Zrilund Town Hostel and a very good man. I told him what had happened and asked him whether any of the leading troublemakers—of which Zrilund has several—had left the island. He called back a short time later. It wasn't dawn yet, so he didn't know whether it was the same red dye, but some early-rising fishermen found the beaches filled with dead fish."

Through most of the year the principal currents about the island of Zrilund were those generated by the gentle winds. They blew east, toward the mainland, at night, and west during the day, and it required no involved calculation for Wargen to deduce that the Zrilund beaches would be awash with poison for days or even weeks as the winds took it back and forth and made the island a quiet vortex of death.

Awash with poison and buried in dead fish and birds. This was the native home of the gulper, and where Mestil Island had mountainous piles, the Zrilund beaches were inundated and the blood-red sea choked with them.

A few painters were at work on the cliffs even though no tourists had appeared or were likely to. Some painted the red sea, a novelty, and some even included the dead fish. Since the souvenir-hunting tourists would be repelled by such a scene, Wargen was forced to conclude that crises sometimes jolted the most prosaic painter into heroic leaps of imagination. One was painting a bird's-eye view of Zrilund, which he envisioned as shaped like an enormous dead fish surrounded by millions of tiny islands. The catastrophe might even provide an impetus that would convert one or two souvenir painters into genuine artists, but it was, Wargen thought ruefully, an excessive price to pay for art.

No local authority or combination of authorities could cope with a catastrophe of such colossal scope. The dead fish would have to be strained from the sea before they became a serious health hazard and an offense to the nose as well as to the eyes. The poison would have to be neutralized. If action were delayed, the first strong onshore wind would pile poison and dead fish onto the mainland.

Wargen sent the necessary messages and had another terse conversation with the World Manager. Then, meditating a problem even more immediate than dead fish and poison, he walked over to the town oval. Something had to be done about the people of Zrilund.

They moved about dazedly, they spoke to each other in whispers, and they did not seem to notice Wargen when he passed them. He circled the oval and entered the Zrilund Town Hostel, and the two men seated at the back of the room looked up at him irritably. One, Arnen Brance, he had seen before. He recognized Rearm Hylat from Jorno's description.

"We're closed!" Hylat called bitterly.

"When did a Zrilund landlord ever turn away a customer?" Wargen asked with a smile. He sat down and introduced himself.

"Zrilund is ruined," Hylat said gloomily.

"Nonsense! It's ruined only if you people persist in sitting around with your mouths drooping. To work, man! Zrilund has twenty registered fishing boats. I want them out there at once seining the dead fish."

"What are twenty boats with a billion billion dead fish?"

"A beginning. A thousand more boats are on the way. Do the Zrilunders expect to sit around and watch while someone else cleans up their ocean?"

"A thousand boats?"

"Right. And every other kind of assistance anyone can think of, but if those fishing boats aren't working in twenty minutes I'm calling the whole thing off. You should know whom to see about it."

Hylat loped toward the door, opened it, and hesitated. "What'll they do with the fish?"

"Dump them in the most convenient place. You'll have to organize some townspeople to help them unload. Higher authority will either figure out a use for the fish or find a way to dispose of them."

Hylat hurried away.

Brance said, "The World Manager's First Secretary? I seem to remember your taking part in a police raid. You do get around."

"Right," Wargen said cheerfully. "At the moment I'm on a different sort of police raid. Can you tell me who dumped the poison?"

"If I knew," Brance said evenly, "you'd have the chore of disposing of him—or them—along with the fish."

"There are interesting points about this poison. It covers a limited area of the sea, but it completely surrounds the island. This suggests that it was dumped on both the windward and the leeward sides, and on one of them it had to be dumped close to shore."

Brance was listening with interest.

"There's a splendid sea view from the cliffs," Wargen went on. "The moons were in the sky from midnight until dawn. I was wondering if any young lovers were admiring reflections in the water and what else they may have seen."

"You don't happen to know a man named Karlus Gair, do you?" Brance asked.

Wargen smiled and did not answer.

"It's a point worth wondering about. I'll ask people."

Bron Demron was seated on a bench on the cliffs, staring out at the stained and death-strewn waters. Wargen sat down beside him, and Demron said glumly, "I suppose we're reduced to asking this Wes Alof where he was last night."

"I'd rather he didn't know we're interested in him. Anyway, he was in Zrilund at midnight, which makes it certain that he didn't dump poison at Rinoly. What bothers me is that I can't find a pattern. Zrilund doesn't fit. The entire world of Mestil has it in for Jorno, and both the townspeople and the artists of Zrilund recently had it in for him, and we have no notion of how many other enemies he may have, but why would anyone go to this length to kill a dying tourist resort?"

"There's got to be a pattern," Demron said.

Wargen shook his head. "Zrilund doesn't fit. I think I'll stay here tonight. Maybe it's my eyesight that's defective. Maybe I can smell out a few answers."

"Smell out a few for me," Demron said.

Wargen checked in at the Zrilund Town Hostel and sat up late with Arnen Brance and Rearm Hylat, drinking adde and talking. Hylat and Brance were stunned and angry, but if they had any answers they weren't aware of them. Wargen slept badly and was routed out at dawn by Bron Demron.

"Do you still say there's no pattern?" Demron demanded.

Wargen, who had a mild hangover, took a moment to reflect. "I don't think I said there was no pattern. I just said I couldn't see what it was."

"Last night," Demron said grimly, "someone put all of Jorno's boats out of operation. With explosives. And at just about the same moment, someone wrecked both underwater

139

ferries and the Zrilund boat. With explosives. How's that for a shot at both resorts' tourist trade?"

"Any reports from anywhere else?"

"None. Are you ready to leave? I'll wait for you in the dining room."

He left, and Wargen sat on the edge of his bed constructing a formula that balanced Jorno's three thousand meszs with Zrilund's poor old nonor, Franff, who no longer lived there; for he instinctively felt that animaloids were somehow involved.

Then he remembered the swamp slug. The thought so intrigued him that when he returned to Donov Metro he told his driver to take him to his office by way of Harnasharn Galleries.

And the galleries stood transformed by people. Two straggling lines of perspiring tourists stretched across the front of the building and converged at the main entrance. The amazed Wargen rushed toward the entrance, and then on an impulse he turned aside to ask a question of a waiting tourist.

The tourist shifted his feet and spoke with obvious embarrassment, as though he knew in advance that his answer would sound silly. "Well, we heard there's these ten paintings by a Zrilund swamp slug, and, well, we wanted to see them."

Wargen immediately confronted Harnasharn, who was exultant about the spectacular growth of interest in his permanent exhibit until Wargen deflated him in scathing tones. "Spread a rumor that you also have paintings by a Garffi wrranel and sculpture by a frost lizard, and they'll tear down the doors to get in. What was that about *ten* slug paintings?"

"I have three new paintings. One of the original eight was sold."

"Then the slug continues to paint?"

"But of course!"

Wargen hurried off to report to the World Manager. "It seems that neither our citizens nor our tourists have much feeling one way or the other about animaloid artists, except that if the animaloid is freakish enough they'd like to see its work."

Ian Korak heaved a sigh. "Of course. We should have expected that. The tourists probably consider *any* artist to be at least slightly animaloid. What does this have to do with the Rinoly-Zrilund situation?"

"As far as I know, nothing at all."

In a town on the Rinoly Peninsula, a merchant was heard remarking to a customer, "They're having problems with the drinking water on Virrab Island. That poison and all those dead fish, you know. They'll have to import pure water or close the resort."

In a stylish little bistro on Tourist Row in Nor Harbor, one tourist was heard to say to another, "That talk about sabotage to the Zrilund boats is just a cover-up. The government closed the place because Zrilund's drinking water is contaminated. That poison and all those dead fish, you know."

Within the hour Wargen had been informed of both conversations. He went to a conference in a thoughtful mood and listened passively while Bron Demron developed the thesis that the new resort association between Virrab and Zrilund had posed a threat to other resorts.

The World Manager heard him out and then turned inquiringly to Wargen.

"All I'm prepared to say," Wargen announced, "is that someone has directed violence against both islands and now is making a devilishly clever attempt to exploit it."

"The immediate question is whether they're finished or whether we can expect more trouble," Demron observed.

Wargen had no answer, which embarrassed him, and he was grateful when a special messenger called him away. Sarmin Lezt was at Port Metro and wanted help. Wargen's duty officer had sent every available man and notified the regular police to stand by.

Wargen rushed off to the port. His men were still arriving, and Lezt had posted one of them to give directions and orders. Wargen found the agent in one of a long row of drinking places that marked the boundary between spaceport and seaport. Because spacers and seamen not infrequently chose to disagree, tables and benches were welded to the floor, and the only containers permitted in the establishment were of lightweight, disposable plastic.

Lezt greeted Wargen with a grin, and Wargen said reproachfully, "Why didn't you let us know?"

"I didn't have a chance. They boarded ship just before blast off, and I only made it by a stroke of luck. I thought I'd better come along and point 'em out to you, descriptions are worthless for something like this, especially when some of the culprits are playing with disguises. Then one of them turned out to be a blood brother or something of the communications officer, and I decided not to call attention to myself by sending a message. If they'd suspected anything at all they could have dumped me easily before help arrived, but obviously they didn't. They marched down here from the terminal as though they were on parade. They're in the bistro across the street."

"Who are *they?*"

"Four would-be thieves. From the way they've operated in the past, two teams."

"Good work. With any luck at all they'll lead us to their Donovian contact."

"They're meeting him now. This scheme has been working smoothly for so long that the principals are getting a mite careless. Ramsy Vorgt happened to have a directional detector in his pocket, and he's over there pretending to get drunk while recording everything they say. They'll split up when they leave, but the scans are ready for them."

A short time later the newly arrived thieves emerged in pairs and went off in opposite directions, each pair trailing a smoothly functioning scan. Finally the contact stepped through the door, pondered the street gravely, and strolled away. Bristling black whiskers hid his face, and he wore the long trousers and tight-fitting jacket of a seaman on shore leave.

"Recognize him?" Lezt asked.

Wargen shook his head.

"He and the one on Rubron got their whiskers from the same wrranel."

"Do you know who he is?"

"No, but on the basis of what's happening on Rubron, I could guess *what* he is."

They followed him at a distance until he vanished into a large hostel. Two of Wargen's men were close behind him. "This is the critical moment," Lezt said. "He'll change his clothes and disguise and leave by another exit. It's what stumped us for so long on Rubron. If they can stay close enough to see what room he's using and what he looks like when he comes out, we'll have him."

They took a front table in a bistro across the street from the hostel, and before they'd got around to sampling their adde a scruffy-looking, brown-whiskered workman in dirty clothing came out of the hostel and walked away. One of Wargen's men followed, glanced about to make certain that others were picking up the scan, and turned in the opposite direction. The workman took his place in line at the first T-stop with two of Wargen's men directly behind him, and the three of them boarded the next airbus.

Lezt signaled to a waiting police transport. "He'll get off in the neighborhood of Embassy Row. We might as well wait there."

"Do you know where he's going?"

"I can guess. Sornorian embassy. He'll be one of the undersecretaries. At least, that's what the contact was on Rubron."

Wargen took a deep breath. "So it *is* Sornor. But what could Sornor possibly expect to accomplish with such a stupid harassment?"

"I figure maybe they'd hoped to stir up a huge amount of trouble in a hurry and then quietly agree to call it off in return for Franff's extradition. It didn't work out, but they kept trying. Now it's dragged on for so long that Franff is pretty much forgotten on Sornor and everywhere else. I was wondering if maybe the idiot who thought this up has forgotten to turn it off, and it just keeps going."

"What I have to decide now is whether Sornor thought the thefts were taking too long and decided to speed things up by dumping poison."

Lezt turned quickly. "What's that about poison?"

Wargen told him. "Even knowing that Sornor is responsible may not help," he added. "We'd never be able to prove it unless they foolishly kept on dumping it until we caught them."

"Do we have to prove it? The instant we catch one of these new teams stealing we'll have a complete and fully documented case, with sound recordings and photographs. The earlier attempt to abduct Franff is obviously a part of the same plot, and so is the poison. Beyond that we don't need proof. Nothing Sornor said in rebuttal would be believed."

"Perhaps you're right." Wargen mused. "We can perform our own blackmail and offer Sornor a choice between overwhelming diplomatic humiliation and a quiet arbitration settlement on the damages Donov has suffered. Very well. You wind the case up and assemble the documents. I'll report to the World Manager. He can have the novel experience of ending a day on a brighter note than the one it started on."

* 16 *

The art colony at Garffi was unique because it belonged to
the artists. Those who discovered the place considered what
an avalance of artists and tourists would do to that charming
village and its spectacularly beautiful surroundings, and, thinking of Zrilund, were horrified. They passed the problem to
the Artists' Council, which took it up with the Donovian government, and the government arranged a long-term lease on
the entire district with the object of keeping it the way it
was.

The villagers continued to live in their homes, farm the
valleys, and pasture their herds. A few of them found employment in the artists' village, which was built out of sight in
a lateral valley. The artists were serious, hard-working craftsmen, given to painting all of their waking hours, and if one
wanted to raise hell he went off and did it at Port Ornal,
where hell had so many more interesting variations than it
did in a sleepy rural village. Villagers and artists got on fa-
mously, and there were no tourists. Because of the remote location only the most passionate of art enthusiasts could have
made his way there, and if he did so uninvited he found no
accommodations.

A novice such as Eritha Korak should not have been permitted at Garffi, where assignments were in such high demand that the Artists' Council maintained a carefully
screened waiting list; but Eritha was only occupying the
quarters of an artist who had returned to his home world for
a short visit. Since the arrangement was temporary, the local
committee first satisfied itself that she really was there to
study and then quietly ignored her. The Artists' Council was
not even informed.

The village of Garffi stood at the head of a deep bay
where a mountain river cascaded into the sea. The entire
region was a scenic wonderland, with the river rushing
through verdant, steep-sloped valleys, with a multitude of tin-
kling, leaping streams seeking it, with the steady pounding of
rapids and falls sounding a dull background for the shrill

coughing of fluffed-out wrranels on the high mountain pastures. In the background were formidable, oranged mountains, their jagged peaks softened with an encrustment of white. Along the arms of the bay, the quiet, warm sea lapped enormous boulders and fantastically shaped monoliths deposited there in some long-forgotten natural convulsion.

The unspoiled beauty and fascinating diversity of the setting offered an endless variety of art subjects, and the light on the beaches of Garffi rivaled that of Zrilund. Many artists painted nothing but the massive chunks of rock that were scattered there. One monolith could inspire months of steady painting. The artist shifted his easel slowly, in a circle, and with each move the rock's shape changed, its facets reflected light differently, its shadows altered, its hues varied, and its background shifted from the open sea to other curiously shaped monoliths to the village framed by looming mountains—and back again.

The artists tolerated Eritha good-naturedly, and they quickly settled on an unspoken working arrangement with her. Mornings she painted, and the artists patiently answered all of her questions and gave her as much help as she wanted. Afternoons she modeled for them. Those artists interested in life studies had been bored to desperation with painting Garffi's peasants. Eritha sent for the latest fashions in rev dresses, and she passed each afternoon posing as the artists requested, with the sea breezes whipping her frilly costumes. She stood on boulders, she waded in the surf, she lounged, she ran lightly along the beach, she stood pensive in the dusk, head lowered, in an attitude that was supposed to signify that the rev was over.

She was being immortalized—for some of these paintings were very good indeed and would certainly find their varied ways into important collections—on fifty different fabrics. During an occasional rest period she liked to wander from easel to easel and see how the different artists were portraying her. The strangest paintings were those by artists whose home worlds possessed raging, foaming seas. They liked to paint the monoliths with gigantic waves breaking over them, their sleek sides wet and glistening, all of which was a flagrant libel on Donov's quiet ocean. Their paintings showed Eritha in heroically defiant poses, doggedly facing adversity while treacherous fingers of water snatched at her.

While she examined the paintings, she listened to the artists talk. As at Zrilund, they talked incessantly, and if Neal Wargen wanted to know what they talked about she could tell him with one word: art.

The first news of the Virrab and Zrilund tragedies was brought to Garffi by one of its rare visitors, an art critic on sabbatical named Mora Seerl, from the world of Kurnu. Eritha, whose work was not such as to inspire visiting critics to seek her out, did not meet the woman until late in the day, when several of the artists were escorting her through the sepulcher—the display and storage room that in art colonies possessed an importance second only to that of the dining hall.

She was a dark, good-looking, vivacious woman in tourist costume—considerably older than she tried to look, Eritha concluded matter-of-factly—and like most critics she exuded conversation about art. Midway through her tour she pounced upon a group of paintings that Eritha had modeled for.

"This," she proclaimed, "dramatically typifies what is wrong with Donov's art. It's an art of *things,* and things have no feelings, no emotions. The emotion must come from the artist, and Donov's artists simply are unable to imbue Donov's outworn art subjects with emotion. The only thing that could save Donovian art is people, which is the sole art subject that has its own intrinsic feeling, but no Donovian artist has found any people worth painting except tourists, and he paints tourists only to mock them. These are the only paintings in this room that include a human figure, and look what the figure is—one of your fellow artists! Donovian art is dying."

Eritha said sweetly, "In your studies at the Institute, have you happened onto any portraits of Anna Lango?"

"Anna Lango was a professional model," Mora Seerl snapped. "Professional models aren't 'people'—they're artists' props."

"And that," a fellow artist murmured to Eritha, "puts you in your place."

Eritha nodded. "There's something to what she says, though. Why don't we paint people?"

"Here at Garffi, everything is on too grand a scale. Look what an insignificant thing you are among all those enormous boulders. What could a person, or a whole group of persons, add to a painting of a mountain? When people are dwarfed to insignificance, isn't it better to omit them? And if the artist tries to make them significant, then there's no room for the mountain. We aren't here to paint people, we're here to paint Garffi's special scenery—the mountains, the amazing seashore, and so on, just as the Virrab artists are there to paint Virrab's special scenery. If we wanted to paint people we'd go somewhere else."

"Where?" Eritha demanded.

"Anywhere people are."

Eritha said nothing more. She knew only too well why *she* didn't paint people—it was because *things* were so much easier to paint. Now, abruptly, she was tired of painting things, and since people were utterly beyond her it was time she went home.

She also was tired of conversation about art. There was stark tragedy at Virrab Island and at Zrilund, and in the sepulcher at Garffi, six artists and a critic were debating whether there was a place in Donovian art for the human figure.

Wes Alof's little coterie of Zrilund artists was already assembled when Arnen Brance entered the room. Alof waved to him and pointed to a chair. "We're talking about Jaward Jorno," he said.

Brance filled a mug and drank deeply, the appropriate response of any artist offered a choice between drinking and talking about Jaward Jorno. He was experiencing an unfamiliar weight of responsibility. He no longer was a volunteer spy for Jorno, or even for the mysterious police officer Karlus Gair. He was a confidential agent of the World Manager's First Secretary, appointed that very afternoon, and he'd noticed the difference the moment he accepted the position. Jorno and Gair made polite requests. Wargen issued orders.

"What about Jorno?" Brance asked.

"Reports say that the poison was spread around his islands and also that his boats were wrecked."

"So?"

"The reports lied."

Alof's plump face carried its usual flush of anger. The other artists seemed in varying degrees overwhelmed by Zrilund's catastrophe and disposed to listen at least as long as the adde lasted.

"Those were official reports issued by the Donovian government," Brance objected. "This business is highly embarrassing to Donov, and if the government wanted to lie it could have avoided no end of unpleasantness by not mentioning Jorno's resort at all."

"That's exactly what I mean."

"Maybe you'd better explain that," Brace said perplexedly.

"Virrab Island and the Rinoly mainland are Jorno's private property. Right? And he could have cleaned the place up and fixed his boats without any outsiders knowing what had happened. Right? Under the circumstances that would have been the smart thing to do. So why did he call in the police and

147

make the matter public and scare away no one knows how many resort customers?"

"I give up. Why?"

"It was much more to his advantage to make it public. Otherwise he wouldn't have done it."

Brance said doubtfully, "I still don't understand—"

"I'm explaining it. Have you seen any tourists on Zrilund today?"

"The ferries and the boat aren't running yet."

"It'll take weeks to repair the boat. Government inspectors have just certified the ferries unrepairable. They'll never run again. Even if both were ready tomorrow we wouldn't have any tourists because tourists don't enjoy looking at a poisoned sea filled with dead fish. The authorities aren't even guessing about how long it'll take to fix that. Zrilund is ruined. Just by comparison, did you know that Jorno's resort didn't close at all? By some incredible coincidence, the poison was dumped in the wrong place and most of it got carried out to sea. The poison dumpers didn't know the Rinoly currents. They knew the Zrilund currents perfectly, and they'd have known the Rinoly currents perfectly, and they'd have known the chart, but they didn't. Jorno's boats were wrecked—he says—but by another incredible coincidence he was able to replace them the following day. Zrilund is ruined. Jorno's resort wasn't even inconvenienced."

"That is something to think about," Brance admitted. He was tempted to point out that the Zrilund trip counted as an ocean voyage and required certified craft that had to be custom built, while the trip to Virrab never took one out of sight of land in any direction. Jorno could use small boats that were readily available anywhere. Brance was tempted, but it wouldn't have been wise for him to come through too strongly as Jorno's apologist.

"That's just the beginning," Alof said. "The person who concocted that poison had a considerable knowledge of chemistry. Did you know that there are two prize-winning chemists among Jorno's meszs? Look here. There's no doubt at all that Jorno is trying to ruin Zrilund. Normal competition didn't do the job fast enough, and he's using his meszs to speed things up. He has to pretend that someone is trying to ruin him at the same time so he won't be suspected. Everything that happens to Zrilund happens to Virrab in exactly the same way, but you'll notice that he cleverly sees that the things happening to Virrab do very little damage. What nasty prank do you suppose he and his meszs will aim at Zrilund next?'

"None," one of the artists said.

148

Alof turned on him angrily.

"There won't be any more," the artist said, morosely gazing out at the deserted oval. "They don't need any more. Like you said, Zrilund is ruined."

It was late when Brance finally left the artists. Rearm Hylat was waiting up for him, and the two of them sat together in the darkened dining room.

"Adde?" Hylat asked.

"Thanks, no. Alof believes a conspiracy should be launched on adde. I floated down here."

"What happened?"

"The usual rubbish. They talk endlessly about Jorno's iniquities and they agree that something has got to be done. They don't say what."

"Few artists are men of action," Hylat observed. "Not that Alof is any kind of artist."

"But he is. He showed me a portrait tonight. Old woman he found over in Fish Town. He's a fairly good artist. Maybe that's his trouble. He keeps getting people together and stirring things up, and then instead of following through on it, he goes off to paint."

"Maybe he's waiting for someone else to suggest the action."

"Maybe. Or maybe he's still cringing over what happened the last time. I'd like to speak up in Jorno's behalf. His mesz chemists have just perfected a process that precipitates the poison. Things may be back to normal weeks sooner than anyone expected. They also worked out a safe method for converting the dead fish to fertilizer, and they cobbled up a vast machine to do the job. It was shipped yesterday. Today Jorno and a few of the meszs were in Nor Harbor looking at the damaged ferries. The meszs think they can build a bigger and better ferry in a third the expected time, and they won't charge anything except for the materials."

"Wargen told you this?"

"Yes. He also told me I wasn't to mention any of it, because I'd destroy my effectiveness if the artists got the notion that I've ever nurtured a kindly thought about Jaward Jorno. They'd assume that I'd been bought."

"Nonsense!"

"True. A plausible lie can be much more convincing than the truth. For example, under Alof's manipulations that bit about the mesz chemists would be offered as proof that the meszs concocted the poison in the first place. Otherwise how'd they manage to come up with a treatment process so quickly? Jorno looks like the sort who'd buy people, so the person who defends him must have been bought. I'm not to

149

say anything to anyone except you. You're to pass the information to discerning townspeople at your discretion, remembering that you yourself are suspect because you're the one who sponsored that ridiculous tourist association with Jorno."

"Maybe that's what's wrong with this world," Hylat said sourly. "Everyone is suspect."

They sat for a time in silence, with Hylat sipping his adde and Brance trying to keep from dozing off. Brance was about to suggest to Hylatt that they postpone the solution of Zrilund's problems until the morrow when he heard a shout.

Footsteps sounded on the worn stone paving, more shouts rang out, and Brance and Hylat sprang for the door. The oval was unlighted, but four widely separated disks gave a dim illumination to the street that encircled it. Only artists would be out that late in Zrilund Town, and three of them were standing uncertainly in the middle of the street.

"Dunno," one responded to Brance's question. "Someone fussing about the fountain. Ran the instant we hove into view."

"Around the *fountain?*" Hylat exclaimed. He and Brance exchanged glances. "We'd better have a look. I'll get a light."

Hylat brought a handlight and led the way as they advanced on the celebrated Zrilund fountain. Suddenly he swore and leaped forward, and Brance hauled on him and told him not to be an idiot.

"Explosives!" Hylat gasped, trying to pull free.

"Then let's handle them so only one of us gets blown up!" Brance snapped. He sent Hylat scurrying for cutters and chased the artists back to a safe vantage point; and when Hylat returned, Brance cut the wires from a complicated timing device and carefully traced them to the four packs of explosive that had been buried around the fountain.

By the time he finished Zrilund was awake. Artists and townspeople teamed up for an exhaustive search of Zrilund Town, and when that uncovered no trace of the culprits, everyone sat around in grim determination waiting for the dawn. At first light they began a carefully organized search of the countryside, but nothing was found except a few strange marks on one of the beaches—proof that a boat had grounded there and that someone whose feet did not make human footprints had come ashore.

Neal Wargen said, "You couldn't be more mistaken. Those footprints are proof positive that Jorno had nothing to do with this."

"Who other than meszs leave mesz footprints?" Brance demanded hotly.

150

"Jaward Jorno is neither foolish nor careless. I don't speak for his moral integrity because I know nothing about it, but I do know that if he'd been connected with this in any way you wouldn't have found mesz footprints. Further, while I can make no guarantee for Jorno, I can for the meszs. Unlike we humans, they hurt no one, they damage nothing, they don't even defend themselves when attacked."

"That isn't the feeling around Zrilund this morning."

"What *is* the feeling?"

"That Jorno's gone too far this time. There wasn't any proof about what he did to the sea and the boats, people were angry, and they could speculate, but they didn't *know*. Now the fountain has been attacked, and that's the heart of Zrilund, it's irreplaceable, and a mesz left footprints. Now the people know, and they're no longer angry. They're enraged."

"There may be another attempt," Wargen said. "I'll ask Demron to station men there."

"They aren't needed. Volunteers are putting up lights right now, and every square inch of Zrilund Town will be under observation tonight."

"Anything else happening?"

"There was a mass meeting this morning. Townspeople and artists. Didn't do much except ask for volunteers to work on the lights and perform guard duty. There's an artists' meeting this afternoon. I don't know what for."

"Call me back when it's over," Wargen said.

Brance thanked the fat com agent on his way out and went to the Swamp Hut for lunch. He regretted having to pass up Hylat's food, but in order to find out what the artists were talking about he had to go where they were.

Wes Alof joined him. "We've called off the meeting," he said. "I'm talking with the artists individually. We're all going to Rinoly."

Brance stared at him.

"We've been studying the map," Alof went on. "There aren't any towns big enough to accommodate all of us, but I understand that every village has abandoned buildings that we could rent for virtually nothing. We'll manage our own accommodations. I've already sent messages, I'm sure some artists from the other colonies will want to join us. Inside of a week we should have a minimum three hundred artists in Rinoly." He grinned. "Three hundred artists are a match for three thousand meszs any time."

"What'll we do in Rinoly?" Brance demanded.

"Paint. We're all licensed artists, we can go to any public place and pursue our calling, the regulations say so. The important thing is to get everyone down there. Then we can study

151

the place and make plans to put an end to the mesz menace. Living expenses will be less there than here. I've raised money to help artists who need it with their transportation and other expenses, and I expect a lot of them will. What about you?"

"I can manage," Brance said. "I'll need time to make arrangements, though. I own a house, you know, and—"

"Just let me know as soon as possible. There may be a few artists who'll have to stay here for one reason or another, and that's all right—we don't want the people of Zrilund thinking we're walking out on them in time of need. They ought to understand, though, that very few of us can earn money without tourists, and there's no point in our sitting here while our paints dry up waiting for Jorno to blow all of us into the ocean."

Brance resignedly returned to the com center and placed a call to Wargen. He explained what had happened, and Wargen said, "The question is whether you'd accomplish more with the townspeople or with the artists. I think with the artists—I can ask Hylat to keep me informed about Zrilund Town. Did Alof give any hint at all of what he plans to do when he gets you to Rinoly?"

"None. I'll go if you want me to, but I'll have to make a few arrangements. You see, I have a pet swamp slug, and—"

Wargen was regarding him strangely. "Swamp slug?"

"Yes. I've had it for years."

"A *Zrilund* swamp slug?"

"That's the only kind Zrilund has."

"You must introduce me sometime. What about it?"

"I'll have to arrange for someone to look after it."

"Work it out, then, and be sure to let me know where you're going and when. Ask Hylat to call me."

Hylat was sitting at the back of his empty dining room, his mournful face radiating gloom and catastrophe. "I hear the artists are leaving," he said. "That'll finish Zrilund."

Brance seated himself and grinned at him. "For years I've been hearing the people of Zrilund complain about the artists, and for years I've been hearing the artists complain that no one person on this whole decaying island properly appreciates them. A temporary separation ought to be marvelously dissatisfying to all concerned. Both the artists and the townspeople will have to find someone else to complain about."

"But will they come back?" Hylat demanded.

"They'll come back. Even if for some strange reason Rinoly welcomes them, which it won't, they'll come back. Like me, a lot of those idiots love this place."

⋆ 17 ⋆

The Zrilund artists vanished into rural Rinoly. For all the news Wargen had, that impoverished land could have blotted them up. He waited for a report from Brance—waited a week, two weeks, three weeks, first in irritation and then in anger and finally with acute alarm. Had Alof discovered that Brance was a spy?

When he could wait no longer, he sent for Eritha Korak. "How'd you like to go to Virrab?" he asked her.

"I couldn't," she said. "Even the lodge for visiting artists has a huge waiting list."

"I'm sending you there as a guest. Intelligence out of Jorno's resort is extremely hard to come by—we get only bits and snatches picked up by eavesdropping on returning tourists. I need a comprehensive evaluation of what's going on there. I also need to find out what the Zrilund artists are doing in Rinoly. I have a man with them, Arnen Brance. Know him?"

Eritha shook her head. "He wasn't at Zrilund when I was there."

"He was, but he wasn't associating with artists. He went to Rinoly with the Zrilund group, and he hasn't reported since. I'm worried something may have happened to him. Most of the artists are harmless fools, but the people trying to manipulate them aren't."

"You want me to go to Virrab as a tourist, give Jorno's resort a careful scanning, and check on the Zrilund artists?"

"That's right."

"Better send someone Jorno hasn't met. Normally tourists enjoy basking in the warm glow of the proprietor's personal hospitality. If one of them turned her back whenever he approached—"

"I've thought of that. Listen. As far as I'm able to determine, business at Jorno's resort is exceeding his expectations with a single exception. He built a couple of superluxury rotundas, and they haven't had a single customer. The kind of people who could afford them already have their favorite resorts, usually places catering exclusively to millionaires, and they aren't likely to visit a catch-all resort like Virrab unless it's ecstatically recommended to them. Jorno can't get an endorsement for his luxury accommodations until someone patronizes them, and without it no one will patronize them. So I suggested to Lilya Vaan that she have herself a vacation at Virrab and take you as her companion. She thought a few days of slumming it at Jorno's resort might be mildly amusing. Then she happened to mention it to Mother, and now the countess insists on going with you."

"The countess—with Lilya and me?"

"Yes. Jorno will be elated. Watch!"

He placed a call to Jaward Jorno. "My mother, the countess," he told him, "would like to visit your resort with two companions. Do you have suitable accommodations for the countess and her guests?"

They could hear Jorno's sudden intake of breath. "Of course. Highly suitable accommodations. Would they prefer the mainland or Virrab?"

"The mainland. They've never visited Rinoly, so—after they've experienced all the charms of Virrab, of course—they'd like to travel about."

"I'm afraid they'll find little of interest in Rinoly apart from my resort, but I'll make every effort to enable them to see whatever they like. I'm sure that once they have visited Virrab they'll find it endlessly fascinating."

"Would you place a limousine and chauffeur on call for them?"

"Of course."

"There's one more thing. They'll dress as ordinary tourists, and they'd prefer to keep their identities confidential. Can you accommodate them in that?"

"But certainly. You said the countess and two guests?"

"The Countess Wargen, the Dame Lilya Vaan, whom I think you know, and Miss Eritha Korak, the World Manager's granddaughter."

Jorno took another deep breath. "When shall I expect them?"

"I'll notify you as soon as the arrangements are completed."

Wargen broke the connection. "It must be galling to build magnificent accommodations for millionaire guests and have them unused. He'll keep your identities secret as long as you're there, but the moment you leave it'll be known all over Donov and several other worlds that the Countess Wargen, the Dame Vaan, and a member of the World Manager's immediate family vacationed at Virrab."

"Is Jorno a snob?"

"That's irrelevant. He's a practical businessman, and socially prominent people are good for his business."

"I thought he was a brilliant man of galactic vision. Now it turns out he has the soul of a village usurer. The real mystery is why the countess didn't cancel out when she heard I'd be along."

"She wants to know you better."

"I don't believe it!"

"It's true," Wargen said gravely. "She wants to be familiar with all of your defects."

"That's more like it. And forever after, when you two are having a quiet conversation, she'll drop in flattering remarks about me. 'By the way, Pet, did you know that the little Korak minx mixes adde and wrranel milk for breakfast?'"

Wargen regarded her with horror. "You do?"

"Of course not. But once she's taken a cozy excursion with me she'll be in a position to know all sorts of things, whether they're true or not. Just you wait—she'll draw up a catalogue of my bad habits, and she'll read it to you every evening at dinner."

"It won't do a bit of good," Wargen told her. "I already know all about them."

The rotunda was screened from the public park by a magnificent grove of trees, and even such a massive building as this one was rendered charming by its mesz architecture. Their suite, which occupied an entire floor and had its own staff of servants, represented the absolute ultimate in plush resort accommodations. They strolled through private gardens laid out in strange and fascinating patterns by the meszs, they swam at their private beach, and they enjoyed a seaside promenade on their private pier. Later they dined in their own dining room on fare as luxurious, varied, and delicious as anything Lilya had ever served at a rev.

All three of them were relaxed and mellowed when Jorno's steward arrived with an invitation to join him for a tour of his estate—even the countess had found nothing to complain about for as long as twenty minutes at a time. The two older women accepted at once. Eritha, who had been instructed to scan Jorno's resort but not his private property, pleaded fatigue. Instead of receiving this excuse with the skepticism that it deserved, the countess seemed to find it flattering.

As soon as the countess and Lilya had been ceremoniously escorted away by the steward, Eritha donned her tourist's cloak and went for a stroll on the public promenade. Then she examined the park that the meszs had created—it hadn't been completed on her previous visit. To her amazement she found a fountain spouting colored, phosphorescent water, and as darkness fell its spray became quite spectacular.

"But it'll never take the place of the Zrilund fountain," Eritha heard a cool voice murmur. She turned and found another tourist smiling at her—Mora Seerl, the art critic on sabbatical. "Good evening, Miss Korak. We met at Garffi—ah, you remember me. It's a pleasure to see you again. On this world one doesn't often meet an artist in disguise."

"Or an art critic," Eritha said.

Mora laughed merrily. "But isn't this as appropriate a costume for a critic as any other?"

"At least it's a costume that excuses anything, which is why I wear it. I take it that you've been to Zrilund."

"Months ago. It was the first colony I visited, and I've known its great paintings for so long that it was like going home—to a sadly deteriorated home, to be sure, but none the less home."

"How do you like Virrab?"

"It's wonderfully scenic, and I suppose there'll be a Virrab vogue for a time, but to me the place is dead simply because it'll never come alive."

"I rather liked it," Eritha said.

"An artist would. It's new and different, and therefore exciting, and it presents the challenge of capturing all that newness in paint. The critic or tourist doesn't look at it that way. Virrab has the only untamed nature I've ever seen that is utterly sterilized. Keep to the path. No stopping except at official lookouts. No standing between the yellow lines or you'll spoil the view for the working artists. I miss Zrilund and the other resorts where you can look over the artists' shoulders. To a critic, just wandering about in those places is a priceless education. You can study a scene and then instantly see it through the eyes of a dozen artists and then look again and think what you might do with it yourself if only you could. On Virrab the artist is behind a bush, and if he's aware of you at all he's waiting for you to go away. In time you resent that, or at least I do."

"I hadn't thought of it that way," Eritha admitted. "Of course the Virrab artists are among the best on Donov, and the best artists feel very little obligation to entertain tourists. The artists at Zrilund invite interruptions from tourists, which may have something to do with their being the worst on Donov."

"I doubt that they are. It's just that those poor souls have got themselves into a frightful rut, painting and repainting scenes that were exhausted years ago. All they need is a rous-

156

ing collision with reality, but the only reality on Zrilund is already petrified. In a sense, all Donovian art needs a collision with reality. All of it is dying. Virrab is just a glitteringly artificial attempt to resuscitate something better left to perish in peace."

Eritha said indignantly, "You can't believe that!"

"Name the great artists working on Donov," Mora Seerl said. "You can't. There are lots of first-rate craftsmen—there are even some at Zrilund—but the greatness is gone forever. Donov has nothing left but tradition, and the tradition is one of subject matter only. Even the most casual student of Donovian art notices that at once—the Zrilund fountain treated in a bewildering variety of styles, for example. Once that subject matter is exhausted, and it's already been exploited to death, those artists had better take their styles elsewhere. Eventually they will."

"And—Virrab?"

"New subject matter, but there are no more great artists on Donov to make a tradition of it. As an art center it won't last a decade. It may last forever as a charming tourist resort. I've no knowledge at all as to the criteria for tourist resorts."

Eritha indicated the fountain. "Someone will make a subject of that."

"Certainly. It won't have the appeal of the Zrilund fountain. There can't be more than one original, and it's a rather blatant imitation, but it'll be painted." She looked about her. "I wish it were being painted now. I miss the artists. When I see them perspiring in the hot sun attempting to give permanence to the most fleeting of visions, I think perhaps I'm catching a glimpse of what human aspiration is all about. I consider it prophetic that Virrab advertises itself as an art resort and yet keeps both art and artists virtually invisible. Donov is well on its way to becoming just another popular vacation world."

"I find it hard to accept that."

"Oh, people interested in art will always come here, both to see the splendid permanent collections and to see what remains of the things the great artists painted. But they won't come to see artists painting those things, because there won't be any artists. There's a limit to the number of Virrabs that any world can promote, and Virrabs have very short lifespans. They are places without feeling. The only art subject with feeling is people, and Donov's artists are afraid to paint people."

"You aren't going to the island again?"

Mora shook her head. "I have three more days here. I

157

haven't decided what I'll do—behave like a normal art-hating tourist, I suppose. How about you?"

"This is my second trip, so I've already seen everything. I'm just an escort for two charming middle-aged women."

"You poor thing!"

"So I don't know what I'm going to do, except that I'll try to escape whenever I can manage it—which is what I'm doing now."

"How'd you like a ride into the country?" Mora asked.

"What's there to see?"

"Absolutely nothing, but we may find some artists. I've heard that some of the Zrilund artists came down here when Zrilund was closed to tourists. I've been toying with the idea of hiring a transport of some kind and trying to find them. Would you like to come along?"

"I'd love to," Eritha said.

In the morning Eritha persuaded Lilya and the countess to eschew the private tour Jorno had planned for them and join a rollicking crowd of tourists from the main resort. She saw them off for Virrab, and then she climbed into Mora Seerl's rented transport, the driver nodded agreeably, and they followed a winding road through the parklike grounds of Jorno's meticulously groomed estate. The road looped around Jorno's new transportation center, and they emerged into the bleak Rinoly countryside.

Mora looked about her with distaste. "Maybe my friends were having their little joke. They swore that the Zrilund artists came down here. I didn't think to ask what the artists were supposed to be doing. Surely not painting—I've never seen anything so inartistic."

After a few minutes of barren, humped hills and decrepit farm buildings, enlivened only occasionally by a plot of the waxy, pink leaves of tarff, Jorno's fiber plant, they topped a hill and floated down to the small village of Ruil. On Eritha's previous visit it, too, had looked decrepit and abandoned. Now the old stone buildings were obviously in use, the few shops appeared to be favored with customers, the streets were tidy, and the village oval had entertained a market as recently as that morning.

Mora spoke to the driver, and the transport settled to a halt. She looked about her and asked perplexedly, "What artists?"

"I'll ask someone," Eritha volunteered.

Mora got out with her. They walked together to the nearest shop, and at the doorway they halted in tense, staring incredulity. Finally they moved inside and continued to stare.

158

The artists were using it as a sepulcher. There were paintings everywhere—on improvised easels, leaned against the room's rickety furnishings, stacked in haphazard piles—and the walls were filled with them.

Eritha was gazing awesomely at a large fabric entitled, "Market at Ruil." The dilapidated, squalid village surrounded dilapidated, squalid people in a scene where the buyers obviously had little money and the sellers just as obviously had little to sell, and those juxtaposed facts gave every transaction a monumental importance.

Mora suddenly burst into laughter. "Souvenirs!" she gasped. "They're still painting souvenirs, but now the souvenirs have a *message!* It's incredible!"

Eritha said nothing—one art lesson she had learned well concerned the inutility of arguments about art—but her entire being wanted to scream, "Beautiful! Beautiful!" She moved breathlessly from painting to painting. Here was the bleak countryside, where a weathered farmer stared disconsolately at a parched field and meditated the nothing of the coming harvest. There a mother, as unfertile as the ground she tilled, ignored the undernourished child beside her who played feebly with the undernourished grain. In a painting of heroic dimensions the cheerless, wasted landscape lay resigned under a stormy sky, awaiting punishment, and in the foreground a threadbare child struggled frantically to lead an enormous wrranel to shelter. It was a stark masterpiece. It was magnificent.

And it could not be. These were *Zrilund* artists, the despised souvenir painters who had nothing to say and said it so badly. They had been trapped between the mawkish taste of the tourists and the heavy weight of outmoded tradition and forced to perform anew something that had already been done better ten thousand times.

Now they were liberated—their talents were liberated. They were free to paint what they saw and felt. More important, they sensed the high drama of a barren struggle for existence, and they were painting what the unfortunate natives of Rinoly felt.

Mora was moving from painting to painting with renewed peals of laughter and enlarging her comments about souvenirs with a message. "What do you think?" she asked finally.

"I like them," Eritha said defiantly.

Mora regarded her with interest. "How odd! But then, you're a rather bad artist."

"Extremely bad," Eritha agreed. "At Garffi the artists said I painted almost as ineptly as a critic."

She was retracing her steps, looking at the signatures and finding many that she recognized. She gave an exclamation of delight when she saw "W'iil" scrawled on some of the larger paintings. "Dear Todd!" she said. "He finally found subjects that made him forget his theories. And look at the prices! If I were wealthy I'd start a Rinoly Museum of Art."

"I can't imagine myself wealthy enough to do a silly thing like that," Mora said.

"If I had any money at all I'd start my own collection, but I've been living a whole quarter in advance. Damn!"

A man had come in quietly, a neighboring shopkeeper. Mora asked, "Where are the artists?"

"Out painting."

"Out where?"

The shopkeeper gestured at the horizon. "They move around a lot."

"Do you sell many of these paintings?" Eritha asked.

"Ain't sold none yet."

When they returned to the transport, the shopkeeper trailed after them. "If you're looking for artists you won't find them in that," he said. "Them back lanes aren't big enough for that thing, and farmers hereabouts won't tolerate people driving over their fields. You'll have to walk."

That day Eritha developed sore feet for the first time in her life and learned to profoundly appreciate the Donovian tourist costume. They tramped narrow lanes, they stopped at time-eroded dwellings to ask questions of elderly, taciturn farmers, they took wrong turnings, they walked in inadvertent circles, they retraced their steps.

Now and again they came upon small groups of working artists. The first such group was gathered about the corner of a crumbling stone wall where a small boy struggled to milk a wrranel, and there Eritha found Todd W'iil. He yelped his surprise, greeted her with a hug, and proudly led her to his unfinished fabric.

"It's wonderful," Eritha said. "I saw some of your work in town, and it's all wonderful. But what are you doing here?"

Todd scratched his head fretfully. "Well, there's this artist Wes Alof, and he thought we ought to come down here and do something about Jaward Jorno on account of Jorno and his meszs ruined Zrilund."

"Do what about Jaward Jorno?"

"I don't rightly remember," W'iil said impatiently.

Mora was examining the unfinished paintings, and Eritha waited apprehensively for a sneering remark about souvenirs with a message. Instead she began to gush an enthusiasm that Eritha found sickening.

"Anyway," W'iil went on, "there was nothing to do in Zrilund, no tourists at all, so I came along. When we got here Alof told us to pretend to work while he got things organized, so we started painting, and—we're *painting!*" He beamed at her. "Everyone is painting."

"Even Wes Alof?"

"Sure. He's not much good except for human figures, but he does them pretty well."

"Know an artist named Arnen Brance?"

"Sure. He's good. He's better than me."

"Where is he?"

"Around somewhere. He's staying in the next village south, but I see him now and then."

"And—he's painting?"

"*Everyone* is painting! We're painting as early as there's light to see by, and as late, and we're finding things to paint that we didn't know existed. Brance has a word for it, he calls it 'the drama of life.' Everywhere I look I see that and I want to paint it. Friend of Alof's—not an artist—comes around every now and then and says the plan's ready and we can get moving against Jorno, and we tell him what he can do with his plan."

"Are you selling any paintings?"

"There's no one around here to buy them. They'll sell when we take them where the tourists are—they'll even sell in the big galleries. We'll work here as long as our money lasts, and it don't cost much to live in Rinoly."

Eritha and Mora finally made their way back to the transport. With the driver consulting a map they drove through a series of decrepit little villages, all of them showing signs of the unexpected prosperity wrought by artists spending Wes Alof's money. Rulong, Reroff, Vuln, Wef—the villages were blurred facsimiles of the first one they visited. In each of them the artists had taken over an abandoned building as a sepulcher, and Eritha wandered through these in bewildered wonderment.

Between villages Mora led her on exhaustive tramps through the narrow lanes in search of artists, with whom she delightedly exchanged verbal jabs and matched theories of art.

"Do you still like the paintings?" she asked Eritha abruptly.

"Yes. It's an entirely new approach to art—new for Donov—and it's amazing the way these artists are inspired by it. I even feel as though I'd like to paint something myself!"

"I don't, but I enjoy watching the artists."

Eritha flexed her aching feet. "The only artists I want to watch now are those I can see from the road."

"Just keep telling yourself that somewhere in the wilds of Rinoly is the one artist capable of raising this art above the level of souvenirs, and you may find him. That's what makes criticism exciting."

They drove and walked through a landscape so repetitive that Eritha had the sensation of passing the same bleak, rocky hills and the same moldy, crumbling buildings again and again.

Suddenly, where the road forked to embrace a village, they came upon a small crowd. It was the first time that day that they had seen more than two people at a time in a village street. Mora signaled the chauffeur to stop, and they dismounted and limped toward it curiously.

Long before they reached it they heard strange, hoarse, whispered utterances, monstrously amplified and tossed to the fitful Rinoly winds. Then they saw the long, silken neck, the sleek, gleaming, golden fur, and they began to comprehend the whispered phrases: "The smallest quickening of being is no less precious to the creature who possesses it. Life is life's greatest gift and life's greatest responsibility. The life that destroys life points the way to its own destruction."

"What is *that*?" Mora demanded.

"Franff," Eritha said.

"The animaloid artist?"

Eritha nodded.

"We have two of his paintings at home, in the Qwant Museum. Who's the old crone?"

"Anna Lango."

Mora stared at her. "That old hag? Excuse me, but I know her face as well as I know my own, her *young* face, she modeled for so many artists. No artist ever used a lovelier prop."

"Every life is a monument to all life," Franff whispered.

Mora Seerl shook her head bewilderedly. "What a day this has been!"

That night Eritha placed a call to her grandfather—the World Manager's communications were equipped with a sensor that screamed a protest when an unauthorized party attempted to monitor—and asked him to connect her with Neal Wargen.

"First," she told Wargen, "you can forget your man Brance."

"What happened to him?"

"He's discovered that he's an artist, and he's much too

162

busy painting to spy. Second, you were right about someone trying to manipulate the Zrilund artists, and you can forget that, too. It's a fiasco. All of the artists are painting furiously, and they're no more interested in sabotaging Jorno than Brance is in spying on them."

"What have they found in Rinoly that's worth painting?"

"I haven't the time to explain it. Third, make a note. Mora Seerl. Allegedly an art critic on sabbatical. Find out if her visitor's or student's permit is in order. Find out if she has any connection with a transport with registration 5494682, which she says she rented for the day, along with a driver. There's no place in Rinoly where one can rent vehicles and drivers except through Jorno, and he doesn't offer transports. His chauffeurs are in uniform, which this driver wasn't."

"Slow down!" Wargen exclaimed. "Mora Seerl, a visiting art critic. What about her?"

"She's as phony as that forged Ghord that Harnasharn hangs in his office once a week to remind him of his one mistake. I've met her twice. The first time, at Garffi, she was from Kurnu. Today she was from Qwant. She knew my name, which she didn't get either here or at Garffi. She has a good patter of art talk, but she knows nothing at all about art. She goes on and on about how the only art subject with feeling is people, and when she encounters some really remarkable paintings of people she has no awareness that *this* is what she's been talking about."

"That makes her suspect?"

"That and the rest of it, including the transport she said she rented but didn't. I suspect she brought it with her for transporting whatever props would be needed in the plot against Jorno. The funny thing is that we were both touring Rinoly for the same reason—no reports! I was looking for your man Brance, and she was looking for Wes Alof, who seems to be the conspiracy's link with the artists. Like Brance, Alof got interested in painting. I was able to write Brance off as soon as I heard what had happened, but she had to spend the entire day looking—unsuccessfully—for Alof. Probably he saw her coming and hid. Someone invested a lot of money in moving the Zrilund artists to Rinoly. Someone was counting on making use of them. No wonder she ended the day in a foul mood!"

"Call me back in an hour," Wargen said.

She did so, and he answered with a note of elation in his voice. "There is no Mora Seerl registered at the Institute or any museum. There is no student, visitor, or tourist register on a Mora Seerl from either Kurnu or Qwant. The transport registration is in the name of Ronony Gynth."

"Say—do you suppose—"

"I think it quite likely that you've met the mysterious Ronony. You say she was at Garffi?"

"She's probably visited all of the art colonies to discreetly test out various undertakings in iniquity."

Wargen chuckled. "And just as she was about to succeed, all of her henchmen turned artist! It's almost a poetic touch. In fact, it's a lovely exit line. On Donov, all of her plots turned to art. Our line and her exit—I've thought regretfully for a long time that the day would come when we'd have to do something about her."

"Yesterday she said she had three more days here. I'd guess that she'll be looking for Alof again tomorrow."

"I'd guess that she won't. Demron will have her picked up tonight. If she's registered under that false name we can hold her incognito while we investigate her various other iniquities. I'll also have all of her employees picked up. Perhaps one of them will talk."

"About what?"

"Sornor has confessed its responsibility for the thieves—with the evidence we have it couldn't very well do otherwise—and the Sornorian ambassador, who I think means well, swears by the teeth of his ancestors that he knew nothing about it, that his government knew nothing about it, that it was a pernicious scheme fostered by the former ambassador in revenge for our kicking him out. He also swears that Sornor had nothing to do with poisoning Donov's oceans. I've wanted to believe him, but I couldn't without evidence pointing to another plausible candidate. Now we have it."

"Ronony Gynth?"

"Mestil. All this time I couldn't see how Zrilund fitted into the plot, and I should arrest myself for stupidity. The idea wasn't to ruin Jorno, you can't ruin a multi-multimillionaire by sabotaging a little resort he runs as a hobby. The idea was to arouse so much antagonism against his meszs that they'd be expelled from Donov. It was damned cleverly done—utter devastation at Zrilund and only a little damage at Virrab, topped off with a forged mesz footprint, and the artists swallowed the notion that Jorno wrecked Zrilund and purposely did token damage to Virrab to divert suspicion from himself." He beamed at her. "And that was when the plot turned to art. You did quite a piece of work today. Do you have anything else?"

"Franff is in Rinoly."

"He's been there for several days. What are the countess and Lilya doing?"

"Eating too much and being fawned on by Jorno."

"Splendid. I take it that you're doing the same?"

"I missed lunch today," Eritha said bitterly. "I walked through all the back lanes in Rinoly looking for your Mr. Brance and keeping an eye on the phony art critic. I haven't even had dinner yet."

"Cheer up! Your grandfather will award a medal to you. He might even raise your allowance—tonight he'll be able to sleep well for the first time since the poison was dumped. And you can drop the scanning and have yourself a real vacation."

"While you're in such a generous mood I don't suppose you'd lend me some money," Eritha said. "No, you wouldn't. Never mind." She cut off.

18

Eritha said wistfully, "Lilya, would you lend me some money?"

The countess turned on them with a disapproving frown. Lilya smiled and said, "Of course, Pet. How much would you like?"

"Would you lend me a lot of money?"

Lilya's smile vanished. "How much is a lot?"

"Two thousand dons."

"Oh." Lilya smiled again. "I thought maybe some gigolo had latched onto you, but gigolos come much higher than that—or so I've heard."

"Eritha," the countess said, impaling her with the frown. "What do you need two thousand dons for?"

"I want to buy some paintings."

"Oh, well." The countess sniffed reproachfully. "I suppose we all have our little foibles."

"Listen," Lilya said. "I asked this innocent to buy me a painting when she was at Garffi, and she did. Cost me five hundred dons, and I thought she'd let one of her friends put something over on the two of us. A week later Harnasharn saw it at one of my revs, and he offered me seven-fifty. When Eritha talks about paintings, I listen." She paused. "Two thousand dons is a lot of money for a painting, Pet. What kind of painting?"

"Paintings. A lot of paintings. None of them is very expensive, but some day they'll be worth lots of money. Why don't you two come along? You might find something you like, and in a very short time these particular paintings are going to be the rage."

"Heaven forbid I should hang anything on *my* walls that's going to be a rage!" the countess said.

But when morning came she was ready to accompany them. Eritha heard her say to Lilya, "When you've seen Virrab Island once, you've seen it."

They boarded the limousine Jorno provided, and the Rinoly landscape sustained the countess's interest almost as far as the village of Ruil. While Eritha was selecting paintings from the village sepulcher—she took six by Todd W'iil—the two older women prowled about restlessly and fixed painting after painting in dual stares of puzzlement.

"You say, Pet, that these things are going to be valuable?" Lilya kept saying.

Tiring of that, they went to look at the village. A short time later Lilya hurried back and called to Eritha. Two lumbering wrranels were passing with an enclosed cart. The single passenger was an elderly woman, and Franff—now almost completely blind and obviously much enfeebled—stumbled along beside the cart.

The shopkeeper, who had watched dumfounded while Eritha made her purchases, momentarily recovered his speech. "I heard he's on his way to visit the Brotherhood Park the meszs built."

"Poor old beast," Lilya said softly. "I'm glad, now, that the count persuaded me to hire him. It was my money that bought his wrranels and cart and supported him all these months, and at least he's been able to live as he chose and do what he wanted to do. If he hasn't helped the cause of brotherhood, at least he hasn't harmed it any—and how many of us can say as much?"

Lilya and the countess quickly satisfied any curiosity they may have had about Rinoly or the paintings, and Eritha sent them back to the resort along with the paintings she had purchased and a crock of fresh wrranel milk that she bought from a farmer. Neither the countess nor Lilya had tasted it before, and its cool sweetness enraptured them. "Not only that," Eritha told them gravely, "but it's a type-two dietetic food and excellent for the complexion." When the limousine returned, she loaded in more paintings and rode to the next village.

She was back at the resort by early afternoon with all of her money spent, and she obtained Jorno's permission to use the unoccupied suite on the floor above to display the paintings. Jorno, the countess, and Lilya came to see them. "You should put together a collection of your own," she told Jorno, "and build a museum to house it. These paintings are going to make Rinoly famous. Not only will they be a fabulous advertisement for your resort, but a museum for them and for the Virrab paintings would attract a lot of visitors."

Jorno favored her with his most engaging smile. "Miss Korak, you take after your grandfather, and no one will ever pay either of you a finer compliment. It sounds like an excellent idea, but instead of riding all over Rinoly and sifting through piles of junk art in the hope of finding a few gems,

167

why don't I just buy the paintings you've already selected? I'll pay what you paid plus twenty-five per cent."

"Nope. I bought these for myself. You'll have to do your own sifting."

The countess said incredulously, "Do you mean to say that you're turning down a profit of five hundred dons on a single day's work?"

"I didn't buy the paintings to make a profit. I bought them to keep. If Mr. Jorno is interested, I'll be glad to go back tomorrow and help him make his own collection, and he won't have to pay me. There are still hundreds of paintings to choose from, and there are some very fine examples that I would have taken if I'd had more money."

Jorno said thoughtfully, "Of all the unlikely places for a new school of art, surely Rinoly would top the list. And of all the unlikely artists, those from Zrilund—it isn't that I question your judgment, understand, but I think I'll ask Harnasharn's opinion before I start acquiring paintings."

"I'll show them to him when I get back to the Metro."

"He's here now, selecting some Virrab paintings," Jorno said. "I'll ask him to stop off before he leaves." He went to send a message, and then the four of them sat down to wait for Harnasharn.

"Did you know you have unregistered guests in the park?" Eritha asked. "Franff and Anna. At least, that's where they were headed."

"Franff wanted to see the sculpture," Jorno said. "It was rather pathetic—his eyesight is just about gone, and of course a nonor doesn't have hands to feel with. I thought he'd just come as a matter of form, being pledged as he is to the cause of brotherhood, but he really wanted to study the statue. Felt the thing with his nose, went over and over it until I was willing to swear that he'd meditated every chisel mark. But they're no longer in the park. I sent them over to stay with the meszs. Poor Franff—his health has failed terribly since the last time I saw him."

Harnasharn arrived in a peevish mood. "This'll make me miss my connection to the Metro," he grumbled. "*What* new school of art?"

At the entrance to the suite he halted abruptly and stared. "The *Zrilund* artists?" he asked incredulously.

"Most of them are very sound craftsmen," Eritha said. "All they needed was subjects they really cared about."

Harnasharn nodded. He made a rapid circuit of the suite and then found a chair and sat down heavily. "You wanted an appraisal?" he asked Jorno.

Jorno shook his head. "The paintings belong to Miss Korak, and she isn't interested in selling. I'd like your opinion of her suggestion that I establish a museum for the art of this Rinoly group and the Virrab artists, and just out of curiosity I'd like an informal evaluation of these paintings."

"How many paintings are there?" Harnasharn asked.

"Fifty-three," Eritha said.

"You couldn't form a collection like this without an enormous number of paintings to choose from."

"There are hundreds," Eritha told him.

"Strange that these sophisticated artists can come down here and instantly achieve such a feeling of empathy for provincial farmers." He began another circuit of the suite and then stopped and exclaimed, "Brance? Arnen Brance is painting?"

"Magnificently," Eritha said.

"Yes indeed. Years ago he was capable only of photographing his subjects in paint. Now he photographs the emotions of his subjects, and all of his vices have become virtues. Well, then—"

The countess and Lilya moved forward expectantly. Eritha, suddenly apprehensive of being thought a fool, wished the pronouncement did not have to be quite so public.

"The museum is an excellent idea. An evaluation isn't so easily managed. If these paintings catch the fancy of art buyers, they could be worth ten times their present value in less than a year." He smiled. "Or a hundred times. *If* they catch on. They are very good paintings, all of them, but it's the market place that determines value, and these are the work of unknown artists exploiting a subject matter that has no tradition. Until they have a tested market value, my best offer would probably average out at about a hundred dons per painting. Keeping it in round figures, I'd be willing to pay five thousand dons for this collection."

"Five thousand!" the countess exclaimed. "You're joking! Why, that's more than twice what she paid!"

"I don't make jokes about art, ma'am," Harnasharn said irritably. "My valuations aren't based upon what someone else paid, but upon what I'm willing to pay. I think Miss Korak has made an excellent investment. She'd be wise to keep the paintings."

"I may have to sell some of them to repay Lilya," Eritha said.

"Never mind, Pet. I don't need the money and I wouldn't want to stand in the way of your becoming independently wealthy. But how about going back there tomorrow and picking out a few for me?"

"I wish I could give the artists more money," Eritha said. "It doesn't seem right that I paid them so little."

"That's noble of you, Pet," Lilya told her. "But wait until I've bought a few before you go around inflating prices."

"I'd like to see these hundreds of paintings myself," Harnasharn said. "Would you mind if I accompanied you?"

"Please do," Lilya said graciously. "Granted Eritha must know something, but when the advice is going to be free I like to get a lot of it."

"I'll come with you," the countess said. "Perhaps a few of those paintings would look attractive in my rev room. Why don't you join us, Mr. Jorno, and make your own selections for your Rinoly museum?"

Jorno beamed at her. "What a splendid idea!"

"And you, Mr. Harnasharn," the countess went on. "Please be my guest for as long as you choose to stay. Tomorrow we'll tour Rinoly together."

"And tonight I'll offer all of you a different kind of treat," Jorno said. "The meszs are holding a fest in honor of Franff, and you can join me on Mestil Island."

"Franff!" Harnasharn exclaimed. "Is Franff here? I haven't had an opportunity to see him since he returned to Donov. I'd be pleased and honored to be present. What does a mesz fest consist of?"

"A very polite, excessively formal, overwhelmingly elaborate dinner. I've been promised every possible variety of mesz food, and mesz food is delicious. Unfortunately all of it is liquefied, but if you find that tiresome the meszs always prepare special non-liquid dishes when guests are present. Shall we make it a rev? Splendid!"

At Jorno's private pier they found a red-bearded artist named Arnen Brance waiting for them. Jorno had sent for him at the request of Franff and the meszs, and Eritha learned to her amazement that Brance had personally planned and managed Franff's escape from Sornor, and also that he'd been one of the artists who instructed the meszs. His familiarity with Harnasharn amazed her more. She had never heard any artist, not even those of stature, call Harnasharn by his first name, but Brance did.

She managed a few words with him in the boat, and when she told him that Neal Wargen had been disturbed because he hadn't reported, he said indignantly, "There was nothing to report."

The mesz village was still unfinished, but its focal point, a vast community rotunda, had been completed. The hundreds of meszs attending the fest were already at their places when

Jorno's party was ceremoniously escorted down a ramp to the place of honor, a circular table at the center of the room.

Looking about her, Eritha saw tier upon rising tier of meszs seated at long, curving tables. She was seeing them in person for the first time, and when she recovered somewhat from the shock of their almost-human grotesqueness, she found herself wondering whether the twilight produced by the room's oddly subdued, indirect lighting was a gracious gesture on their part to spare their human guests the stark reality of their appearance.

Huge ceramic tureens in vivid and glowing patterns stood in formation along the tables. In front of each diner was a wide, shallow bowl. In addition the guest table was provided with an array of goblets and platters of small cakes.

"Each tureen will have a different combination of liquefied vegetables," Jorno explained. "Try as many as you like and have as much as you like. The cakes are the same kind of food, they deliquefy it and compress the residue." He smiled at Franff. "Everything is vegetable. The meszs eat no meat."

Anna ladled liquid from the nearest tureen into Franff's bowl, and he cautiously dropped a long tongue into it. "My teeth aren't *that* bad," he whispered. "They didn't have to chew it for me." Anna slapped him playfully and fed him one of the cakes.

The others began to fill their goblets. Eritha, pausing before she drank, looked up at the meszs. They ladled liquid into their bowls, leaned over them, and with their strangely shaped mouths seemed to soundlessly inhale the contents. In the dim light and with the rims of the bowls partially concealing their faces, she could not discover how they did it. Obviously no napkins were necessary when one entertained meszs—none of them got so much as a drop of liquid on his face.

The countess and Lilya were having a delightful time. They sampled the meszs' liquid concoctions with all of the deliberation of a professional adde taster, comparing impressions with Jorno and mildly arguing the virtues of one blending over another. Their mesz attendants changed the tureens often and kept the platters of cakes filled, and Eritha agreed with Harnasharn, who was seated beside her, that everything was delicious. Privately she had written the evening off as one unending appetizer for the meal she intended to have the moment she got back to the resort.

She contented herself with listening to the others, with vicariously enjoying the enormous pleasure Franff was experiencing in this reunion with his friends Harnasharn and Brance, with watching the meszs and admiring the tasteful

171

decor of their community building. The one sobering note was supplied by the six moons that swam the lofty, star-flecked dome—Mestillian moons. The building was a haunting monument to a lost world.

Suddenly, above the rolling murmur of a vast roomful of quiet conversations, a dull boom sounded. Jorno turned quickly and leaped to his feet. Eritha followed his gaze and saw a man standing in a distant entrance. At that instant he threw something and stepped back, and the massive door rolled shut.

There was a flash, a boom that rocked the building, a concussion that swept dozens of tureens from tables, a poof of acrid smoke that brought tears to the eyes and left the nostrils stinging. Something slapped against the table, and Eritha looked down upon a cluster of bleeding mesz fingers.

No one screamed; no one even spoke. The humans leaped to their feet and then stood in stunned immobility. The meszs acted with calm resignation—except for those who remained to assist the wounded and dying, they were quietly filing toward numerous exits that opened magically beneath their feet as they pushed the tiers aside. A mesz was plucking at Eritha's sleeve and motioning her to follow him.

The distant door rolled open again. Arnen Brance saw it first, and he hurled his way up the tiers of tables. As he ran he shouted something, and then, still in full stride, he caught what was thrown and flung himself through the closing door and into the night. Eritha saw the flash but no sign of Brance.

"This way!" Jorno called.

A moment later they were moving along a dimly lit tunnel, and the only sound was the click of Franff's hoofs. The tunnel branched in several directions; Jorno, after calling to them to follow the meszs, turned off and vanished around a corner. He rejoined them almost at once, announcing that he'd sent for help, and took the lead. At intervals they passed heavy metal doors, and they began to hear them being slammed behind them. Finally the tunnel floor pointed upward, and they emerged in the waterside warehouse.

From the direction of the village came blasts that made the flimsy building shudder. Leaping flames cast remote, flickering shadows. Jorno hurried them the length of the pier to where their boat was tied. Then he halted and swore bitterly.

"What are we waiting for?" Harnasharn demanded.

"There was supposed to be someone waiting here to take you back." Jorno hesitated, looking about him. "I can't leave the meszs now, I simply can't, and none of them will want to leave while their brothers are being murdered. I don't suppose you—no, it would be too risky."

The countess and Lilya were looking longingly at the boat, which heaved gently at its mooring. Harnasharn, fretfully peering down at it, muttered that he had never operated a boat.

"Help is on the way," Jorno said. "You can wait in the tunnel until it gets here. You'll be safe there."

They turned back.

From the direction of the village a shout rang out, and footsteps pounded toward them. Franff, standing beside Eritha with drooping head, suddenly tensed as they began to clang on the pier. Eritha heard him hoarsely cough a word, "Brothers," and he bounded forward.

But he had no microphone, no amplifier to carry his message, and the first man he met raised a weapon and slugged at him viciously. Franff toppled into the water.

Anna moaned and hurried to help him, but Jorno was ahead of her. Snarling invectives, he swung a killing blow with his fist, but it never landed. The weapon crashed onto his head, and he crumpled to the pier.

The man turned toward Anna.

Eritha leaped between them. In the shallow pier lights she had begun to recognize faces. "What do you think you're doing, Benj Darwill?" she called. "Striking a poor defenseless beast—bully right to the end, aren't you?" The weapon raised again. Eritha kicked his shin viciously. "You try that on me," she snapped, "and I'll claw your eyes out. You, Cal Rown. I hope you're proud of yourself, throwing explosives at the meszs. It takes a really brave man to attack something that won't fight back. Get out of here, all of you."

She gave Darwill's face a resounding slap, and the men turned and fled precipitately. Eritha and Anna leaped from the pier and stood waist-deep in water trying to help Franff, but he was quite dead.

So was Jaward Jorno.

The meszs came, then, and helped them to pull Franff's body onto the pier, and the sobbing Anna flung herself onto him.

The explosions continued; the fires had spread, and the village became a caldron of swirling, crackling flames. In the mélange of terrifying sounds they did not hear the boats approaching until the first swung alongside the pier. A man climbed out and confronted Eritha.

"Where's Mr. Jorno?"

She pointed to his body.

Confusion surged about them while boats tied up and men

173

clambered out brandishing weapons. Then someone shouted an order, and they moved toward the shore; and each one, as he passed Jorno's body, faltered momentarily and bowed his head. A moment later they were moving up the slope toward the village.

One of the pilots called, "I'll take you people back." The meszs carried Franff's body to the boat, and then Jorno's, and Eritha handed a pale countess over the side and helped her to a seat. They pushed off, leaving behind them a ghoulish pattern of blood-red flames.

"Who were those men?" Harnasharn asked.

"Men from Zrilund Town," Eritha said. She was not frightened—at no time had she been frightened—but she had to struggle to master her overwhelming anger.

"Artists?" Harnasharn asked.

"If they'd been artists, I'd have done more than slap a face," Eritha said grimly.

"Arnen Brance—do you suppose—"

"As far as I could see, he had it in his hand when it exploded."

More men were waiting at the mainland pier, and they helped them from the boat and carefully laid out Franff's and Jorno's bodies before they embarked. A short time later Jorno's chauffeur arrived. There was no room for Franff's body in the limousine, and they had to coax the still-sobbing Anna away. The chauffeur promised to bring it to them later.

At the rotunda the resort's doctor was waiting for them. He gave sedatives to the countess, Lilya, and Anna, and ordered them to bed. Then he approached Eritha.

"None for me," she told him. "I still have things to do."

"Are you sure? You look somewhat overwrought."

"I'm not overwrought. I'm *mad!*"

Harnasharn said, "Where can I place a call to the Metro?"

"For millionaires, Jorno did things in style," Eritha told him. "The rotunda has its own communications center, but I'm first."

With her grandfather, Neal Wargen, and Superintendent of Police Demron listening, she described the situation tersely.

"From Zrilund Town?" Wargen asked. "You must be mistaken. They couldn't have planned such a massive attack without Rearm Hylat finding out about it, and he would have told me."

"I recognized at least six, and I know four of them by name."

"Casualties?"

"We didn't stay to count them. Several meszs were blown up in front of us. Likewise your man Brance. Franff and

174

Jorno died from blows on the head. That was just the beginning. The explosions were continuing when we left, and the fires were tremendous. They must have poured flammables all over the place. The building exteriors are of stone, but obviously the interiors aren't. Jorno's men were well armed, and there may be a war going on there right now with the meszs in the middle of it."

Wargen said, "Bron?"

"I've already issued orders," Demron said. "I'll fly in every available man."

"Are you people all right?" Wargen asked.

"The doctor put the countess and Lilya and Anna to bed. We're all right, except that I'm as angry as I've ever been in my life."

"We'll get there as soon as we can."

Eritha turned the communications center over to Lester Harnasharn. By that time Jorno's servants had arrived with Franff's body, and with their help she laid him out in an unused bedroom and smoothed the wonderfully soft, glowing fur.

Then she dismissed them, and after they left she sat beside Franff's body and wept.

Gerald Gwyll, aroused from his bed by an urgent call from Harnasharn, made a frantic dash to Port Metro and at dawn was searching the Nor Harbor quays for his chartered boat. He had an uneventful trip to Zrilund across a smooth sea, and the pilot tied up at the disused ferry pier.

Gwyll hurried up the steps and set out at a run through the deserted streets. He passed the oval, turned onto the Street of Artisans, and finally reached the court where Arnen Brance's house stood. There he panted to a halt. The door was unlocked—no one ever locked a door in Zrilund Town—and one glance told him that the house's interior had not been disturbed.

He turned aside and followed a path around the house and through a sagging gate. There he halted again, and with a cry of horror.

The enclosure Brance had built was smashed, the stones tossed about haphazardly. The mud it had contained was scattered and completely dried up. In a momentary frenzy Gwyll pawed and kicked at it, and then he turned slowly and walked back to the ferry pier.

175

19

An appalling reek of devastation hung over the fire-blackened mesz village. The buildings were rubble-choked shells, their stone walls split and crumbled by the heat, and the shrubs and young trees were charred.

But the most unnerving thing about the village was its silence. There were meszs everywhere, seated motionless amid the ashes or on the seared grass in attitudes of repose and meditation.

Neal Wargen supposed that they were mourning their dead.

"No," Eritha Korak said. "They're mourning our dead— Brance, and Franff, and especially Jaward Jorno. First Jorno rescued them from Mestil, and now he's given his life for them."

"How many meszs were killed?"

"Only fourteen. Twenty-one were seriously injured. Minor injuries were too numerous to count. Even so it's unbelievable, but we have to remember that they've been through this before. Just because they won't fight back doesn't mean that they're fools. They built fireproof, explosion-proof shelters under all of the dwellings, and they lived in them. It's a habit they acquired on Mestil. The village wasn't a place to live, it was a monument to their past."

"How many human casualties?"

"Jorno and Brance. A few critical injuries among Jorno's men, one is expected to die. Five known dead Zrilunders, they took their injured and maybe some of their dead with them. The battle didn't last long after Jorno's men arrived with weapons. The Zrilunders didn't have any."

"They had plenty of explosives and flammables," Wargen observed.

"Demron is trying to find out how many boats were used. The Zrilunders he's caught won't talk."

"I want to see them," Wargen said.

As they walked toward the pier, he stopped once and looked back. "I suppose, being meszs, they have no anger."

"Being meszs, they don't judge us by the humans who at-

176

tacked them, but by the humans who died in their defense. It's just as well. They can't get angry at us and leave, they have no place to go."

Three Zrilund fishing boats were tied up at Jorno's pier. The sullen Zrilunders, those who had not been injured, were under guard in Jorno's warehouse.

Wargen spoke to one sitting near the door. "Among your other good works of last night you managed to blow up the engines and the keel of the new underwater ferry the meszs were building for you."

"Generous of them," the Zrilunder drawled, "considering that they blew up the old ones. It costs them nothing to say they were building it for Zrilund—they know Zrilund is ruined and couldn't pay their price anyway. Actually, they were building it for Jorno's resort."

"It was to be a gift," Wargen said. "A gift of gratitude for the alleged hospitality of the people of Donov. Now they'll rebuild the motors and try to finish the thing before you grateful Zrilunders blow it up again."

The Zrilunder met his eyes with a mocking grin. Wargen turned away.

"What was it you wanted to find out?" Eritha asked.

"Whether the madness of the riot worlds has come to Donov. It has."

Bron Demron had set up his headquarters in Jorno's mansion. He was energetically directing the search for the missing boats and at the same time wondering what he was going to do with them when he'd caught them.

"Those characters claim they were fishing last night," he said indignantly. "They haven't been able to explain what a Zrilund boat is doing fishing off Rinoly with a capacity load of passengers, some of them wounded, but I'd feel better with a few witnesses."

"Eritha can identify some of them," Wargen reminded him.

Demron smiled at her. "So she can. I'd forgotten about that."

"Have you found out where they got the explosives?"

"No, but I will. Say—would you two like to hear a confession? One of Jorno's men is dying upstairs, he was caught in an explosion, and he keeps saying he wants to confess. Then he talks gibberish."

Wargen nodded agreeably. "Gibberish is just what this situation needs."

Eritha suppressed her shattering memory of the mesz fingers and followed the doctor and Wargen into the dying man's room; but this victim appeared to be untouched.

"His legs were blown off," the doctor whispered. "Many fragments of stone penetrated his body."

Wargen stepped to the bed. "What is it you have to confess, fellow?"

"The riots!" the patient gasped.

"What about them?"

"The riots!"

Wargen coaxed patiently, but the man kept repeating the same two words. Finally they withdrew, and the doctor said, "It sounds as though he was on one of the riot worlds, and he thinks the same thing has happened here."

"What happened last night must have been a very palpable imitation of the rioting," Wargen agreed.

"He hasn't been rational since he was brought here, and he's under heavy sedation."

"I understand. Just the same, I'd like to have a servant stationed here. If he says anything more, it should be written down."

Demron was waiting for them. Two more Zrilund fishing boats had been captured, and he wanted to find out whether Eritha could identify any of the men already in custody. Wargen left her there and went to pay his respects to his mother, the countess.

She had found herself obliged to assume the role of hostess under circumstances as trying as any that had perplexed a Wargen in all of that family's illustrious history. In one bedroom lay a dead animaloid. The countess had refrained from pointing out that its fur would make the most magnificent garments she or anyone else had ever seen. She sensed that some would consider the remark in bad taste, and a Wargen did not make remarks in bad taste. In another bedroom reposed an elderly woman of dubious character, worthless ancestry, and precarious health. She seemed likely to expire at any moment and the countess accepted this fact as confirmation of her lack of breeding. The carnage of the previous night had produced casualties much more urgently in need of medical attention than a woman afflicted by old age and the loss of a friend, so the doctor had been forced to leave Anna's fate in the hands of the countess, who received it unwillingly. In the third bedroom lay her own long-time friend and companion, Lilya Vaan, who had chosen a most inconvenient moment to go completely to pieces. This offended the countess less than the fact that Lilya was so obviously enjoying it.

As a hostess must, the countess was coping. Relentlessly

she made the rounds: Medicine and a surface bath for Anna, fresh sheets wrapped about her perspiring old body, a servant left to keep watch over her. A quick look at Lilya Vaan, an exchange of insults, Lilya accusing the countess of being a parasite that fattened itself upon the misery of its friends, and the countess answering that she was running the flesh from her bones looking after a lazy hypochondriac. She darkened the room, told Lilya to rest if her conscience would permit it, and left her. Next she glanced at Franff's body, wondering what sort of death rites such creatures observed. Perhaps none. She could think of nothing to do with him or for him, death was such a risky thing to tamper with, so many silly prejudices existed. For herself, all she wanted was flowers, music, and a whiff or two of incense, something to please the sight, hearing, and scent of the mourners if there were any; but there were humans to whom all three would seem offensive. With another covetous glance at Franff's fur, she left him.

Then her son arrived.

"I don't suppose," she told him bitterly, "that you came down here to succor your poor old mother in her time of trial. You merely came on some silly government business."

"Very serious government business," Wargen said soberly, "and you're a part of it. You had a narrow escape last night. Eritha says you were heroic."

"Does she, indeed!" The countess sniffed haughtily. Then she said, a touch of awe in her voice, "Eritha—did you hear what Eritha did?"

"No. Obviously it's something I'm not likely to hear from her, or she would have told me. Did she disgrace herself?"

"Disgrace herself? Eritha?" The countess eyed him indignantly. "She's a remarkable young woman. All she did was save our lives. Sit down, please."

Wargen did so, wondering.

"Neal, I've been thinking for some time that you should be getting married. And I think the little Korak girl would make an excellent wife for you. She has neither wealth nor lineage, but surely we Wargens already have ample of either. There was something quite—quite regal about her, the way she faced danger. I don't know how she comes by it, but she certainly has it. Those men had just murdered Franff and Mr. Jorno, and I knew we would be next, and she just stepped forward and *ruled* them. She told them to go away, and she slapped their faces, and they went! No queen could have done it better. Would you like me to speak to her grandfather, Pet?"

Wargen smiled at her affectionately. "Mother dearest, ever since Eritha was sixteen I've been asking her to marry me at every suitable opportunity. I have confidence that eventually she'll consent. In the meantime, she keeps telling me that one of us still has some growing up to do. I have the uneasy suspicion that she may mean me."

"Perhaps if I spoke with her grandfather—"

"No, Mother. Eritha will decide when she is to marry, and whom. No one knows that better than Ian Korak."

"I see. I do have one piece of advice for you. If, after you marry, she's ever afflicted with one of these silly whims about buying paintings—let her!"

Wargen felt both irritated and concerned because the attack on Mestil Island came without warning. His first act after Eritha's call was to attempt, unsuccessfully, to reach Rearm Hylat. His second was to send men to Zrilund to find out what had happened. Now, using the rotunda's communication center, he managed to get in touch with them, and he learned that Hylat, alive and furiously angry, had been a prisoner in his own adde cellar since before the fleet left Zrilund.

Wargen returned to Jorno's mansion. Demron reported the capture of another Zrilund fishing boat, and added, "Oh, about the man who wanted to confess."

"Did he succeed?"

"He died. He babbled about riots right to the end, but he never actually said anything. Eritha's waiting for you in Jorno's study."

She looked very small indeed seated behind the vastness of Jorno's ornate worktable, with the rows of book drawers looming behind her. She had lost her anger; now she seemed saddened and perplexed.

He smiled at her wistfully. It had been some weeks since he last proposed, but this seemed an unpropitious moment for resuming a courtship. "What are you doing?" he asked.

"Exercising my curiosity."

"On what?"

She indicated the heavily bound tomes scattered about the table. She had sketched something on the table's work screen, and Wargen regarded it with puzzlement. "That looks like the chart on the wall of my office. Did you memorize it?"

She shook her head. "Jorno made the same study you did, only he didn't visualize it."

"He studied the riots?"

She nodded.

"Did he get any further with them than I did?"

"I don't know how far he got, but he studied them in person. The man who wanted to confess was a long-time employee of Jorno's and a crewman on Jorno's private yacht—

when the yacht is in port much of the crew works at odd jobs here on the estate. So if that particular employee of Jorno's knew anything about the riots, it very likely concerned something that happened while he was on duty on Jorno's yacht. I found the yacht's logbooks here, and I checked the dates and plotted them, and the result is a chart like yours."

"That's interesting."

"Jorno was extremely concerned about the refugees, you know, and he seems to have visited almost all of the riot worlds. We may never know what he learned, but if one of his crewmen was experiencing hallucinations about the riots—"

"Let me see that," Wargen said. He seated himself beside her and scowled at the chart. "Are you certain these dates are correct?"

"They're what the log says."

"You didn't go back far enough. Or maybe Jorno started too late. He visited worlds long after the rioting started and in reverse order. Let me have a look." He opened one of the heavy volumes, found the date at which Eritha had started charting, and began leafing the pages backward. "No," he said finally, "he followed the riots right from the beginning."

When Demron came in he found them gazing at each other perplexedly. Eritha said to him, "This employee of Jorno's who just died—the one who wanted to confess. What was his name?"

"Jac Grawla."

"Since he was a crewman on Jorno's yacht, don't you think it might be interesting to find out if any of the others have anything to confess?"

Demron seated himself on the opposite side of the table. "How would I go about finding out a thing like that?"

"Have one in and ask him."

"From what you saw of Jorno's men last night, you ought to know that it'd take more than a stern look to make one confess."

"Maybe it wouldn't if he thought Grawla told you all about it."

Demron nodded thoughtfully. "Yes. Jorno's men don't know that Grawla spoke nothing but gibberish. I don't suppose there's much to lose by trying." He stepped to the door, snapped an order, and returned to his chair.

Minutes passed. The yacht crewmen had their quarters in a separate building, and they were being detained there—not because their defense of the meszs had violated any law, but because Demron thought they might be needed for further interrogation.

Finally one of them shuffled in—an enormous hulk of a man who had faced far worse dangers than a world superintendent of police without quailing. He said, "You want me?"

"Name?" Demron asked.

"Sair Rondil."

"Have you heard that Jac Grawla died?"

"I heard he was going to."

Demron nodded. "The doctor did his best, but there was no chance at all of saving his life. Grawla knew it, and before he died he made a full confession about the riots. Since you were with him—he named you and several others—"

He broke off because Rondil was gone. Without a word he wheeled and sprinted for the door, flung it open, and disappeared. Demron sprang after him to shout an order; Wargen and Eritha stepped to a window and saw Rondil speeding along the drive with panicky, leaping strides.

"Give him time to tell the others before you catch him," Wargen suggested.

"Right. Then I'll question them one at a time. Sooner or later one will talk, though I can't imagine what it is you expect him to say."

"Neither can I. The one thing I do know is that we need to look closely at Jorno's personal affairs. His attorney is Medil Favic."

"I'll send for him," Demron promised.

"Before you go off to chase the crewmen, would you send in Jorno's steward?"

The steward shuffled in quietly. His eyes were red with weeping, his lank old body stooped under a blow from which it would never recover. He had served the family more years than Jorno was old, he regarded Jorno more as a son than an employer, but he was bearing up bravely. The police, the doctors, the injured persons had to be considered guests, Jorno would have wanted it that way, and there was work to be done.

Wargen greeted him courteously, got him seated, and explained the problem. "We need to know a few things about Mr. Jorno. Perhaps you could help us. Are you familiar with his Good Works?"

"Certainly, sir."

"Could you tell us something about them?"

"There are the meszs, sir."

"Before that. Just a few examples."

"Yes, sir. Did you know there is a world named Jorno?"

Wargen shook his head.

"It happened many years ago, when Master was quite young. He took a long tour on his yacht, and he happened onto this world—it was called something else then—where the settlers had caught an epidemic. Those who weren't dying from it were starving to death. They'd come from a number of worlds, and their governments were arguing about which was responsible. Master hired doctors and brought all the supplies the world needed and saved the colony. He wouldn't let them pay him anything. They changed the name of the world to Jorno."

Wargen stepped to the referencer, punched the gazetteer code, and a moment later was reading a description of the world of Jorno. "That was quite a long trip that your master took," he observed.

"Yes, sir. He was gone for several years, and he did many Good Works along the way. I may be the only one who knows about them. Sometimes late of an evening he would invite me to have a glass with him, and then—" His voice broke. He swallowed and continued hoarsely, "Then he'd reminisce about things he enjoyed remembering."

"Tell us some of the others."

"Yes, sir. Somewhere he kept a list of all the young people whose educations he financed. There are at least four universities named Jorno—he gave handsome gifts to many, but these four could not have survived without his help, and all of them changed their names to Jorno. Master felt very strongly about the value of education. I doubt if he knew himself how many Jorno hospitals there are—he founded so many, on so many different worlds."

Wargen stepped to the referencer again. "How many?" Eritha asked.

"Three Jorno universities, but that's only in this sector." He returned to his chair and said awesomely, "The Jorno fortune must be enormous!"

"It was, sir. I've heard it said that Master's father was the wealthiest man in the galaxy. His financial interests were galactic in scope."

"To be sure. He amassed the money, and his son gave it away like a saint."

"That's true, sir," the steward agreed. "I've had the pleasure of serving him and observing his generosity throughout his life. I wonder if the galaxy has ever had another man who has helped so many people in so many ways. He was entirely selfless where the needs of others were concerned. That's what put him on the verge of bankruptcy."

"On the verge of *what?*"

"Bankruptcy. That's why he had to sell his space yacht to finance the mesz village and his resort. But both projects are unqualified financial successes. He was well on his way to accumulating another fortune."

"To give away?" Wargen asked politely.

The steward looked surprised. "But of course. What else would he do with it? You said yourself that he was a saint."

Wargen thanked him and let him go. The two of them remained silent for some time, and finally Wargen asked, "Did you have an inkling of a suspicion that Jorno was a saint?"

"I didn't and I don't. That's your word."

"What's yours?"

"I won't offer one. I'll just say that I have one thing in common with Donov's millions of overcharged vacationers. I'd be utterly astounded to find a saint running a tourist resort."

⋆ 20 ⋆

Neal Wargen had a report to write. The Interplanetary Tribunal had requested full information, as had the twenty-four riot worlds, and a staff was at work sifting the accumulated evidence and preparing copies for the oppressive number of appendices the report would have to have. The analysis, the explanations, the conclusions were Wargen's responsibility.

First he had a report to think. He had to understand before he could explain, and he began by placing a new star chart on the wall of his office. Resting both elbows on the thick files that littered his worktable, he studied it, traced the order of cruises up and down the spiral of riot worlds, and contemplated the malignant Odyssey of Jaward Jorno.

For Jorno, assisted by the crew of his space yacht—Jorno had caused the riots.

No one wanted to believe it.

The World Manager exclaimed, his face ashen, his sightless eyes peering incredulously, "*Caused* the riots? You mean he deliberately brought them about? Made them happen?"

There was the yacht's log, there were the confessions of the crewmen, and once it became clear that Donov was working, not to embarrass individual worlds, but in the interest of the entire galactic community, the governments of the riot worlds reversed themselves and supplied volumes of supporting evidence.

What Wargen had called a spiraling galactic wind had been the cruise of a single ship. Jaward Jorno had studied the populations of twenty-four worlds until he plumbed their hatreds and discovered depths they themselves had not envisioned in their foulest nightmares. For more than a year before the riots, he moved up and down the spiral, spreading rumors with diabolical ingenuity, playing upon fears as a skilled lumeno virtuoso manipulated his keyboard. Finally he was ready, and he caused the riots.

On Skuron, where according to rumor industrial wastes had poisoned a reservoir, Jorno's men had done the job with bacteria. "We went at night with unpowered boats and

185

dumped cultures of Gelon 12 directly into the intake pipes," one confession read. Gelon 12 did not occur on Skuron, and Skuron's water-treatment procedures merely encouraged the bacteria to proliferate.

One of Jorno's crewmen was an expert chemist. "Gelon 12 rarely has fatal results," he said protestingly. "Why, if we'd wanted to kill people . . ."

Hundreds of thousands became ill; hundreds died. Chemical analysis of the polluted water found Gelon 12. The government suppressed that information, not wanting it known how easily the world's water supplies could be sabotaged, and blamed industrial pollution, but the people were not deceived. Rumors, astutely planted and spread by Jorno and his crewmen, placed the blame on the animaloids, and the riots followed.

On Sornor, enormous tracts of grazing land were sprayed with chemicals. It wasn't necessary to kill the vegetation, but only to produce a reaction that made the natives think it was dying. One of Jorno's crewmen invented an apparatus that produced a spray fine enough to taint an area miles wide. "We rented winged transports and did several thousand acres a night for a week," he confessed. The nonors were blamed, with Jorno guiding the rumors.

On Proplif, Jorno damaged grain crops with the same spraying apparatus. On Mestil, explosives caused the landslides and cracked the dam. A hundred thousand humans died; no one bothered to count the dead meszs. The Bbronan fires *were* arson, they were set by Jorno's crewmen.

On world after world after world . . .

A light flashed, and Wargen started irritably. The World Manager said, "Eritha's coming with Lester Harnasharn. They want to know if you can join us."

"When?" Wargen asked.

"When they get here. They're about to leave the galleries."

"Let me know when they arrive."

He got to his feet and paced back and forth, pausing from time to time to look at the new star chart.

Jaward Jorno. A good man. A saint. The author of more Good Works than his own steward had time to catalogue. Jaward Jorno had caused the riots. With no compunction that anyone was able to notice, he performed inconceivable evils merely so that he could go on doing good.

His dedication to Good Works had so reduced his father's enormous fortune that he found himself rapidly approaching bankruptcy. His remaining assets were a space yacht, a devoted and talented crew, an estate on Donov, and a diminishing amount of capital. His eye fell on the animaloids, many

186

species of them brilliant, all of them abused minorities. They could be an invaluable economic asset for the man who knew how to make use of them.

Jaward Jorno knew how. Everyone had been so pleased at the possibility of low-priced textiles for Fonov that no one had stopped to ponder the fact that Jorno would have a textile monopoly for an entire world. His daily profits would amount to a fortune. With ingenious animaloids to achieve automation miracles, expansion of the monopoly to other worlds would be inevitable. Already Jorno had moved toward a dominant if not domineering position in Donov's fabulously profitable tourish industry. He had taken options on properties with resort potential all over Donov, and with the meszs to construct quality resorts without labor costs, he soon would have been taking another daily fortune from that source.

And that was only a beginning. Nothing was known about Jorno's long-range plans, but Wargen was certain that he'd had some. He'd established tarff in Rinoly years before his animaloids arrived to make use of it. He committed enormous evils, but it was enormous stakes that he was playing for.

Perhaps he hadn't expected success on all twenty-four worlds, but he achieved it, and he selected the animaloid refugees with the most potential value for him. His project almost foundered on Donov's immigration laws and the unexpected coolness of its officials toward accepting the refugees, but a trick saved him.

And he acquired three thousand uniquely valuable slaves. No other individual slaveholder in history possessed such brilliant servants. They could build anything, they could do almost anything, and all of them were willing to die for the man who rescued them from Mestil.

And yet—Jorno certainly returned the meszs' affection, he respected their culture and traditions, and he was conscientious about his responsibility for them. He made them his heirs, and they now owned his entire estate.

Anyone doubting that Jorno had caused the riots had only to contemplate the fiendish efficiency with which he crushed the island of Zrilund. The poison used was the same that simulated the poisonous alga on Cuque, stained red instead of green. On Donov, Jorno was so certain of himself that he saw no need for subtleties.

Neither did he see any need to make the cost higher than absolutely necessary. His men dumped just enough poison at Virrab to divert suspicion from him, and the boats they blew up there were worthless hulks that Jorno acquired for that purpose. He reasoned that a wrecked boat looked very much the same as a good boat after an explosion, and he was right. Demron's men never suspected a thing.

Jorno ruined Zrilund in a childish fit of temper. He was performing such splendid Good Works for Donov—prosperity for Rinoly farmers, low-priced textiles for the entire planet, a revitalization of Donov's tourist industry that would benefit Zrilund and every other resort—and instead of being properly grateful, the stupid people and artists of Zrilund were subjecting him to every petty harassment they could think of. He lost his temper, he determined to show them that no one crossed Jaward Jorno with impunity. It took him just two nights to smash Zrilund utterly.

He forgot that his own animaloids were as vulnerable as the animaloids on other worlds, and he forgot that such enemies as Ronony Gynth were capable of clumsy but effective use of the same forces he himself had unleashed so skillfully. Ronony so little understood what she was doing that she aimed all of her efforts at Zrilund's artists—and she still succeeded in arousing the townspeople and fishermen against Jorno.

Ian Korak signaled. "They're here," he announced.

"All right," Wargen said.

The thing that disquieted him most was that so much good could result from Jorno's evil. Rinoly would prosper as soon as the meszs rebuilt their factory, Donov would have its low-priced textiles, the meszs, despite their shattering experience, were much better off than their brethren on Mestil and possessed an incomparably brighter future; and Zrilund, which Jorno had utterly destroyed, would benefit most of all.

On Wargen's suggestion, the arbiter had ordered the Zrilunders to help rebuild the mesz village. For several days an awkward silence prevailed on Mestil Island, the meszs being unwilling to believe that Jorno was a villain, and the Zrilunders being unwilling to believe that the meszs weren't. Now friendships were developing, and the meszs had become interested in Zrilund's problems. They'd resumed their crash program on the underwater ferries, they'd taken charge of Zrilund's massive cleanup, and they were planning new attractions to make the town more interesting to tourists. The Zrilunders needed all the help they could get, and more than anything else the meszs desperately needed to be needed. It looked like a promising partnership.

But in an objective report on Jorno's iniquity, how could one balance in that paradoxical good?

Ian Korak signaled again. "We're waiting."

Wargen took a final look at the star chart before he resignedly turned away.

The World Manager's lair had the appearance of an art shop. Nine easels stood in a semicircle about him, with a painting on each. Korak was resentfully ignoring them.

"They're the slug paintings!" Wargen exclaimed.

He touched wrists with Harnasharn, bowed deeply to Eritha, who made a face at him, and then he stepped forward for a closer look.

He had forgotten what they were like: The strange, woven texture, the unreal shapes, the dazzling mélange of light and color.

"I was just explaining to the World Manager," Harnasharn said. "Arnen Brance left a will, and I'm his executor. Under its terms I was awarded one of these paintings. I have made my selection, and nine remain. These nine I am to offer as gifts to nine worthy individuals. I consider the World Manager an eminently worthy individual, and I'm offering him first choice."

"And I've been explaining that they all look alike to me," Korak grumbled.

"That's one reason I brought Eritha," Harnasharn said brightly. "She can made the selection for you. The other reason I brought her is that I want her to have one of the paintings for herself. And you, sir—" He turned to Wargen. "I want you to have one."

"That's very kind of you."

Harnasharn smiled. "Kind, and also crafty. I'm hoping that all of these paintings will eventually find their ways into the Institute, they constitute a unique collection, and frankly I'm giving them to the people who are most likely to make that happen—though of course those receiving them are under no obligation whatsoever."

"Did you find out anything more about the slug?" Wargen asked.

"Yes and no. A few days before Brance left Zrilund he hired a boy to care for it, and then because there was so much bitterness against the artists for leaving Zrilund, the boy's parents wouldn't let him. The boy has now confessed. A couple of days after Brance left, he and some of his friends smashed the slug's pen. They spread the mud around the garden, but they found no slug."

"Then Brance made other arrangements?"

"It seems so. The day before he left he drove a hired wrranel cart down to his farm. There he borrowed swamp shoes from a neighbor—they're special shoes the kruckul

189

farmers wear, they're like having a boat on each foot, and those who know how to use them can travel about a swamp with remarkable speed. The neighbor paid no attention to where Brance went with them, but the implication is obvious: He took the slug into the most remote part of the swamp and released it."

"Good!" Eritha exclaimed.

"Yes, though of course we're left with the same mystery we started with."

"But you have an opinion," Wargen suggested.

"I have an opinion, yes. I find it suggestive that when Brance went to Rinoly and resumed painting he was a very fine artist indeed and perhaps even a great one. I think that during those dreary years when he was running his kruckul farm he was also painting as much as he could, experimenting and practicing. I've found evidence that he purchased enormous quantities of art supplies. I think the slug paintings were one of his experiments. He was so embittered by his previous lack of success that he obtained a measure of sardonic satisfaction in attributing them to a Zrilund swamp slug."

"It seems logical," Wargen agreed. "Still—you said you'd actually seen the slug painting."

"I think what happened was that Brance chanced to place his paints and fabric in the slug's pen. The slug found something attractive in the vegetable paints and also found the art fabric a very convenient place to clean its filaments. As a result it 'painted.' Probably it produced a mishmash, but the texture was so unique that it intrigued Brance into experimenting to see if he could reproduce it. And I think he succeeded. He showed the paintings to two of his artist friends, telling them that the slug was the artist, and doubtless these friends were responsible for the rumors. Both saw the slug 'paint,' but in each instance Brance placed an untouched fabric in the pen. That's very significant, it suggests that the slug never produced more than small disconnected areas. The sight of a slug painting anything at all was so startling that neither the friends nor I thought to question Brance's assertion that the slug was an artist.

"So I think Brance used the texture produced by the slug and did eleven paintings showing the universe as he thought the slug could have seen it. I also think he would have destroyed them if he hadn't needed money for Franff."

"I suppose we'll never know for sure," Wargen said.

"No. I'm positive of that. I've searched all of his possessions, and he didn't leave a clue. We'll never know." He smiled. "But we have the paintings, and they're great art. Would you make your choices, Eritha?"

"I insist that she report to me first," Ian Korak said.

The three of them faced him. "Report what?" Harnasharn asked.

"The Countess Wargen informed me an hour ago that I'm about to experience the supreme good fortune of having a Wargen as a grandson-in-law. I congratulated her on her superlative luck in acquiring a Korak as a daughter-in-law, and to my intense surprise she agreed with me. There are days when a man doesn't know his own granddaughter."

His voice droned on, but the beaming Harnasharn was inundating Wargen and Eritha with congratulations. "Then the paintings will be a wedding present!" he exclaimed. "I think that would have pleased Arnen. He had a terribly difficult life, but he never lost his perspective—he realized that he'd chosen that life himself, it was the price of doing what he wanted to do, and he never begrudged happiness to others. In fact, he gave whenever he could, as much as he could. Look what he did for Franff and the meszs. Would you make your choices, Eritha?"

Eritha turned to the paintings and said thoughtfully, "If you don't mind, I'll send mine to the Institute at once."

"You're of course free to do what you like with it. I would have thought, though, that you'd first prefer to enjoy it yourself."

She shook her head. "Ever since I first saw these paintings, I've been puzzled as to what gives them their unique quality. Now I think I know. It's purity. Innocence. Goodness. Those virtues shine there like a radiant light, and I don't think there are intelligent beings anywhere in the universe that can face it without flinching. Not even the meszs. Not even Franff. Not after what has happened. I used to think that everyone, human or animaloid, had an inextinguishable spark of that light within him. I don't want to be reminded of how wrong I was."

Her grandfather said dryly, "If you want to think that, go ahead. I've lived a few years longer than you, and I've found no definite evidence to the contrary. I think it's probably true. Look at Jaward Jorno. He spitefully ruined the island of Zrilund, but the moment it was ruined it needed help, and there he was, pushing his meszs to devise a means of disposing of the dead fish and removing the poison, and starting them building new ferryboats, and if he'd lived he would have personally restored the island and made it prosperous. You can count on it—the spark exists."

Eritha shook her head again. "A spark, perhaps, but not

that spark." She faced her grandfather resentfully. "I thought my understanding that meant that I was growing up. It seems to me that only a mature person can face the fact of what he really is."

"Let her have it her way," Wargen said. "Otherwise she'll revert to childhood and make me wait another five years."

"She can have it any way she likes," the World Manager said, "but she needn't assume responsibility for all the evil in the universe."

"I wouldn't think of trying," Eritha said. "I'm just assuming responsibility for my own. The appalling thing isn't that a good man—I think Jorno was a good man—was capable of such horrendous evil, but because so many men, on so many worlds, had sufficient evil in them to make Jorno's evil possible. Great evils are only chance combinations of lesser evils, I think, and if the lesser evils weren't so universal, no great evil would be possible. So I won't keep the painting. It's a beautiful, a magnificent light, but I won't keep it."

Wargen took her hands and smiled down at her. She said nothing more, but their eyes met, and he understood. She was not disturbed by the possibility that the light had never been, but by the fear that it could never be.